THE SECRET OF SNOW

Tina Harnesk is a writer of Sámi descent born in northern Sweden. She works as a library assistant and lives on a mountain outside Arvidsjaur, Sweden, with her husband and children. *The Secret of Snow* is her debut novel.

Alice Menzies holds an MA in translation theory and practice from University College London, specializing in the Scandinavian languages. She has translated, among other works, *And Every Morning the Way Home Gets Longer and Longer* by Fredrik Backman. She lives in London.

THE SECRET OF SNOW

TINA HARNESK

Translated from the Swedish by Alice Menzies

ORION

First published in Swedish as *Folk som sår i snö* in 2022 by Bokfabriken

First published in Great Britain in 2026 by Orion Fiction,
an imprint of The Orion Publishing Group Ltd.
Carmelite House, 50 Victoria Embankment
London EC4Y 0DZ
An Hachette UK Company

The authorised representative in the EEA is Hachette Ireland, 8 Castlecourt Centre,
Dublin 15, D15 XTP3, Ireland (email: info@hbgi.ie)

1 3 5 7 9 10 8 6 4 2

Copyright © Tina Harnesk 2022
English translation © Alice Menzies 2026

The moral right of Tina Harnesk to be identified as
the author of this work has been asserted in accordance
with the Copyright, Designs and Patents Act of 1988.

Alice Menzies has asserted her right to be identified as the translator of this work.

All rights reserved. No part of this publication may be
reproduced, stored in a retrieval system, or transmitted
in any form or by any means, electronic, mechanical,
photocopying, recording, or otherwise, without the
prior permission of both the copyright owner and the
above publisher of this book.

All the characters in this book are fictitious, and any resemblance
to actual persons, living or dead, is purely coincidental.

A CIP catalogue record for this book is
available from the British Library.

ISBN (Hardback) 9781 3987 1777 0
ISBN (Export Trade Paperback) 9781 3987 1778 7
ISBN (Ebook) 9781 3987 1780 0
ISBN (Audio) 9781 3987 1781 7

Typeset by Born Group
Printed and bound in Great Britain by Clays Ltd, Elcograf S.p.A.

www.orionbooks.co.uk

For the kids
Ejvind & Flora
Jon-Ánte, Joar, Máhtte, Erik, Signe,
Dag-Biehtar, Antaris, Edith, John & Daria

. . . and for you, the man who promised me a dog if I wrote a book.

Your move.

Prologue

"Tell me the story about the herder who met a *háldi*, Uncle!"

The boy's voice was bright and insistent, spilling across the floor like a handful of frostbitten lingonberries.

From where she was lying in the next room, Máriddja heard Biera slurp coffee through the lump of sugar between his teeth, followed by the sound of china on wood.

"Ah, you've heard that one plenty of times, but I'll tell it again," he replied with mock resignation.

His wife knew he loved to tell stories. He had inherited that from his parents, who had themselves inherited it from those who'd walked life's path before them. It was their way of remembering, a way for a people without words on paper to leave a mark on an Earth they did their best not to change.

More than anything, Biera loved telling stories to the boy, who was perched on the cushion atop the storage bench in the kitchen, eyes eager yet weary, spinning the birch bark sugar bowl in his hands on the table between them. Máriddja tugged at the pillow beneath her cheek, adjusting her plait so that she was lying comfortably in the darkness. She closed her eyes.

She loved his stories too, especially the ones that were drawn out of him like this: at a child's request. Lying there, she could just picture the distant look in his eye as he searched for the words inside himself, trying to find the young reindeer herder. When Biera eventually managed to locate him, his voice belonged to someone else. It fumbled through the glow of the stove in the kitchen and made its way out into the darkness on the other side of the window. His voice was soon reverberating through the shadows in the room, summoning figures out of the gloom. Máriddja listened as Biera conjured the sound of thudding hooves, reindeer moving across the open landscape, wind tugging at their fur and caressing their muzzles. And there was the herder boy, constantly but silently communicating with his dog, practically running to meet Biera's audience. His lasso swung as he moved across the rocks, his knife smacking against the side of his leg.

"There once was a young reindeer herder . . ." Biera began, his voice as rich and heavy as a church bell. Each word was clear, filled with the memories of his people. It was impossible to say whether he had been possessed by the force he had invoked, or whether it was Biera himself who possessed that force, the reindeer herder – all of them alive in that moment. Even the old clock on the wall seemed to be holding its breath as he read aloud from a book of stories that had never been written down.

"That reindeer herder and his dog were out in the mountains one summer, alone with their herd. It was hard work, and they were both tired when they lay down to sleep in the *lavvu* he'd pitched. The fire had died right down, but the hot embers were still smoldering between the rocks. Sleep had almost caught up with the young herder as he lay with his eyes closed and his head on his bag. That was when he heard a scraping sound against the outside of the tent. He opened his eyes, squinting in the half-light, and saw something push against the fabric. The reindeer herder sat up. He could hear bubbling laughter, soft voices – spoken in a girl's teasing manner – and as he listened, he saw three silhouettes emerge outside. They were squabbling, and he saw the outline of a body fall against the hide of the tent. A voice said: 'You've been peeping from a distance all day. Go and get a proper look!'

"The reindeer herder realized that the voices outside must belong to *háldi* girls, for there wasn't another soul for miles. Everyone knew that these secretive creatures were always close by, living side by side with humans, yet only visible to those with the gift. There were countless stories about the *vitterfolk* – that is what we Sámi call our mysterious cousins – and the young herder had heard every tale passed down through his family. He knew there were ways to make contact with them, to persuade them to stick around.

"The reindeer herder's dog had woken, and was staring tensely in the direction of the three girls. A low growl rumbled from his throat, but he settled down when the herder stroked his raised fur. The young man reached for the knife on his belt, gripping the antler handle and pulling out the sharp steel blade without making a sound. The next time the *háldi*'s body fell against the side of his *lavvu*, he was ready. He pricked her gently in the buttock, making a small flower of blood bloom across the tent's hide.

"Outside, silence fell, as though a thick fog had descended over the mountain. The wind held its breath, the brook stopped singing, and the soft crackling of the embers hushed, as though frozen.

"That was when the heavy hide was pushed to one side and a figure leant in through the opening. Moving slowly, she sat down on the other side of the fire and looked up at him. The *háldi*'s eyes were as deep and dark as a mountain tarn, and she held the herder's gaze until he felt like he could no longer breathe.

"She spent a long time studying him like that, as though she was searching for his very essence. Then she smiled. In a musical voice, she said: 'You wanted to hold me. Now let's see if you can keep hold of me.'

"She spoke in an old-fashioned dialect, but her voice was calm and steady. She went on, 'I shall be your wife, and you shall receive my entire herd as a dowry; I will give you healthy sons and strong daughters, and we will be happy together. But you must promise me one thing.'

"The reindeer herder's heart was racing. All he could do was nod, overcome with joy and anticipation.

"'You must never tell anyone how I became yours or what I am. You must never call me by any name that does not belong to your world.'

"The young herder cleared his throat and made a solemn, eager vow to do as she said. He then went to his family's sacred rock, their *siedi*, as the girl had told him to, and he squinted out into the bright summer night. Not even the mosquitoes seemed to stir at that hour.

"That was when he heard the reindeer approaching, lots of them. With his lasso in his hand, he followed the movements of a powerful white bull, just as the girl had told him to do. He cast his rope. And when he managed to catch the strong, proud reindeer, the herd split in two, with half following him. Necks outstretched, the animals seemed to automatically flow in the direction of the dominant bull, moving toward the young man.

"And everything happened just as the *háldi* girl had foretold. They married, but throughout the ceremony they both moved counter clockwise and his *siida*'s shaman read the Lord's Prayer backwards. The powerful elder no doubt saw what the bride was, but he knew better than to say a word. In the years that followed, the couple welcomed one child after another, and they grew rich from her substantial herd. Life went well for them, and they had great fortune with their reindeer."

A sudden silence filled the kitchen. Biera idly turned the coffee cup in his hands, gazing down into it with a seer's eyes.

"But then what happened?" asked the boy.

"Ah lad, you surely know. One evening, as the man ran his hands through his wife's black hair, he whispered in her ear. *My darling wife, my love . . . my háldi . . .* And his wife froze. As slowly as a cloud drifts over the sun, she turned away from him, gathered her children, and they strode silently through the flap in the *lavvu* without once looking back. To his horror, the man watched as his family – and the herd of reindeer grazing nearby – grew fainter and fainter, eventually becoming one with the first rays of sunlight."

Máriddja shuddered where she lay beneath the covers, waiting for the spell to break, the way it always did when Biera finished his story. She heard the snap of the snus pot opening, his callused fingers pinching a wad of the loose tobacco to push beneath his lip. The boy sat quietly for a moment, and then he asked:

"But why did she go? If she loved him, why couldn't she and the children stay?"

Biera seemed to consider his answer carefully before he spoke. "Deep down, even though she loved him, I think she probably missed something else. I don't think a person ever stops longing for the place where they belong. No matter who we become or where we end up, our hearts have a root."

I

Green Light for Jábmemáhkká, Goddess of the Dead

In the depths of darkest midwinter, the old woman received her sentence. In a room filled with drab art, she had stubbornly refused to meet the doctor's eye. They had probably picked these ghastly landscapes specially for framing conversations like this, Máriddja thought cynically. Doctor Skruvlenius waited patiently for her reaction, squinting at the patient with her green-tinged brows knotted in pity. Her eyebrows really did look a little seasick, in both shape and color, perched above the top of her glasses like a pair of hungover anchovies. Or lizards, possibly. Lively little lizards darting across her forehead as she spoke in a calm, studiously sympathetic tone.

Was it the light? There was a strong smell of hand sanitizer and lilies in the room. Máriddja raised her chin to get a better look. Red hair could develop a greenish hue if you washed it in acidic water, she knew that. Or was it the other way around? No! It was saltwater that turned body hair green. She had seen it on TV, so it must be true.

The doctor continued to mumble softly, reassuringly; the old woman in front of her had just received an upsetting diagnosis, and she was clearly in a state of shock.

"I know this is hard, Maria, but I'm afraid there's no easy way to break such *terribly* sad news."

The doctor's eyebrows sagged in slow motion before returning to their compassionate green A-shape above her eyes.

Máriddja raised her own eyebrows as high as she could in an attempt to check whether they felt like reptiles, but alas, no. It was a pity; she would have loved a skill like that. Her nostrils flared in exertion as she tried to mimic the doctor's magnificent facial movements. The woman's precision-plucked brows had now dropped impossibly low as she tried to catch her patient's evasive gaze.

I wonder if that's the kind of trick you can learn, Máriddja thought, leaning forward with interest in the uncomfortable and unnaturally deep armchair. She could see that her lack of response was starting to trouble the doctor.

"Tell me, how are things at home?" Doctor Skruvlenius asked, cocking her head. "Do you have a partner or anyone else who can help you through this?"

The doctor had a particularly irritating way of articulating every word, as though she thought Máriddja was a simpleton.

"Naturally we'll do everything we can to support you and make this difficult time as easy as possible. We can offer counselling, and I can also prescribe antidepressants if you think that would help?"

Her voice was soft, but Máriddja was immediately on her guard, fully present in the room once again. Any analysis of the doctor's eyebrows would have to wait.

"I'm married, and the old man will take fine care of me. Now that I know what's what, we don't need anything else." Máriddja moved to get up. "Thank you kindly for your help."

Doctor Skruvlenius held out a cool hand to stop her. The two lizards crept closer, sniffing each other over the bridge of her nose. Her dainty little doctor's paw lingered on Máriddja's crooked fingers, like a petal on a gnarled tree trunk.

"I know this must be hard to take in, Maria, but once you feel ready I'd really like to discuss your options. If nothing else, perhaps we can arrange some counselling for your husband?"

Máriddja was so horrified that she forgot to bristle at the doctor getting her name wrong yet again. She shook off Skruvlenius's hand.

"No, no, the man's never been much of a talker, but I'm sure he'll take this in his stride. I don't think it'll be a problem for him, no."

Now the lizards recoiled, making the doctor's forehead crease, sinking into the furrows of her face as though to hide their surprise — or horror.

Amazing what talents this woman has been gifted, Máriddja thought, so impressed that she forgot what she had been saying.

"I . . . obviously this is going to be difficult for him . . . getting by without support in a situation like this, that really isn't something we'd recommend for an elderly person." Skruvlenius's slightly monotone voice had begun to reach a refreshingly higher pitch. "The prospect of losing one's other half after so many years is a *serious* trauma!"

Máriddja rocked her head back and forth in a conciliatory nod, then said: "Well, he managed to deal with all our old dogs when the time came, and let me tell you: the man's a soft touch! He was far too fond of most of them, so of course he blubbed a bit when he thought no one was looking — but it never took long until he was back to his old self again."

The doctor's jaw had dropped. "Surely you can't be comparing this to putting a pet down? I mean . . ." Her eyes were the size of dinner plates, and she was on the verge of losing the last of her professionalism. ". . . you're not a dog; you're his wife. I'm sure it won't . . ." She trailed off, then composed herself and continued in a much more sober tone, determined to follow the established routine for delivering a death sentence. "OK, Maria. Tell me about your living situation. Do you live in a care home, or are you still living independently? With home help, perhaps?"

Máriddja's heart skipped a beat. She could taste hay, and when she next spoke her words were curt and rapid:

"No, none of that. We don't like having strangers poking about the place. We're doing just fine on our own. Damn well, actually. Never needed help with anything. We're not the least bit confused or sickly, neither of us," she informed the doctor, forgetting what she had just been told about her own state of health.

Skruvlenius cleared her throat, then pressed her index finger to her forehead in a contemplative manner.

"I still think we should keep in touch, Maria, just to see how things go. Like I said, there are many ways we can help – even if the outcome is inevitable," she said, gently but clearly.

"Are we done here, then?" said Máriddja, gracelessly rising from the unergonomic chair. Her knees cracked as she bent down to pick up her woollen hat from the floor and pulled it onto her head.

"Yes, if that's what you like. We've got your contact details, so we'll be in touch again in a few days, once you've had time to process everything."

The doctor held out a hand. Máriddja responded by blowing her nose into the handkerchief the doctor had begun the meeting by giving her – then handed it back. The small, shiny lizards on the redhead's face seemed puzzled, but she quickly came to her senses, took the tissue and said goodbye. Oncologist Runa Skruvlenius watched as the old woman flapped across the linoleum floor, muttering to herself, coat open, like a shabby crow in a headwind. Her body probably wasn't the only thing wrong with her, the doctor thought, lizards slumbering languidly in the glow of a hot flush.

★

Máriddja hurried down the hospital corridors as fast as her crooked little legs would carry her. While making her way to the bus shelter, where the bus was due in forty-five minutes, she dug her ancient mobile phone out of her quilted pocket and tossed it into a bin.

Not a single soul would find out about any of this. There would be no phone calls from the doctor. No, this crap was between Máriddja and her creator.

No one would answer any of the seasick doctor's calls. The phone, which sounded like a bunch of over-enthusiastic mosquitoes whenever it rang, would echo in its musty plastic grave of cigarette butts and empty candy wrappers. Its damn battery would die before Máriddja did.

That was one thing she knew for sure.

Máriddja woke with a whimper that night, her wrinkled cheeks wet and tender. Biera had turned to face her, and his heavy hand was resting on her waist.

"You were dreaming." Her lawfully wedded husband studied her with a solemn look on his face, like a Catholic priest who had just received a particularly difficult confession. "About him, I think . . ."

Máriddja's breathing was still heavy, and she put her all into calming it down.

There was nothing to say, so she simply gazed into his eyes, her soul laid bare. She squeezed his aging hand, and Biera gently gripped hers back.

"I miss him too." His voice was as dark as the dawn.

They lay quietly beneath the covers, face to face, both thinking about the child-sized gap between. Máriddja thought about how his hot little foot should be pressed to her palm – though that foot would be much bigger now, and would neither fit in her hand nor offer an especially comfortable sleeping position. It also assumed he would still sleep in their bed, which he wouldn't. Of course he wouldn't. By now, he'd be a grown man. With a beard, a mortgage, probably wearing a uniform he put on to go to work. He'd always liked to play with toy fire trucks and police cars. Maybe he even had a family of his own. Who knew. Not Máriddja, that's for sure. No, if anything he would be sleeping on the storage bench in the kitchen. It was probably a bit on the short side, but Máriddja would have tucked a cushion beneath his calves to stop the blood from getting cut off as they hung over the edge. Given him thick socks, too. If he had no choice but to sleep with his feet hanging out of bed all night, she would have made sure they were warm at the very least. Cold feet as a child meant aches and pains once you got old, everyone knew that.

"It went well with the doc today, like you said, didn't it?" Biera sounded like he was already half asleep again.

Máriddja squinted at his face and then pretended to yawn. She gave him a reassuring pat on the back of his hand.

"It was fine, just fine. I'm fit as a fritter, don't you worry!"

She kissed his thumbnail and then turned away from him to prevent him from seeing what was hiding in her eyes. Her husband's hand was still resting on her waist as he drifted off to sleep, making old man sounds and breathing heavily between trembling lips.

Biera Rijá was now sleeping like a baby, and his wife found that both reassuring and alarming.

As she turned her pillow over and her own breathing deepened, she could have sworn she felt Heaika-Joná's downy little head against her lips. That she could smell him.

Máriddja breathed him in like an animal sniffing the scent of her sleeping young. She let her thoughts become air: carbon dioxide and aching quiet.

2

Biera's Missing Knife and Máriddja's Missing Marbles

They lived some distance from town, on a mountain that rose to a considerable height above sea level. Along the crooked little road that ran through the hillside hamlet of Sarvesoajvve, a handful of cabins and cottages were dotted among the equally crooked birch trees and aging spruces. You could see all the way to Guovddo, the only built-up area in the region, and in winter the lights on the slalom slope looked like strings of Christmas lights.

This was where Biera and Máriddja Rijá owned a house. It wasn't much to look at – small, with a couple of outbuildings – but they did at least have a functioning bathroom and a satellite dish. The wooden panelling could probably have done with a lick or two of paint, particularly on the south-facing wall, but the Rijás found that kind of thing trivial, bordering on unnecessary. The driveway could also have done with a few more spadefuls of gravel – but again, that wasn't something that concerned them. Their home was, and always had been, good enough as it was.

No, the somewhat dilapidated state of the house wasn't worth worrying about. It was something else entirely that was on Biera's mind.

He was on his knees by the firewood box, using the wing of a wood grouse to sweep the ash and hay dust from the hearth plate. Biera's fingers were crooked and aching today, which usually meant a change in the weather was coming – though the thermometer on the other side of the glass was barely visible for all the snow that had drifted up against the window. In the sky above, the daylight had failed to break through yet again. Nothing but the dull reflection of the clouds on the snow. Glittering softly on the dry snowflakes, infecting everything with its pale gloom. The mercury in the thermometer agreed; it was bitingly cold.

Using the strap wound around the feathers, Biera clumsily hung the wing on a nail. It twisted a few times in the heat from the stove, feathers catching the light. As was custom, he had taken the bird's wing for use as a brush, especially around the stove, but it was starting to look a little the worse for wear. He would have to shoot another young grouse that winter. The fire crackled behind the hatch, and he glanced over to his wife, who was sitting beside the shrill old radio on the kitchen counter, doing the musical crossword. He swept the dirt into the shovel and carried it over the rag rug to the bin beneath the counter. Máriddja absent-mindedly moved her sock-clad foot, which was bobbing in time with the music, to make room for him. She looked so happy where she sat perched on her chair, like a little crow on a nice branch.

Biera's mood was the polar opposite of his wife's, and that was largely down to the fact that he couldn't find his knife. It was practically an extension of his body, always within reach on his belt, and he felt oddly naked without it, stunted without its weight against his left hip. He reached for it several times a day, to gut fish, butter bread or any anything else a good knife could do. Biera had made it himself, and he knew its shape and form like the back of his hand. He always pushed it back into its leather sheath without even thinking, and he simply couldn't work out where it could have gone. The whole thing was incredibly strange, even a little unsettling. Yes, its absence bothered him – but that wasn't the only thing chipping away at his peace of mind, leaving an ever-growing pile of wood shavings.

Biera glanced back over to Máriddja, who was holding a pencil to paper as though she were deep in thought. She had a woollen hat on her head like always, and her two plaits meandered down her back like a couple of frozen winter streams. She was wearing a flannel shirt and a skirt, plus an apron that looked like it might have been used to wipe the floor. He had asked her if she knew where the knife was earlier, and she had absent-mindedly replied that it was on the *Norrbottens-Kurir* newspaper beside the dried meat. Which was odd, thought Biera, because they both knew that the smoked meat was hanging on its hook in the shed like it always did, and that the only newspaper they subscribed to was the *Norrländska Socialdemokraten*. Máriddja had got a funny look on her face when he pointed that out, and then she had started talking about his tatty gloves.

There was a chance the *háldi* could have taken it, of course, Biera mused. They did that kind of thing from time to time. Nothing to get worked up over. If he knew them, it would turn up again before long.

"Go on and borrow it, but I'll need it back soon," he mumbled, just to be on the safe side. So softly that his lips barely moved as he pushed his foot into his boot. But the truth was that he was far from sure the underground creatures had taken his knife – nor what was really going on with his wife. Because Máriddja *had* been different lately. Brooding and . . . strange. Biera couldn't think of a better word for it. Máriddja had been acting strangely of late. She kept talking about the past, even the parts of it they never usually mentioned. The hidden, painful bits. She had brought up all that business that had gone practically unmentioned for years, too – several times. Biera whispered the syllables to himself. He felt the spirit of the boy stir inside him, and his old heart whispered the first few notes of the *joik* he had sung so many times before. He then rubbed his forehead with his rough, sinewy hand and pulled on his hat.

"I'm going out."

The cold air was like a haze around him on the porch, and Biera thought back to Máriddja's visit to the hospital a few weeks earlier. She'd claimed it had been just for a check-up, but could it have been for something more serious? The icy January wind sank its sharp teeth into him, inside and out. No, she really wasn't her usual self. Biera shivered. Imagine if it was one of those dementia doctors she'd been to see.

Hearrá don áiga, she wasn't about to go back into childhood, was she?

3
The End

Lines of ink instruct command
Fettered families fettered land
Royal seal seared like a brand
Tumbled from a furrowed hand

Every time Kaj had visited his mother over the past year, he had been hoping she would die. That wasn't something he was ashamed of. In fact, his mother seemed to understand it, to want to grant his wish, because she rounded off every visit with an apologetic sigh through her nose. As though she was saying: *Sorry, not this time either.* And the proverbial fat lady had pursed her lips and refused to sing, again and again.

It wasn't that Kaj wanted to see his mother suffer. On the contrary, he wanted her path towards the departure that all seriously ill people probably hope for, deep down, to be as peaceful and painless as possible.

And he had been genuinely anxious to make things better for her, too. He played soothing tunes about sparrows' eyes, about women who wanted to throw open their windows, and about how heaven is around the corner, whenever he sensed her life flame was flickering. He held her hand and mumbled comforting words – both for her benefit and his own.

But then he always heard the same resigned sigh from her sickbed, and he gave her a kiss goodbye on her grey head. He packed up his book, his half-eaten bag of candies and his phone charger, and as intensely as he had just been urging his mother over to the other side, he now prayed that she would hold on a little longer. Until the next time he visited. Because it wasn't just a question of nobly hoping for a loved one's suffering to end. He was fully aware of that.

No, Kaj wanted to be there at the end. He needed to be there.

And so, day in and day out, he trudged up to her hospital room in Borlänge with his tote bag from the library. It wasn't much of an inconvenience. Since he was a doctor at the same hospital, he had no real excuse not to see her. Kaj visited her during his breaks, after work, sometimes even with his lunch from the cafeteria. He sat in the armchair by the window, faded curtains framing the view, and gazed out at his old high school on the other side of the road. Waiting, drawing up a wordless balance sheet. Over the summer the street outside had offered up dog walkers in raincoats, leading small spaniels with sad eyes; blustery days that made the flags flutter outside the petrol station, like young boys' ears being tugged by the instructive hand of a stiff breeze. And every day, he took careful note of the lives that were going on outside. The backdrop, the very last one, to a life that included his mother.

As he was sitting in the window one afternoon in August, Kaj became the unwilling witness of a middle-aged man, wearing nothing but a towel beneath his rounded belly, running by and jumping into a cab. With his long limbs, the man looked like an overgrown daddy long legs, and his tight grip on the towel – with liver spotted hands, no doubt – was almost certainly all that prevented a flashing scandal.

Watching the spectacle, Kaj felt a rush of gratitude towards the poor taxi driver. He had zero desire to see any more of the man's pale flesh than he already had. What could have caused his sudden sprint? It couldn't be anything good, that was for sure.

No, he didn't feel any sympathy for the wearer of the thick gold chain, thudding against a hairless chest. Dirty old bloke, Kaj concluded glumly, picking up the book he had open in his lap: a slim volume of poetry by a local writer that his partner Mimmi had given his mother for Christmas.

He continued where he had left off, picking up on the word where he had paused, straightening out the verses and letting them hang in the air like delicate little baubles on a Christmas tree. All to make his sleeping mother happy. Kaj was relieved she didn't die that afternoon. She deserved more than to stop breathing on the same day a half-naked man who was up to no good could lay claim to even a single nanoparticle of the same air.

His brother Gustav, seven years his junior, spent almost as much time in the worn armchair by the window. They took it in turns, like roving drone bees in a hive.

In the end, she died during one of Kaj's shifts. Though he very nearly missed her departure from her earthly resting place. He was in the bathroom at the time, attempting to rinse off the orange juice he had, as usual, spilt on the neck of his sweater. It was doomed to fail, of course – who could wash something from their collar without first taking off the garment in question? Only someone working in a circus, thought Kaj. No, a cat. He stopped dabbing at his upper body when he heard a sound from between the sturdy metal railings and starched hospital sheets: the clearing of a throat.

Like rugged peaks under a thin layer of snow, his mother's cheekbones protruded from beneath her pale, wrinkled skin.

Her hair was thick and heavy on the pillow, her teeth peeping out from beneath her half-open lips. She was a handsome woman. Even in that moment, when it no longer mattered, she was elegant. Her hands, whose nails he had painted only the day before, were resting gracefully on her chest, as though she were about to fill her lungs. Kaj half expected to see her exhale, hands moving down her torso in a yogic manner, demonstrating how to optimize one's oxygen intake. But she didn't, even though she was still breathing. Unevenly, shallowly, the air was still seeping out of her.

Kaj pulled the chair closer and sat down beside the magnificent woman. She should have been slumped low in bed, but instead – true to habit – she seemed to be floating above, *on top* of all the things that might weigh the average person down. Gravity had never quite managed to work its magic on his mother's cool sense of aloofness. Her footsteps had always been snowflakes on warm rocks, her restrained movements carrying her through life with an almost dancelike elegance – like a fairy.

Unfathomable, untouchable.

Her red glasses were folded on the bedside table, and Kaj felt a sudden urge to put them on, to view the world through the same prescription as the woman who had given birth to him. He wanted to see through her eyes. He wanted to see *her*, to meet her for the very first time now that it was their very last chance.

Instead he stroked the blanket covering her body – completely free of creases, of course.

"Do you want me to call a nurse? Or Gustav?" he asked in a voice made of rust.

His mother closed her eyes for a moment and then gave a slow shake of the head. Her breathing was strained and uneven, but she didn't seem to be in any pain. Kaj tried to meet her eye, and found it waiting for him: pale brown, like a cup of milky Earl Grey.

Between them were layer upon layer of silence and secrets. Mother and son gazed at each other, and she did him the honor of not looking away. For once. She cracked open the door to everything that was hidden inside, just enough for him to make out something stirring behind the facade of distance. Resting against the pillow, her thin neck seemed swanlike, so swanlike in that moment that the pillow suddenly resembled rippled water.

"This is the end, Kaj," she whispered, as though she was pointing out that the credits for a pleasant, if unremarkable, film had just started to roll. Her amber gaze seemed to be thawing as the curtain of her lashes rose and fell.

Nothing, that was what he said. His mind was racing, everything he had decided to say and ask tumbling around in his head like a couple of playful fox cubs. He swallowed. His mother's fingers crept slowly across the blanket towards him, and he took them in his hands. Her nails may have been cold and hard against his fingertips, but her wedding ring was solid and warm. He stroked it with his thumb and felt his own pulse sting and throb.

All this waiting, and still he wasn't ready. He thirsted for something from her, desperately needed to hear her say something before she left – before the mother's hand that had never offered a completely steady grip let go of his sticky child's hand for good. But right there and then, with his last ever chance within reach, gazing peacefully at him . . . he just couldn't do it. His lips were dry, like something that had been left lying in the sun for so long that it had lost all elasticity.

He felt, rather than saw, the swan in his mother's soul steeling itself for the effort of kicking off and trying to get some air under its wings. He gripped her hand again and shifted in his chair.

"Mum," he said softly.

With every blink, another layer fell away. One by one they disappeared, the membranes that had separated them for so long, in time with death's creeping footsteps through the room. Her irises became crystal clear, and she looked up at him, her gaze direct and close, and started to talk.

Her words were low and melodic, her voice gentle. It broke through all of Kaj's defenses, spilling from her lips with a naturalness and an intimacy he had never heard from her before. And it wasn't just the language that was so new to him; she also spoke so quietly, with a completely different nuance and tone. Sitting with his cheek to her mouth so that he could hear every word she said, he couldn't help but feel astonished. His mother had never spoken to him like this, and it felt completely alien – yet oddly familiar. He didn't even notice that she had stopped speaking, not until his ear grew cold. When he pulled back he saw that she had closed her eyes, sailed away with beads of water glittering on her wingtips.

It was Kaj, rather than his younger brother, who got to be there for the end. There was a justice in that, even though his heart felt as tender as a bruise when he picked up the phone to make The Call.

Gustav had got his beginning, but the end belonged to Kaj.

Two weeks later, wearing not nearly enough layers, the brothers stood shivering in the cemetery as Laura's coffin was lowered into the gaping hole in the ground. Gustav's daughter sang *Day by Day,* her bright, innocent voice floating through the air for a moment or two, and Gustav gripped the flowers he had brought in the way a jaw might clench around something that shouldn't be said.

All around them, the headstones stood as monuments to people's lives and deaths. Their hopes and dreams, their hard work and graft, summarized in a few short lines carved into stone. A quiet collection of silent mourners, of granite.

Kaj's scarf was itchy, and he did up the zip on his coat. His sister-in-law rubbed her eyes with her palms.

He looked down at the headstone where his mother's life had been reduced to a handful of letters and numbers. It was beside his father's, which had already been weathered by the elements. Her remains would be laid to rest beneath the weight of the granite.

In the sadness of that moment, Kaj found himself wondering whether his mother would be at peace now.

His eyes stung, and he asked himself whether his mother would actually remain in the ground, or whether she would continue to hover above it the way she always had in life.

He pushed his shoulder-length hair back from his face and took in the small group that had gathered: sad toy soldiers standing in ragged formation around his mother's final resting place. It wasn't that there weren't enough of them – the funeral had been confined to immediate family only, in line with her wishes. No, it was something else that was niggling away at him, something other than the fact that she was no longer around, and it *hurt* so damn much.

He reached into his pocket and found a forgotten apple core wrapped in tissue. With some care, he dug out a pip from the exposed heart of the fruit and threw it onto the lid of the coffin. The priest gave him a confused look, and Gustav raised an eyebrow, but the gesture brought something to Kaj. Was it peace?

4

Contemplation in His Birthday Suit

Kaj felt drained the evening after the funeral, heavy and empty. He was relieved not to be at work, didn't think his mental health was up to taking care of anyone else. As a doctor, he needed to keep his own anxiety in check. He knew that, and could generally manage it, but right now he was more wreck than man. Whenever the grief rained down on him, he found his thoughts swirling into a downward spiral.

He called Mimmi before he got into the shower, and her voice was like a caress down the line.

"How was today?" she asked.

"Yeah, pretty tough," he replied with a tender sigh. "But I also think it was nice."

"Mmm."

"It's good to know she's not suffering any more, if nothing else."

He peeled off a stubborn sock that seemed to be doing its best to become one with his foot.

"I can understand that, Kaj. She was in so much pain towards the end."

"Yeah," he agreed, turning his attention to the next obstinate sock.

"I'm sorry again that I wasn't there, but I—"

"I know, don't worry. It was the only way to get the keys in time, so it was for the best."

Kaj unconsciously rubbed his chest, as though he was trying to massage whichever part of him was aching.

"Yeah, it was just such bad timing, with your mum, the funeral and everything. But our colleagues did a great job with her, didn't they?"

"Definitely. Don't worry about it; tell me about the house instead! Did everything go OK? Is it cold up there?"

"Ha, yup, definitely makes your cheeks sting a bit. But the sun did actually come out for a while earlier, and the house is still just wonderful. I think we'll have to pay someone to clear the driveway for us next winter, though. There's no way we'll be able to keep the yard clear ourselves, not with the amount of snow everyone says they get round here."

"We'll see," said Kaj. "Maybe we can ask the seller once she gets back from Crete. She might know someone with a snowplow."

He was quiet for a moment, his mind sluggish after the emotion of the day, in no fit state to make any great promises about clearing snow. He changed the topic to something less demanding.

"What about Abel? Does he approve of his new kingdom?"

Mimmi laughed. "He hasn't come out of the carrier yet, he's still just lying there, glaring at me, all . . . arrogant. But I'm sure he'll like it once he realizes that this house comes with the opportunity for outdoor activities."

Kaj wondered how their spoiled, slightly overweight city cat would fare with his hardened, and likely much tougher, new neighbors in the far north. Maybe they would have to buy him one of those studded collars to help boost his reputation and give him more street cred. To stop the other cats from messing up his neat white fur. Kaj smiled at the thought and turned his attention back to the call.

"I'm sure . . . When is your first day again? Monday?" he asked.

"Tuesday," Mimmi said.

He could hear running water, which meant she was probably in their little bathroom, and he tried to picture the toilet, to remember whether it was the kind with a button or a handle.

"They haven't given me my login details yet – maybe you could remind them? You're going to be my boss, after all," he said.

"Mmm," Mimmi replied, the tap squeaking in the background. Kaj continued:

"How are you feeling about starting work, then?"

He couldn't remember the toilet, and that bothered him. Maybe it was actually the old-fashioned kind, with a pull chain? God, why hadn't he paid more attention? What else had he missed?

"Yeah, I feel good. A bit nervous." A hint of Mimmi's mother tongue came out in her rolled R, *nerrrvous*. Cute, thought Kaj, not for the first time.

"It'll be great and you'll be amazing. They'll be patting themselves on the back for making such an incredible hire by lunch." He smiled encouragingly – people often said you could hear a smile, even over the phone – and despondently flexed his muscles in the bathroom mirror.

More pancake than beefcake, he thought, trying to remember where he had heard that description before. From someone who had got much too close a look at his upper body, clearly.

Sure enough, he heard Mimmi's smile down the line. "I miss you a little bit," she said in her sing-song accent.

"I miss you too, but I'll be there as soon as the estate is settled and everything else is done."

He turned his back to the mirror and inspected himself over his shoulder.

"Yeah, I know. Hey, don't forget to water my plants! There are some in the office, too."

Kaj wondered whether she meant the entire forest of vegetation on the windowsill, or whether it would be OK just to splash a bit of water onto the pots he could reach from the doorway. He decided not to ask, pleased with his narrow approach to the task at hand.

"Got it. Listen, I'm going to jump in the shower. Speak tomorrow."

They hung up, and he got into the shower and turned the hot water up high. He needed to feel it burn to wash the misery out of him.

Kaj thought about Mimmi, all alone in the new house he had only seen once, during the viewing a few weeks earlier. He wondered whether she would remember to bleed the radiators in the living room. They had started spluttering like cholera patients when Kaj gave in to the urge to turn a knob as the estate agent showed them around. Mimmi had shot him a look that made him turn it back in panic, but that had only made the radiator wheeze instead. It sounded like its illness had taken a turn for the worse, like it was gasping for breath in an oxygen mask.

Kaj was looking forward to his new life with Mimmi, the woman who could rein in his bad habits, including his inability to let things lie, with a single glance. She was strong and straightforward, and the way she said his name, as though it were a Finnish love poem . . . Well, maybe not. A declaration of love in Mimmi's mother tongue had a tendency to sound like a death threat. Still, of all the things he loved about her, her Finnish accent was right up there. It made him feel all soft and fuzzy inside.

His mother had had an uncanny ability to mimic the way Mimmi said her own name, pleasingly melodic and with warm, weighty consonants. She would grin mischievously as she let it bounce between the walls whenever she greeted them in the hallway at home. She had liked Mimmi, liked both her sons' partners. Embraced them both as part of the family, and enthusiastically welcomed the two grandchildren his little brother and his childhood sweetheart, Evelin, had gifted upon the world.

Mum.

He allowed his to mind wander, enveloped in a cloud of steam, soap and melancholy.

5

The Phone Machine Device

The wretched knife still hadn't reappeared when, a few days later, Biera heard muttering from the bedroom. It sounded like a lemming grappling with a boot – or something else a lemming might disapprove of.

"Useless piece of junk!"

Máriddja repeatedly jabbed a finger at the object in her hand. A cat that had just been served a bowl of spinach would probably have looked more enthusiastic than his wife did right then.

"Smart? You could have fooled me. I've never come across a more brainless lump of rubbish in my life. Pff, let's see, if I . . ."

Biera hurried over to help with a: "Hmm?"

Máriddja got such a fright that she almost dropped the pricey little gizmo.

"Who are you talking to?" her spouse asked.

"This phone thingy! It doesn't work!" Máriddja snapped, pointing an accusing finger at the object on the bed.

"You shouting at it's not going to help," the old man snorted, picking it up from the checked blanket. He sat down and tried pressing the screen with a grubby finger. It lit up obligingly, and Biera didn't even attempt to hide his sense of triumph.

"There, you see! It does work!"

"But they forgot to send the buttons with it," Máriddja sulked. "I told you to buy a phone, not one of these infernal contraptions, these . . . *amás masjijnna!*" Her voice had gone up an octave, splitting the air with its shrill affect.

"No, no," Biera mumbled, squinting down at the technology in his hand. "The lad I spoke to said you could ring people on it, so it must be a phone."

Máriddja snorted. "I bet they're all laughing at you down in town, Biera Rijá. You mark my words! That Swedish boy tricked you out of half your pension, for a . . . a . . ." She studied their latest purchase as though she was sizing it up for use in other areas. ". . . it could be handy for scraping the windows."

But Biera was no longer listening. His wife had moved on to less polite language, muttering to herself in Sámi, and she wandered through to the kitchen to show just how unhappy she was by banging the pots and pans. He peered down at the bright screen and decided that its presence in their lives would make everything much more exciting.

Máriddja would thank him once he had worked out how to navigate between Spottyfight, Goggle and all the rest of the exciting, interesting things the salesman had promised. What they would use those dizzying features for didn't matter; it was all so shiny and *new* that Biera felt like an overjoyed magpie who had just filled his nest with treasure for no reason.

"We're going to be good friends, you and me," he whispered, smiling contentedly. Máriddja, sharp-eared as ever, snorted disapprovingly from the next room. They both knew she wasn't angry, not really. She just thought that a good lecture and a few mood swings from time to time helped to shake some life into the pair of old fossils. And she wasn't wrong, Biera was willing to admit that. But she definitely wasn't happy about this purchase of his, either.

★

Máriddja gritted her teeth.

The phone machine device was completely useless, and he'd paid a fortune for it!

It was also wrapped in a case covered in psychedelic mandala patterns that made her go cross-eyed and get lost in existential brooding. She found herself wondering whether they were alone in the universe, how long a piece of string was, and why it was considered cute when a child said what they were thinking, yet when she called the bus driver a damn bloodsucker she was a "troublemaker" and had to "get that damn goat off this bus right this instant."

The incident with the bus driver had occurred several years earlier, after Máriddja asked to see the fare chart. All she had wanted was to prove that there was no mention of tickets for goats, which clearly meant they could travel for free, but that hadn't made the bus driver any more cooperative. Not at all.

The man's attitude had robbed her of the ability to acquire said goat, which had to be returned to the seller. It was an injustice Máriddja wouldn't forget in a hurry, and yet another excellent argument in favor of boycotting the local buses.

Biera sighed contentedly from the bedroom, and Máriddja did the same, with decidedly less commitment. She trusted their expensive new machine and its mysterious uses about as much as she trusted bus drivers lacking any competence when it came to ticket prices.

6

A Changeling and Her Goat

People said it was the underground dwellers who had lured the Skájddes' girl out in the boat that late summer's day all those years ago.

Young Máriddja herself had calmly explained that it was the goat's idea. An entirely different goat to the one she would later try to board a bus with, of course. This particular goat was white.

Who the goat in question blamed remained to be seen, but given that she was the worst sort of turncoat – a creature who would do anything for something to eat – it isn't hard to imagine that her judgmental hoof would have pointed straight at Máriddja. Assuming anyone bothered to ask, that is.

Regardless of where the blame lay, Máriddja and the goat climbed into the little wooden boat and eagerly set off for the other side of the water.

The goat stood in the bow, beard fluttering in the breeze, bleating in time with Máriddja's oar strokes. That was what Ola Råmåk claimed, anyway, though no one gave much weight to what he said – he was a bit of a simpleton. But several others from the tents nearby had heard wicked laughter and strange singing. These supposedly echoed around the foot of the mountain, accompanied by the sound of triumphant bleating, but again: no one took what the Råmåk boy said seriously. Other eyewitnesses were also deemed unreliable, because no one in the area had managed to get a full night's sleep in weeks. The Gávvels' twins had colic, and their screaming was so loud at night that even the mosquitoes were considering permanently relocating.

Whatever the truth, after a worrying number of hours without a single sighting of either Máriddja or her goat, the girl's relatively hardened mother eventually began to feel a bit anxious. With the dog hot on her heels, she went from tent to tent, asking after her daughter. No one she spoke to had seen her – and thankfully, they might have added, though they kept that to themselves, shrugging apologetically instead.

Ibbá could be quite short tempered when it came to less than flattering descriptions of her little girl, which is probably understandable – as was the fact that less than flattering descriptions were often quite tempting when it came to Máriddja. The telling off she had given the merchant from Luleå when he claimed that young Miss Skájdde was about as happy as a cornered pine marten was still fresh in everyone's minds, for example.

A couple of members of her immediate family eventually stepped up to help Ibbá search the area, but Máriddja – and, as they would later discover, the goat – had vanished without a trace. Yet again, someone might have remarked on the girl's origins at this point, speculating that the underground dwellers had simply taken her back, but no one wanted to upset her mother. Nor risk being given a box around the ears.

Still, the fact of the matter was that it was common belief among the men and women of Máriddja's community, her *sijdda*, that the girl was a changeling. Most chose to ignore the fact that, with her broad mouth, she clearly resembled the other Skájddes – especially her old *áhkko*, Sara. The prospect of having a *vitter* child in the community was much more appealing than an ordinary, unruly little brat, so they clung on to their conviction.

Those who claimed to be in the know said that Máriddja's mother had forgotten to put a silver coin in her girl's bed before the priest got round to blessing the baby, and that one of the *vitterfolk* had swapped her own youngster for the beautiful Sámi child. People had long known that such things could happen if you were unlucky.

Whether there was any truth in that or not, the changeling had been missing for hours, and the rest of the *sijdda* eventually went out to help look for the little rascal. She was one of them, after all; Sámi take care of one another, they help one another and they look out for their own. Even the *vitter* children in the community.

Ola Råmåk's uncle was the one who eventually spotted the oars bobbing among the reeds, with no boat anywhere in sight.

It was somewhere around this point that the dismayed whispering began, about the beings who lived on the other side of what ordinary people could see and why they might possibly need a little brat – and a goat.

No one had told Máriddja's mother about the oars, and she was still busy searching among the boulders at the foot of the mountain. But further out, practically on the far side of the water, an eagle-eyed old woman eventually spotted the boat drifting in the oppressive July heat.

Two young men who knew more or less how to swim waded out into the water, each with a throw rope around their shoulders. The one boat in the community wasn't available at that moment, after all, what with the missing duo already having borrowed it.

By the time the boys reached the boat, Máriddja's mother had made it down to the shore. She came running, her *gákti* swinging around her legs like waves. Tense and pale, she saw young Abmut, with a shove in the backside from his friend Nils, clamber up into the boat.

Behind the brave first man, the horrified villagers looked on as something terrible rose up from the depths of the hull. Long, lank hair hung over the face of a creature each of them swore was more grotesque than anything they had ever seen before, and on top of its shaggy head were two long devil's horns. It was a Stállo, the terrible beast they had heard so many stories about, come to eat them all.

Anna Riebme was so startled that the stout old eighty-year-old – a woman who was capable of carrying an entire reindeer on her back after slaughter – collapsed to the ground, eyes rolled back and drooling.

The local children darted beneath their parents' trembling *gáktis* at the sight of the Stállo that had risen from the depths of the lake. Unlike the rest of the community, Abmut was blissfully unaware of the danger at hand, and was busy trying to pull his friend out of the water. As Nils's legs flailed, the little rowing boat swung around so that the side was facing the shore.

Those who dared glance over saw a girl's head pop up in the bow, accompanied by a couple of horns atop a calmly chewing goat. The two adventurers gazed across to the crowd of people on the shore and had the good sense not to wave, either of them.

Once the second exhausted swimmer had been pulled up into the boat, Abmut and Nils managed to throw their ropes over a spruce tree that was drooping like some sort of suicidal giant on the little islet in the middle of the water.

The crowd on the beach cheered, and the two boys' mothers nudged each other in their plump sides, barely managing to hide their proud grins at their sons' bravery and exceptional throwing arms.

The lads pulled the boat towards the little islet with a few firm tugs on the ropes. Several of the older men, keen to enjoy their own slice of glory, boldly waded out into the water to grab the rowing boat and its crew.

The two young heroes nimbly hopped out at the water's edge and helped to drag it ashore, with Máriddja and the goat tumbling around like two drunk sailors inside.

Old Anna Riebme got back onto her feet and spent the rest of her life convinced she had fallen because someone had cast a spell on her.

Safely back on dry land, Máriddja found herself facing tellings off and shaking fists from the rest of the *sijdda*, which had gathered around them. A few people muttered about the oars, which could have drifted off downstream towards the rapids on the strong currents. Others, who caught the murderous look in Ibbá's eye when the fate of the oars was mentioned, instead lamented what might have happened to little Máriddja if they hadn't spotted her in time.

The girl herself didn't say much, the goat even less. She simply took her mother's hand in a display of uncharacteristic tenderness and followed the rest of the community as they set off along the narrow trail.

Máriddja's mother was far from the only one whose legs shook during the walk home that day, and the majority cast anxious glances back over their shoulders to make sure the terrible Stállo from the depths of the lake wasn't following them.

The explanation the girl gave later that evening, when pressed by her mother, once her father was home from his work with the herd, was that the goat had been beside itself with hunger. The hay stuffing that Máriddja had dutifully pulled out of her shoes to feed her was all gone – as was the hay from her parents' shoes, and that which they had hung to dry outside the tent.

And so Máriddja Skájdde, apostle of virtue, had simply decided that she and the goat would find a solution to the problem: she would get into the boat to row over to the other side and pick more sedge. To the far side of the water, where they often did that kind of thing. She did it for the goat, in other words; the hay her parents had collected to keep their feet warm that winter didn't seem to concern her all that much.

In a state of bliss at clearly having died and gone to a heaven full of the most delicious food, the goat had started jumping around in glee. That was when Máriddja accidentally knocked the oars, making them fall out of their locks and bob away across the water.

And when the goat, showing no remorse whatsoever, decided that the best course of action was simply to sleep off its hearty meal, Máriddja had decided that sounded like a good plan. She had curled up beside the shaggy, happily farting goat and dozed off.

The pair had only woken when their heroic rescuers arrived and had then calmly allowed themselves to be brought back to dry land.

Máriddja admitted that it hadn't been the most carefully considered of plans.

The goat admitted that she probably could have turned to a more local source of food, enabling them to avoid getting into the boat in the first place – at risk of suffering even more flatulence as a result of eating shoe bands and rough woollen material.

That was what Ola Råmåk claimed the goat thought, anyway, but as we've already established, he wasn't quite all there.

Máriddja had only just turned five at the time, the goat barely two, but to the horror of the entire *sijdda* it was only the first of their many adventures together.

"That's the trouble with a lax upbringing," Biera would say about his wife's wild temperament years later. Her mother Ibbá had laughed with delight at the provocation, eyes wide.

That was just who Ibbá was. She had been that way since Máriddja was a wild young thing who, like an untrained dog, ran between the tents on all fours, and she was exactly the same as an old woman. She let things lie, taking them for what they were rather than allowing them to weigh on her soul. If the girl wanted to climb trees and leap fully dressed into the cold spring, then she was free to do so. Her clothes would dry.

But woe betide anyone who tried to criticize her daughter for her behaviour. As Ibbá's son-in-law, Biera was an exception to that rule, and Ibbá herself simply sighed and shook her head at the person she had pulled from her own body so long ago. Because Máriddja was crazy, there was no doubt about that.

She had been an enterprising and imaginative child and had been given the freedom to be that way. Máriddja had always said what was on her mind, laughing too loudly and swearing whenever she needed to – all with her parents' permission, if not blessing.

Perhaps it was because they could see a hint of something inevitable in her; a new era in which a person no longer had to bow their head, in which they no longer had to be easy-going and agreeable.

Or maybe that was just who her parents were: peaceful and content with their strong, beautiful girl. Máriddja's childhood had been one long adventure, and it had shaped her into a woman with a wild spirit, paying no mind to the rules and norms of society.

★

Perhaps that was why things turned out the way they did. Perhaps it was God's hand – taking the form of a stubborn bus driver with a bellyache – that had stopped Máriddja in yet another attempt to own a goat many years later. Because with a partner in crime like that, things could have escalated even more – if that was possible.

That was Ola Råmåk's assessment, anyway. Though by that point he was already dead, and no one heard him. Besides, the man was no less dim-witted as a ghost.

7
Roadkill

Just over a week later, a car pulling a trailer backed up onto the driveway outside Kaj and Mimmi's new house. Number eleven was a red split-level building, and they had bagged it for a great price. Mimmi watched from the window as the trailer arrived. She couldn't stand still, so happy to see the little white bug of a car – the rust spots on the white paintwork only reinforced the image of an overgrown ladybird – that she almost felt sick, and she drummed her fingers on the rough surface of the radiator.

Backed up probably wasn't the right term for what the car was doing, because it spent about as much time going forward as back. In the pit of her stomach, her eagerness and impatience began wrestling like a couple of unruly kids as she watched her partner's attempts to pull up outside. From the corner of one eye, she could see a china figurine she hadn't yet unwrapped, mummy-like in its protective plastic shroud, and she moved it away without letting the car out of her sight.

Jesus Christ, could he go any slower around that heap of snow? What was he doing? He just needed to go for it now; he had a clear line of sight and the trailer was at the perfect angle. Mimmi felt the cold draft as she leant forward to get a better view over the window ledge, saw the snow glittering like sequins in whipped cream. There, Kaj! Use the rear-view mirror. Look in the mirror! You're not going to be able to see through the cover on the trailer, no matter how hard you try! She shifted impatiently and managed to bash her ankle on one of the moving boxes. *Älä helvetissä*, had he even bothered adjusting the wing mirrors? They were so high he wouldn't be able to see the wheels on the trailer even if he did glance down at them from time to time! Did she have to go out there and do it for him? Seriously, he'd clipped the heap of snow now. Mimmi clapped a hand to her forehead and ran out onto the porch. The cold air was like a slap to the face, but she was relieved to see that Kaj had stopped trying to force the car over the pile of snow and was now driving normally instead. With a level of caution worthy of a heavily pregnant ewe, he backed up in front of the house. Mimmi's heart tumbled slowly from her throat to its rightful place beneath her ribs, beating hard and rhythmically.

As Kaj got out of the car, she bounded towards him, throwing herself into his arms like an over-excited golden retriever, still in her stockinged feet.

The obvious risk of letting her partner make the long drive north on his own wasn't something Mimmi felt the need to discuss any more. She didn't even need to think about it. He had survived, and fortunately – though it had been far from guaranteed – so had his fellow road users. And now he was here, he was home! With her. She gave him peck after peck on his nose, stroking his loose man bun and kissing him properly. His lips were dry, already tasted of winter.

Kaj laughed and spun her around in the air – a little awkwardly, but with good filmic effect – before putting her down. His girlfriend was at least half a head taller than him, but his arms seemed to have survived the effort. He didn't look like he'd hurt himself, anyway. And she was still in one piece, too.

Kaj noticed her unusually colorful socks – they were strange, like something a three-year-old would wear, covered in cheery Moomins – and he rolled his eyes.

"I take it you haven't noticed how cold it is?" he said. "One glance at your feet and the neighbors will be able to tell we're city people!" His sarcasm was undermined slightly by the joy of reunion that took over his face, radiating from the corners of both his eyes like sunshine.

Mimmi replied with a hearty laugh, picking up Kaj's backpack and grabbing his arm. She felt an urge to open the car door and put it into gear, releasing the handbrake to stop the brakes from freezing, but she decided that could wait. Instead, she stroked Kaj's arm and felt the tension loosen in every muscle in her body.

It had seemed to Kaj that he'd only just driven past the blue sign bearing the name of his new hometown before he was heading out of the community again. After he'd passed the speed limit signs, he made a U-turn and drove back, feeling slightly downhearted. The place really was tiny. Still, his heart rate – which he had been struggling to keep in check during the drive – had settled a little amid the calmer traffic.

Tractors driving back and forth, buckets heaped with snow; houses that looked as if they had been scattered at random, like a handful of dice. There were still fairy lights and garlands on the streetlamps, presumably a leftover from Christmas, and every car he had passed (all four of them) on the main street had enormous extra headlights mounted at the front. He would have to get himself a set of those at a local garage, he had thought. That was probably the kind of thing you needed up here, because it would be incredibly dark at night. But he forgot all about that as he and Mimmi stepped over the threshold into their new home. He paused and filled his lungs with the unfamiliar scents. Drew the crisp, unfamiliar air between his lips and let it loosen his jaw, which had tensed up during the last stretch of the drive.

Mimmi closed the door behind them and watched as Kaj collapsed into the rattan armchair. He slumped into its firm embrace like someone who had just survived a catastrophe, disproportionately relieved to have spotted a familiar face among the crowd. The man had never even liked that armchair, she thought with a wry smile. He'd fought until the last to take it straight to the recycling center rather than their new home. But now it seemed it was good enough after all.

Kaj tugged his hair tie loose, shook his head and pushed his hair back from his forehead. It was cool beneath his hot hands. A sense of expectation began fizzing through him, racing towards his giddy head like champagne bubbles. It could finally begin, it had *already* begun. Everything he had been longing for, to the point where he felt like he was going mad with impatience; it was all finally within reach. This: Mimmi, the house, the future. And the awful fucking drive was over. If it were up to him, he would never get behind the wheel of another car.

Mimmi sat down in his lap without making any effort to lessen or offset her weight, and he loved her for it. She lowered her forehead to his, and they sat like that for a moment or two, mute and blind, in quiet perfection. It felt so good, but Kaj didn't even have the energy to stroke her back in the wake of all his overwhelming emotions.

He was no good at waiting, knew his impatience tended to verge on being unashamedly overwrought. His restlessness, which had buzzed in his ears and left him irritable, had made him a lousy moving guy – and definitely a terrible travel buddy.

If he were honest, the end of their time in the city hadn't really been so bad. It was the waiting, the longing that was worst. The torture of not being where Mimmi was. Kaj hadn't longed to get away, that wasn't it. He had longed to come home. To everything Mimmi represented to him. A calm epicenter; the eye of the storm when everything else was hazy and unclear. Safe, soft and comfortable, and with terrible taste in socks.

Mimmi got up. Strange that it was possible to feel lighter with the weight of someone else in your lap than without. Kaj watched as she tidied away the shoes he had kicked off, gazed around the home that was now theirs.

He debated taking a picture of the jumble of boxes, uploading it to social media with some sort of quick, witty caption. But why? All those miles behind the wheel had drained his capacity, eaten up every last particle of productive power at the same rate that the fuel gauge ticked lower. There were no intelligent thoughts left in there, not a single word that could be polished into something smart or enlightening. It felt so damn good just to sprawl in the chair, catching his breath like a regular animal.

He hadn't mentioned the squirrel – may it rest in peace – that his bumper had taken out just a few dozen miles from his final destination, but that was a good description of how he felt after the drive: like a flattened squirrel on the E45. Roadkill. A happily departed squirrel, in a heaven without any foxes or competition for nuts, lounging on a soft bed of moss. But dead as a dodo all the same.

Abel, Kaj noticed, was curled up on one of the seat cushions, emphatically ignoring the new arrival. As the long-lost father figure, Kaj would simply have to take his punishment for his absence – being treated as though he didn't exist, a barely noticeable gust of air between the cat's whiskers – until further notice. And judging by the subtle look of disgust on Abel's face, Kaj was an unpleasant gust of air at that. But that was OK. Kaj barely had the energy to follow Mimmi's movements; in his current state, he would have made a lousy belly scratcher anyway.

8

Packing and Unpacking

Gustav and Kaj had raced through all their legal obligations, quickly and amicably dividing up their mother's estate as they emptied their childhood home. It had already been sold, to a small business owner from Dalarna. The name of the company – Älvdalen Animal Showers – had come up during a Skype call with the buyer. Kaj and Gustav had been forced to fake a dropped connection in order to laugh and speculate about what services the business might offer. Cow-sized shower cubicles? Washing incontinent dogs? Or maybe, and this was Kaj's personal favorite: specialist raincoats for four-legged friends? Who knows, maybe the company was the official outfitter of Princess Victoria's beloved pooch. Breathable, Dalarna-made rainwear for a blue blooded cavapoo with moist dermatitis? It sounded plausible enough. The brothers agreed that anything was possible, then called the buyer again to complete the deal and get back to the deeply prosaic – and difficult – task at hand.

The laughter they had shared felt like breaking the surface for a moment before diving down again into murky depths. They were like two seasoned archaeologists at a dig site they felt no real enthusiasm or eagerness to explore, yet both had been surprised by their emotions and the joy they uncovered once they eventually started digging.

Their father's collection of teak cranes and knife rests shaped like dachshunds had been nothing but embarrassing when they were younger, especially when Hans insisted on showing them off to their friends. But as they took them out of the china cabinet now, each one covered in a thin layer of dust, the reunion was warm and tender.

Gustav kept the little dachshunds for his daughter; she could add them to the vast collection of plastic junk and small glass frogs in her room. Their old man would have loved that.

Kaj surprised himself by deciding to take the entire flock of wooden cranes. They would look right at home on the mantelpiece in his new living room, alongside the geometric fifties wallpaper. They would be happy there, with their pretty, delicate necks and their soft lines, basking in the glow of the fire. Kaj could just picture it.

He imagined they might help him conjure up the musty scent of his father's pipe, his constant humming of Frank Sinatra, an army of comforting memories and stability against all the unfamiliarity of his new home.

So much of what they found was familiar, yet it felt alien in their own hands. Her mother-of-pearl hairbrush and matching mirror from the dressing table, his neatly stacked packs of tissues in the bedside table. Her half-empty bottle of fancy soap, his wedding suit in a protective bag with sprigs of lavender at the bottom. Special and mundane, high and low. Each of their parents' habits, known and unknown; their neat facades and their worn-out nail clippers. All of it.

It was a strange feeling, almost like they were doing something illicit by cracking open the door to their parents' most private moments.

Kaj felt a near constant ache in his chest, but that didn't stop him from growing restless at the occasionally monotonous work. Going through the eighth file of receipts in his father's office, for example. What made a person save the receipt for a box of nails or a carton of rosehip soup for decades on end?

There were times when Kaj just wanted to leave everything where it was, untouched in its cupboards and drawers, behind the magnets on the refrigerator door. He didn't want to move a single thing from the place it would always reside in his memories of childhood, both happy and those that had been wounds, forming scar tissue.

Because the truth was that the absence of fresh coffee in the kitchen, the lack of background noise from the radio and their parents' low chatter: it cut through the brothers' often silent work. Deeply familiar, choreographed scenes from life when their mother and father were both still alive, liberated of all chronology, were performed by shadow figures from their childhood. Among the personal items and everyday objects, props, Kaj could hear his father's voice. *Are you finished with the culture section? Could you turn off the fan for me, Laura?* All so clear and so close. The pear popsicles in the freezer compartment and the flapping flag visible from the bathroom window when he brushed his teeth.

But the same wasn't true of their mother. Never her entire being, and never just her. She remained elusive. So different from when she was still alive, filling every room with her presence, thought Kaj, tearing off a long strip of tape and roughly sealing the lid of a box full of candles and reed diffusers. The sense of loss and rootlessness pecked at him like vultures on a carcass.

In the evenings they shared a few beers at the kitchen table, and he and Gustav talked about life in the broadest and narrowest of senses. Rounding off the day this way was wonderfully relaxing; no thoughts being interrupted by the shouts of young children, in Gustav's case, and no energy left to get worked up or start brooding in Kaj's.

They grew nostalgic, of course, in fits and starts. Their bodies ached from the physically demanding work, arms shaking from hauling everything that was going to the junkyard out to the trailer. Guilt weighing them down with every load they threw away. The beers didn't help to loosen their muscles or the knots of grief in their guts, but they did soothe their tight throats, enabling the brothers to say things that had never been said between those four walls.

"Dad was always so fucking patient, wasn't he. Do you remember how he used to play Lego with us?" asked Gustav. Kaj replied with a musing of his own, as though he hadn't heard his brother: "I wonder if Mom knew how much I missed her when she turned out the light and closed my bedroom door."

They went to sleep early – or went *to bed* early, in any case – each in his old boyhood room. Kaj had no idea whether Gustav was managing to get much sleep. He wouldn't have been able to say whether he was even doing so himself. When morning came round, they got straight back to work.

It was time for them to deal with their mother's things. Her books, her art, her materials, her curiosities; everything her hands had made, everything that had formed her being, her *life* . . . Things that, for Kaj, represented the gateway to her very soul. Being among her half-finished projects, still waiting for her finishing touches, he had felt close to her. Understood his mother. The brothers had saved her studio until last. They had made a decision, as unspoken as it was self-evident, to put off dealing with everything she had accumulated over the years for as long as they could.

But to their great surprise, their mother had already done most of the work for them, especially when it came to her private art collection.

She had divided everything up and packed it away, neatly writing her sons' names on the various boxes. Exactly when she had found the time to do so was a mystery, but it certainly made their job easier. Kaj and Gustav carried their allotted boxes and crates through to their rooms without examining the contents. Her sorting and clearing meant they could put off at least one of their tasks, and that left them feeling more relieved than they had during the entire process so far. In his heart of hearts, Kaj hoped that the things he had inherited from his mother would be objects that reminded him of their best moments together, in her little studio. He wasn't sure he would be able to handle taking any memories of her many locked rooms to his new home in Guovddo.

All that was left for the brothers to do was shake their heads, drain the last of the beer from their bottles and drag themselves up to bed.

Perhaps they would drift off to sleep feeling satisfied with their work that day. Perhaps they would toss and turn surrounded by bare walls and stacks of boxes, thinking about what would happen next, once they had drawn a line under the chapter called "When We Had Parents" and it was time to start the next.

Kaj was confident that Gustav would manage the next part of his story without any real trouble, that he would overcome any minor bumps in the road without panicking or breaking a sweat. Maybe he would use common sense and logic to build himself a sturdy little bridge that could carry his family over any rough patches, and then he could stop to admire the view from his high vantage point.

But in his own next chapter, Kaj couldn't shake the idea that he would cobble together a leaky hot air balloon and crash land, terrified, filthy and alone, with no one to hold his hand as he died. Or something like that.

His little brother's ingrained sense of security made Kaj's inner demons feel dark and overwhelming in comparison.

Where Gustav had certainty, Kaj had almost nothing but questions. Gustav's weary mind touched upon the subject before he drifted off into a deep, exhausted sleep. Sweaty and restless between the sheets, he thought about his big brother and asked himself: What the hell would happen to Kaj now?

While the two boys imagined futures that might or might not await them, another plan had already been set in motion. In one of the boxes labelled neatly with the word "Kaj," his mother had placed a group of carefully wrapped objects side by side, like a crisp new set of jigsaw pieces. The items slumbered quietly in the brothers' childhood home that night, the last of their old lives. And in that same box, on their first morning in their new home, they began to stir.

9

A Third Party

She asked the question during a brief respite from the sound of tape being ripped from cardboard and the rustling of packing paper and trash bags. Outside, dusk had already begun to smooth out the creases in the light, buttoning it safely inside its dark woollen coat.

They were drinking sharp white wine and listening to reggae on Kaj's phone, its tinny speakers butchering every soft backbeat.

"Huh?" said Kaj, pulling his upper body out of a box of kitchen items. He was holding a kettle.

"I asked whether we should maybe get married," Mimmi repeated.

The thick white cable swung in the air as he straightened up, eyes wide. He looked almost comically startled, like a child caught red-handed beside a broken window, slingshot in hand. Mimmi laughed. Kaj then grinned and, in three long steps, crossed the floor awash with plastic bags and discarded packing materials to wrap his arms around her.

"Christ, Mimmi," he muttered into her thick hair. "I thought you'd never ask . . ."

The thought had crossed Kaj's mind before, it had crossed his mind many times, but it had never become anything other than a hint of a wish, a direction lacking any real intent. Of course he wanted to, but *should* he? Was he really worthy of a blessing of that kind?

His recent emotional and physical turmoil had also got in the way of any declarations of intent. Obviously, he wanted to spend the rest of his days with Mimmi, for better or worse – that was the only conceivable option for Kaj – but he would also never be presumptuous enough to ask something like that of her. The life they had planned together was one thing, steps in a dance that wasn't hard to predict once you had nailed the first few; it was virtually automatic. But bringing Mimmi's attention to the pattern their feet were taking, asking her to pick him, that was another matter entirely. Kaj had always worried that those words would cause her to wake from her trance, opening her eyes to the sleepy, habitual rhythm they had created for themselves, and realize what she had done.

But he would say yes now that *she* had asked the question, of course he would; he was wild about Mimmi. And now that she had taken the initiative, he was hardly going to do anything other than accept, even though he knew he should stop her. Wake her up and turn her down, precisely because he loved her so much.

The glass of cola on the windowsill was illuminated by nothing but the street lights and a small table lamp as Mimmi crossed between Kaj's many bags to reach it. The lamp's embroidered shade diffused its glow, giving the room the aura of a porn studio. They hadn't got round to putting up any more suitable lighting yet, but they would do it over the next week, she promised herself.

This would be a light, bright house, a place where they ate breakfast, fell asleep and vacuumed together every day – at least if it was up to her. If they fell out, one of them (Kaj) would sleep on the uncomfortable retro sofa, its fabric so prickly that a film evening on it felt like some sort of terrible acupuncture session. But then they would make up again, they would cook something together or read in the armchairs, toes touching across the Persian rug. They would have a shared bed and a shared home.

They would also have a cactus-green sofa that was about as comfortable as the color suggested, and all because Kaj had looked at her like she'd just proposed wringing a puppy's neck when she diplomatically suggested throwing the wretched thing away. Mimmi would never admit it, but she had been longing for his things in the new house. His strange little secondhand finds; his wardrobe, which smelt like cardamom and mothballs. Even the damn sofa. It looked good, if nothing else.

She had also longed for Kaj, of course. Her *fiancé*. He wasn't hard to love.

If she were really honest, Mimmi had had to make a bit more of an effort when it came to liking his mother. Laura was a difficult woman. So shut-off and distant at times, so distracted that it made you wonder where her mind was. Laura had always been polite and warm, but Mimmi still felt like she might need to pull her hand back to avoid being scratched – or to avoid doing the scratching herself.

Despite all that, the two had developed a decent enough relationship over the past half-dozen years. Not close, exactly, but she had come to feel a good deal of warmth for the woman who had brought her partner into the world. Towards the end of her life, Laura had been admitted to the hospital where Mimmi and Kaj worked, and she had gone to see her regularly. They hadn't got into any particularly deep or meaningful conversations; they mostly just watched repeats of *The Bold and the Beautiful* together, with Mimmi sitting uncomfortably in the visitor's chair and Laura tucked up in bed. Both knew better than to open Pandora's box and air their views on whether Taylor or Brooke was best suited to the polyamorous Ridge. In fact, they had once fallen out so badly over that very subject that Kaj had had to buy Laura a bottle of liqueur and pretend it was from Mimmi in order to restore the peace.

The very last time she saw Laura, Mimmi had had something she wanted to get off her chest. During the ad break, she spoke up. "There's something I'd like to tell you. A good thing, I think."

The woman in the bed had waited for her to go on with a watchful glint in her eye. She looked like she was expecting Mimmi to say that she was dragging her son off to the south coast to live in some kinky collective.

"I've . . . been thinking about proposing to Kaj."

The two women sat quietly for a moment. Mimmi studied Laura's thin face and felt a sense of relief – on par with finding a brilliantly clean toilet when her bladder was full to bursting – when Laura's full lips curled into a smile.

"Thank goodness for that!"

"So . . . so you think it's a good idea?"

Best to double-check that Kaj's mother really understood the full weight of her intentions. Should she record their conversation, maybe even call for a nurse to come in and witness this moment in case Laura later denied all knowledge of it? Though why on earth would she do that, Mimmi thought, feeling ridiculous.

Kaj's mother nodded, a slightly ambiguous smile on her lips.

"And now you've said what you wanted to say, it's my turn."

During the brief coughing fit that followed, Laura's future daughter-in-law managed to grow anxious. Mimmi had half expected some sort of request, something along the lines of

Laura's blessing being contingent on the inclusion of her collection of stuffed birds. To keep their beady glass eyes on them and their sex life from a spot in the very heart of the home. Anything but that . . . . . .

"About children," said Laura.

Oh Christ, this is even worse than the birds, Mimmi thought in a mild state of panic. *I'll take the birds, I'll take the damn birds!*

"You'll be a wonderful mother to the grandchildren I'll never meet," Laura said softly. "I haven't always been . . . but I hope that Kaj and Gustav know that I did my best. Despite everything."

Mimmi listened quietly with her hands in her lap.

Laura cleared her throat, steeling herself, and then went on: "Tell your children, if you have any, that . . . their granny meant well. And tell him, tell Kaj, that there was always love. He never went without, not even when I wasn't around."

If Mimmi was surprised by her future mother-in-law's words, she didn't show it. She intuitively knew that the circumstances didn't leave room for questions, so she simply stroked Laura's hair and said:

"I promise. Now get some sleep, my friend."

Laura's gaze had been as warm and bright as the setting sun in September.

She and Kaj were now engaged, and Laura had drifted off to sleep, never to wake again. Mimmi suspected that Kaj, who was much more romantically minded than her, would have opted for a more rose-tinted proposal – assuming he ever decided to pop the question, that is. She was only too happy to admit that all that stuff wasn't really her thing. And in the long run, she reasoned, it was precisely that strong-willed woman he would have to live with. May as well start their marriage in the same vein she had every intention of going on for the rest of their lives. She knew what she wanted, and what she wanted was Kaj, not a load of romantic nonsense and harp-filled fairy tales. No, as things stood Mimmi preferred to pass on all that, but he would have the rest of his life to try to convince her otherwise, so she didn't feel too guilty about having hijacked the big moment.

"You've really done it now, missy . . . Are you sure you want to spend your life with this wreck of a man?" Kaj tried to mask the seriousness of his question with a self-deprecating smile as he cut their takeout pizza.

Abel took that opportunity to hook a paw across the table and help himself to his rightful share of pizza – all without spilling a single drop of tomato sauce.

That cat has *skills*, Mimmi admitted to herself.

"Yeah." She shrugged nonchalantly. "I guess I'll take pity on you." Her pale eyes glittered, the corners of her mouth turning downward the way they always did when she smiled quickly and tenderly. The light from her smile seemed to linger in the room as they ate.

"As for the rest, we'll see . . ." Mimmi said, so softly that her real hopes materialized as a third party in the conversation.

A tiny third party, one with Mimmi's beautiful cheekbones and Kaj's lactose intolerance.

Kaj's heart began to beat so fast that it felt like his entire upper body was trembling. Like a panicked bumblebee being shaken in a jar without enough air holes.

Mimmi studied him quietly, solemnly. She saw him lower his head and watched his gaze drift across the patterned rug. Saw a small figure between them, growing fainter around the edges yet again. It then crawled back inside her, like a VHS tape being rewound.

★

Mimmi picked up the free pen from the pizzeria and drew a few test scribbles on the receipt.

"OK then, what should we write?"

"Huh? What are we writing?" Kaj asked, with a dry mouth and melted cheese on his knee.

"In the notice. We'll have to send an engagement notice to my *ämmi*'s local paper, otherwise she'll bring down all sorts of terror on us."

Kaj could just picture his furious future grandmother-in-law up in Tornedalen, by the Finnish border, and he realized Mimmi was right. She would.

"Does she even speak Swedish?" he asked.

"Idiot, she's been living on the Swedish side for forty years. She only pretends not to understand when you're around."

Kaj mumbled something beneath his breath, and Mimmi's voice smelt like oregano when she leant in and whispered in his ear.

"The poor thing just wants what's best for me, you know. And obviously that would be a Finnish hunter living within walking distance of her. Someone who could keep her freezer fully stocked."

Kaj gave a resigned laugh. He really had done his best to make a good impression on Sirpa, Mimmi's *ämmi*. Efforts that, if possible, had only made her despise him even more than she already did. In an attempt to humiliate him – and Kaj was utterly convinced that was her aim – the old woman liked to torment him with various hunting-related questions whenever they met. Did he prefer hunting with a Hellefors or a Laika? Did he want to borrow the car and drive over to the range to practice, so that he'd be able to shoot in a straight line when the time came? And would he do her a favor and fetch the meat for the *tjälknöl* – a dish he had never even heard of, but which Mimmi later explained involved slow cooking and then soaking elk meat in brine – from the freezer in the basement? The bags weren't labelled, but surely he would be able to see which hunk of meat was right.

He had fallen into her trap the first few times it happened, admitting that he didn't have a hunting licence. But that just made Sirpa turn to Mimmi with a knowing look on her face, pursing her lips so that she looked like a mean little bird.

His next approach to her stubborn questioning had been to self-deprecatingly exaggerate his non-existent hunting exploits. Once she saw the disarming glimmer in his eye, he reasoned, she would realize he was joking and decide he was actually quite sweet in his ignorance.

Instead, with what felt like biblical anger in her shrivelled little eyes, Mimmi's grandmother had forced everyone at the table to bring their hands together and pray for his deceitful soul. That was what Kaj assumed, anyway – his ability to understand Meänkieli, the Finnish dialect spoken in that part of Sweden, was limited to say the least. Either way, he was fairly sure he was the focus of her pre-meal prayers.

Kaj had refused to close his eyes like the others and had seen Mimmi's bowed head shaking with laughter.

His plans for gaining Sirpa's approval should have been idiot-proof after that, but yet again his efforts had fallen flat. He had called in a greeting to the old dragon's favorite radio show on her eightieth birthday, dedicating a song to her and everything. The choice was between Siw Malmkvist's *Bergsprängartango* and a Finnish psalm. Sirpa and her late husband Ari had gone to the local pensioners' dance sessions every Saturday for decades, so he thought a lively tango would probably go down well . . . though on the other hand, she had also become much more religious since she was widowed. Maybe she thought it would increase her chances of a one-way ticket to the same final destination as the devout Ari whenever her time came?

Looking back, Kaj had occasionally thought that she should have saved herself the trouble; she would surely be going straight in the opposite direction.

He had settled on the psalm with Mimmi in mind, convinced she would be proud of the thought he had put into the gesture. Using the criteria *beautiful* and *solemn,* a quick google search had led him to the title he eventually requested for Sirpa.

When Mimmi picked up the phone a few hours into her *ämmi*'s eightieth birthday, the old woman's voice had been loud and heartfelt. Kaj assumed he must have achieved his aim, and he gave himself a mental pat on the back. He'd gone and done it! He had her on the hook now, and all he needed to do was reel her in . . . The rest of his internal celebrations were drowned out by the sheer volume of the phone call. Sirpa really did sound exultant; she was practically screeching in delight. It felt *so* good to have made an old woman happy on her birthday, Kaj thought to himself, and he and Sirpa would probably end up with a decent relationship after all.

But when Mimmi hung up, Kaj's proud grin quickly faltered.

Sirpa wasn't happy.

She wasn't happy at all.

In fact, she claimed she had never been so *unhappy* in all her eighty years, not now that her granddaughter's partner had humiliated her in front of the whole of Tornedalen, dedicating a funeral psalm to her on the radio.

Mimmi laughed so hard she got cramp in her belly, and Kaj realized that he simply couldn't win, that Mimmi's beloved grandmother was a witch with a heart as dark as a lump of salty liquorice.

Kaj gave his fiancée a quick peck on the lips. The truth was that he couldn't help but agree with Mimmi's *ämmi*, at least partly. Maybe a God-fearing Finnish hunter in full camouflage gear would be best for her after all. Maybe that way she would get everything she wanted and deserved. Everything Kaj was too cowardly to say he didn't want to give her, and too in love to say that he couldn't.

10

Vipers in the Mailbox

Biera dreamt that he was down by the road, swinging his axe. The sun-bleached post beneath the mailbox was mute as it felt the methodical blows of the blade.

The damned wood fibers were so hard, it was a nightmare to cut! Useless thing had probably gone off like a lump of old firewood, but that couldn't be helped. The mailbox was full of vipers that might slither out and bite the dog! He needed to chop it down so that he could stamp the baby snakes to death before they escaped and scattered across the garden. The whole mountain would be covered in them within a few years otherwise; the sneaky devils multiplied like crazy if you gave them half a chance. Biera would probably have to set the whole box on fire once he brought it down, bills and all, but the stick was frozen solid in the ground. He tried to pull it loose from its icy bed, but it clung on tight. *Wretched thing, what kind of dream is this!* Or was it? A dream? It felt precariously close to waking life.

Biera was drenched in sweat, and he pushed back his traditional hat, complete with big red pompom, before adjusting his grip on the axe and letting it bite into the post – bit by bit, chunk by chunk.

Snakes on the mountain? No, he wouldn't stand for that. Like hell!

★

Several hours after he woke, he could still feel the tiny splinters making his palms sting. The dream must have been a warning, he thought, studying the furrows in his hands like ant trails on loose ground. Whenever the dream world broke through to the other side like this, it could only be a sign that his forefathers were trying to tell him something important.

Biera would have to stay on his guard and keep his senses open to the signs he knew would be coming, in one way or another.

He pulled a splinter from the pad of his finger and peered down at it, as though this fragment of a dream could reveal what lay ahead. Biera still wasn't sure whether he had picked up the splinters while he was sleeping, or whether he had been awake.

11

Skájdde-Máija and the Premonition

In the old days, back when they were both young and sprightly, they often went fishing together on Giettek. Máriddja was a good rower, with calluses on her palms, and Biera liked to balance in the front of the boat with the tackle.

Those fishing trips brought them a few hours of fresh air, the numbing scent of the boat's tarred wood in their noses. Life should have been all sweetness and light – they had each other, after all – but their childlessness had left a gaping hole that filled their days with a gloomy background noise. Like the fat in a piece of marbled meat, it infiltrated every thought, and it was only when they were out and about, surrounded by nature, that they found some respite from those niggling thoughts. They took strength from the white breasts of the osprey, diving over their oars; they found a sense of calm in the tiny pike darting around their feet when they launched the boat. The birch trees provided shade for the dog, who was waiting for them on the shore like always. Even he was at peace – and happy for it.

Biera had been teasing her like usual that day, peering down into the cold, dark water from the front of the boat. The pompom on his hat at a jaunty angle, singing as he worked.

Skájdde-Máija, lei jo . . . Máriddja snorted dismissively as ever, but before she turned away he caught a hint of a smile at the corner of her mouth.

He paused for a moment to tug on a net that had got caught before he went on, almost inaudibly this time. *Golmma gieldda fávru* . . . At that point Máriddja threw the halved juice bottle they used as a makeshift bailer at his feet. He laughed so hard that the wrinkles on his face emerged and he took a step towards the seat in the middle of the boat. She remembered that his boots were untied. It was a warm morning, and the ends of the laces swung against the thwart as he pushed the bailer to one side with his toe.

Máriddja had always thought he was so damned handsome, and never more so than in moments like that: hard at work, with the morning sun glittering in his eyes; with the broad knife belt resting on his hips.

The song he was singing, *Skájdde-Máija* – his own version of *Deatnu Máija*, a *joik* by Tanabreddens Ungdom – was an old joke of his. She had been Máriddja Skájdde before she married – a surname that meant "where two rivers meet" in Lule Sámi – and she and the Máija of the song were namesakes, bound by the Christian Maria. It was a common name among Sámi people, with a number of variations, and there was a belief that those who shared a name also shared special ties.

Being compared to the woman from the *joik* – *Deatnu Máija*, or Máija from Deatnu, the prettiest in three towns – was far from an insult, but acting like it was had become a part of their ritual. Máriddja pretended to be annoyed and Biera laughed, spurred on by her reaction. They bickered like two old dogs that no longer cared whose bone it was, fighting mostly out of habit – and happy for it.

★

Máriddja was back in the past, reliving their conversation that day in the boat. Their words. The dark mood that suddenly seemed to descend on them like an area of low pressure. In her mind's eye, she saw Biera slump down so heavily that the boat rocked from side to side. She had taken out a Thermos and poured his coffee into the carved birch cup, hers into the lid of the flask. Or was it the other way around? Did Biera have the metal lid?

Either way, the coffee was hot, warming them up nicely from within that early morning. She was right back there in the boat, sitting opposite Biera, and could almost taste the bitter heat of it.

"I'm worried about Risten," he had said as the coffee swilled down his throat.

He gazed out at the surrounding mountains, flanking their boat and the tarn where they were drifting slowly. Máriddja sighed.

"I know, she's not a baby anymore . . ." she said.

"But she's just got so much damn *chaos* inside her. Messing about with boys already – that could spell trouble. She's so careless, wide open like a baby bird's beak. I don't like it."

Biera pursed his lips, and Máriddja found herself smiling at the picture he had painted. Imagining her husband lovingly dropping worms into Risten's gaping beak.

"You've always worried about her. It's natural, she's your little sister."

He nodded impatiently, as though there were more to come, so she hurried to add:

"It's because she's so much younger than you . . . I doubt she's any worse than the other youngsters. You just don't understand them and everything . . . going on inside them," she said, as though her own insights into the emotional lives of teenagers were particularly nuanced.

"Mmm," he mumbled to himself. "I think that's the problem. I remember it all too well."

Máriddja pretended not to have heard him.

"I just . . . I feel like it's my responsibility. We're all she's got now. They were so old when they had her, and with *Eadni* gone and *Isá* in no fit state . . ."

Yes, all those facts were fresh in Máriddja's mind. Her mother-in-law had been visibly pregnant when she and Biera first started courting – a fact that Ella-Márge denied, right up until the contractions had her lowing like a cow elk and the girl came tumbling out.

"I've just got a bad feeling, that's all. It's as though . . . as though this isn't going to end well, any of this." Biera shook his head ominously without making the pompom on his hat move.

"Careful the evil ear doesn't hear you!" Máriddja shuddered.

Biera's lively and cheerful sixteen-year-old sister could be a spoiled brat at times, but she would never wish her any ill. He mumbled into his cup, muting his voice as he emptied his mouth of words and filled it with black coffee. When he next spoke, his words seemed to bounce off the mountains on either side of them, rumbling over the surface of the water, even though his voice was little more than a whisper.

"I've seen tears in her palms."

Many years later, when Máriddja thought back to the warmth in her chest that day, to the words that had put a damper on the rest of their fishing trip, she regretted not taking the ache in her gut more seriously. Not having taken better care of Risten, protecting her – protecting them. Perhaps things wouldn't be quite so topsy-turvy now if she had just paid more attention to Biera's instincts that day.

Old Máriddja clutched her belly and rocked back and forth on the bench in the kitchen, like a small bark boat in a storm. The day smelt like rotten meat.

The pain was bad today, and she could barely keep her face in check. Biera didn't seem to have noticed anything yet – and just as well, she thought with a heavy heart.

She didn't want him to know, so she only had herself to blame. Her, Skájdde-Máija. What would be would be. There was nothing she could do about it.

12

Steps

The garbage bag was so full that he barely had enough handle left to tie a knot.

Cold water seeped through Biera's socks as he trudged through the snow in his wooden clogs, and he kicked one heel against the other to knock out the slush. His turquoise long johns were well-worn, with a diagonal rip across one knee, and he was wearing a thin knitted scarf that only just covered his Adam's apple – a garment that was at constant risk of being thrown out by Máriddja.

Biera moved heavily, taking great care with each step, just like he did with his words. As though he were walking across rough ground, carrying a heavy sack on his back, when in actual fact he had pavement beneath his feet. The same way every member of his family had walked before him: weighed down by meat, birch bark backpacks laden with cloudberries, ropes slung across their chests. That was also how Biera had moved through life: in forests and fields, across mires, woodland and mountains. His footsteps had been shaped by the life he had lived; that was natural.

Other tongues might have said that his worsening knees and hunched back were proof of the heavy oppression his people had endured for so long. But Biera didn't pay much mind to that sort of thing; he simply forged on, his stride unchanged.

Maybe he should get out on the ice and set a few traps to catch a salmon trout, he thought, adjusting his grip on the garbage as he squinted up at the clouds. The heavy plastic bag cut into his fingers. That would be good, and the weather was surprisingly mild for so early in the year. In another few weeks it wouldn't even matter if he caught a pike – that would enable him to predict the weather. He didn't think much of eating junk fish like that, but the spring pike's liver was a useful indicator of the seasons to come. *Exciting to see what the water levels will be like this year*, Biera thought to himself. Winter had arrived late, and it had been mild, but with plenty of snow. The pike liver would tell him everything he needed to know; they weren't hard to read. If the liver was big, the spring floods would be significant, and if it was small that meant they could expect a cold spring and summer.

There was more sense putting your faith in nature's signs than in the meteorologists on TV, Biera believed; those people gave a single forecast for the vast expanse of Norrland.

Clogs squeaking in the snow, Biera reached the green bin and lifted the lid. It was a wretched state of affairs that his body was in such poor shape that a simple movement like that could hurt so much – he'd always been as strong as a young bear, but these days his stiff shoulders groaned like an old wooden floor. No wonder the handicraft he had put so much time and effort into was behind him now; he was too weak! Gathering the materials he needed from nature was too much for him these days. Biera missed making things with his hands. He even missed the way his fingers used to ache after working with the leather needle, stinging so much that it wasn't even enjoyable towards the end. But worst of all were his wrists – ho! Getting old and feeble was awful.

Biera got ready to swing the heavy bag into the bin, but just as he was about to let go he noticed something metallic catch the light. He reached inside and felt the barrel of his elk rifle.

What the damned devil, he thought. How in the name of his forefathers had *that* ended up there?

Biera pulled the rifle out of the bin and anxiously brushed a few coffee grounds from the stock. The magazine wasn't loaded, at the very least, but that wasn't enough to stop his questions.

He felt chilled to his very soul as he slowly shuffled back towards the house.

Biera put the gun just inside the garage and secured the door with the crossbar. As he turned around, he saw the thin curtain in the attic window stir, as though someone had just moved suddenly.

He had to spit out his snus tobacco, giving him an excuse to slow his inherited footsteps. The ones that left deep marks in the snow behind him, evidence of the family's – and his – heavy burden. The way they always had.

13

Creatures in the Attic

Salty tears metal taste
Icy wind that bites the face
Wayward herd the dogs guide forth
Turn hearts and antlers to the north

With a tobacco-stained thumb, Biera turned down the volume on the TV and peered up at the yellowed ceiling.

What was that? He could hear something thudding and scraping above his head. The discovery in the trash bin was troubling, and he wasn't sure whether to blame the underground creatures or his wife – both were perfectly capable of that sort of mischief and devilry.

This noise didn't leave him any the wiser. Were the invisible *vitterfolk* up to no good after all? Trying to get into the house from above? What on earth would he do then?

There certainly was a creature in the attic, but that creature was making a racket in the name of tidying.

Máriddja had stuffed a wad of paper into each nostril to avoid breathing in any dust or germs, and as the heap of trash by the hatch grew taller, she spat and mumbled "*Ale boste!*" to scare off any disease or nasties that might be lurking in the junk she and Biera had accumulated over the years.

She dragged a large broken sled, a wooden *akkja* that had once been pulled by reindeer, into the pale light of the window, then removed the wads of paper from her nose to fill her lungs with the scent of old leather. Departure, she thought as she stroked the scarred wood. It smelt like departure, like a lack of freedom. The leather straps felt dry and brittle beneath the lifelines on her palm. Cracked, like the blood ties after the long journey Biera's family had been forced to make, so long ago now.

It would be a shame to throw away an heirloom like this, but who would get any enjoyment out of it now? It wouldn't even be any good as firewood, Máriddja decided, sadly but rationally.

They didn't have anyone to leave their family memories to, that was just how life had panned out.

She and Biera would only have each other during their last few years on earth.

They had no children or grandchildren to turn to.

They had no one.

According to Sámi custom, the elderly were never useless or unwanted. Those who carried an entire lifetime's wisdom and experience on their shoulders were needed more than ever. Unlike the way some people treated their elders – like flotsam and jetsam, washed up on the shore – the Sámi saw the old as sturdy ships that would carry the family forward, and they were given the care and attention they needed in order to stick around for as long as possible.

Crooked fingers were welcome to join in, boiling coffee and wiping descendants' noses. They were allowed to keep doing what they could, sharing the things they knew. Their knowledge and presence were both welcome, and Máriddja had often thought that was probably the reason why so many Sámi lived to such an advanced age. They were the link between the past and the present, their stories the family's womb, and they were involved in shaping the future of the family, too. But that required there to be a younger generation, a future. For the branches of the family tree to be full of life, for there to be young, healthy people to grow old.

Máriddja made a real effort to force back those dark thoughts and pushed the old *akkja* towards the hatch. She dodged a bag full of insulation and then moved back and stood with her hands on her hips, gazing around the space as she stood tall beneath the low ceiling.

Her parents' traditional *gáktis* were hanging neatly between the low beams. The blue material had faded in the light from the window, and she carefully shook the dust from them with a sense of melancholy digging into her heart.

No one would wear these *gáktis* and their woven bands again. The beautiful pewter embroidery would never again sit around anyone's neck.

All the stories, customs, memories and their family line, they would be buried in the same ground they had once walked. Máriddja too. She was now an old woman, and whether she liked it or not she was facing her own imminent departure. The Skájdde family would come to an end with her.

Her forefathers were from the old guard, grown from the land where Lule Sámi was spoken, unlike Biera's, who had been forced to relocate southwards. It had been her parents, her *Ieddne* and *Áhttje*, who had faced the new arrivals and their herds.

Those days hadn't been easy, for them or for us, she thought. The displacements had sown division, forcing people to live side by side on land that had traditionally belonged to her family. Their customs were different, as was the way they lived alongside their reindeer, and yet they were ultimately one and the same people. The boundaries that were drawn up in the south, and the edicts that followed, made them forget all about about how much they had in common.

Máriddja pursed her lips as she thought about the injustices her people had faced. It wasn't something she really liked to talk about – nor think about, for that matter. The rules laid out on paper, stamped with the royal seal, they had been more than words to the people up here; they represented a shift in destiny. And yet her people had been unable to read the proclamations, never mind respond to them. They had changed everything, but no one up here had suspected that those slim documents would have the power to tear the land apart.

Máriddja's choice of partner hadn't gone down well at first, but Biera had courted both her and his prospective in-laws in the traditional way. Her mother and father were good-natured people, and they had seen through to the man beneath the gaudy northern Sámi *gáktit*. Soon enough, they gave their blessing by setting the coffee pot on the fire.

But despite all that, there was still talk. People whispering about Skájddes' girl getting involved with one of *them*, a northerner in a red pompom. Resentment and suspicion sprouted like poisonous mushrooms in the village, and her parents had probably heard their fair share of gossip. It hadn't been easy for her and Biera in the beginning, oh no. The discord drove wedges between people, making it difficult to work together in the way life demanded. Still, they had managed. It hadn't been easy, but the high walls had gradually been worn down – to razor-thin boundaries and wide ditches. The kind of thing it was possible to live with if you really put your back into it.

Perhaps that was why they hadn't been blessed with children, she thought sadly. Because the ground beneath the snow, where those tiny seeds were supposed to grow, was so full of strife and misery. Perhaps Biera's offspring would have been as unwelcome in this area as his parents had been when they arrived.

Or perhaps her flesh was just barren.

Máriddja could feel rather than hear Biera's anxiety from the ground floor, and she called down to reassure him that it was just her.

Clearing out, chucking away.

The past — and the future.

She kept that last part to herself, knew there was no point burdening Biera's mind with everything that was plaguing hers.

Hidden behind her parents' *gáktis*, she had found a beautiful old trunk, the kind that people from the north had taken with them when they went out with the reindeer. She could almost hear the thudding of the hooves, the dogs barking and the scraping of the sleds as she untied the stiff leather strap holding it shut and opened the lid. It was among *her* things, everything that had been left behind when she took the boy and left.

Even if Máriddja and Biera had known where to send her possessions, they wouldn't have done it. They would have gone over there to bring her and the boy home. Back here, to them. Where they belonged. They would have drawn a line under all the harsh words and then gotten on with their lives. There were so many things that could have been done differently, though hindsight was easy half a lifetime later. Several decades had passed since Risten left, but her things were still here; they had never been able to bring themselves to go through them. It had been too painful, both of them too wounded after the deathblow that tore their lives apart.

Inside the wooden trunk was a messy pile of books and papers. Máriddja took out one of the notepads and opened its thin cover. Page after page of her sister-in-law's handwriting, ink the color of the river during the last snow of spring. She let out a whimper when she realized they were diaries, the words sketching and mapping out the mind and soul of an unhappy, broken young woman.

It would be wrong to intrude into someone else's secrets, thought Máriddja. *Obviously* she would never think of doing such a thing. Yet as she told herself that, she also pulled the trunk towards her, making it easier to lift down from the attic at a later date – or another day soon.

Perhaps it was time to find closure. Perhaps it was time to forget. To forgive Risten.

Good grief, maybe she could even forgive herself. Because the future was lost to them; all they had left was the lingering warmth of the past.

14

Brown Politics and Blue Fingers

One Saturday in February, Kaj decided to get better acquainted with the local community. He wasn't due at work at the hospital until that evening, and Mimmi was sleeping off the night shift, so he made his way out into the slowly brightening morning on his own. He hadn't needed to put on too many layers; it was a relatively mild day, and the sun was peeping over the treetops. He paused, closed his eyes, and took a few deep breaths of the crisp air. It almost felt like he was inhaling the rays of sunlight, like he was being illuminated from within.

He hadn't made it very far before he found himself chatting to an inquisitive neighbor. The older gentleman was wearing an orange Helly Hansen jacket, and he leant against his snow shovel as though he was congratulating himself on having found an excuse not to move any more compacted snow for a moment or two. He shook Kaj's hand over the snowbank left by the plough, so hard that Kaj felt like he had been left with dozens of microfractures. The old man then used the back of his hand to wipe a frozen droplet from the tip of his nose and scrunched up his face to get the wad of tobacco beneath his lip back into the right position.

Kaj noticed that the man – who introduced himself as Micklas – wasn't wearing gloves, even though the mercury was hovering just below zero. And it didn't seem to be bothering him.

He peered down at his own gloves, a fluffy new pair of Lovikka mittens, and felt a rush of shame over the colorful cuff tassels that swung every time he moved his arms. Kaj found himself taking them off and holding them in one hand instead, though his fingers quickly grew cold and stiff.

"Warm out today," said Micklas, squinting up at the sunlight between the rooftops.

Kaj nodded, unsure of the next steps in this dance. Unsure of the local definition of warm. The old man stood quietly for a moment, studying him.

"Just hope the temperature doesn't drop again," Micklas continued after wiping yet another drip from his nose.

Kaj hesitated, wondering what he meant, whether he was talking literally or figuratively.

"No, that would be bad," he said, still unsure of himself. "It'll be really slippery and hard to walk. On the pavements and that kind of thing. For the elderly, I mean," he added, showing just how well he understood the implications of any sudden change in the weather, assuming that must be what the old man was getting at.

Micklas gave him a quick glance, as though he was trying to work out what old folks had to do with anything, then responded with two sharp intakes of breath – the locals' way of indicating agreement, Kaj had learned since his arrival.

"Hell for the animals too, of course," he said, looking at Kaj as he shook his head in apprehension and crinkled his nose to readjust the tobacco again.

"Yeah, obviously they can slip and hurt themselves too," Kaj conceded, attempting a similarly concerned expression of his own.

Micklas stared at him for a moment, bushy Elkhound brows raised on his weathered face.

"Yeaah . . . I was thinking more that it'll be hard for them to find anything to eat under the crust . . ." he said.

Kaj felt as if he had just melted into a shameful heap of slushy yellow snow in front of the old man. Mercifully, his neighbor seemed to realize that neither the weather nor the local fauna were among the shivering newcomer's areas of expertise, and he changed the subject.

"So, you're the one who's moved into the Lundmans' house, are you?" he said, nodding towards number eleven. "Nice place, that."

Kaj stood taller. "Yes, it is."

The man hummed and then mumbled that they could probably settle on a good price for clearing the driveway.

"Wait, so we've already spoken!" Kaj blurted out when he realized that he was talking to the tractor owner who had promised to help clear the snow.

"Correct," Micklas said with a grin.

Right then, his eyes came to rest on something behind Kaj, and the corners of his mouth curled downwards, as though they were being dragged down by gravity. Kaj turned around and saw a man with a bare head and eyes the size of flaxseeds trudging along the other side of the street.

"Stinkurt," Micklas muttered once the man had passed. "Politician," he said with a disapproving shake of the head.

"People call him Stinkurt?" Kaj asked.

Micklas sucked affirmatively and grinned. "Yup, old Kurt's a modern-day brownshirt," he said, his grey brow raised. "You know the ones I mean – obsessed with keeping Sweden 'Swedish,' or something," he said, wiggling his fingers in a kind of rabbit ear gesture. It looked more like a two-year-old trying to wave.

"Ahh," said Kaj, still trying to make sense of the olfactory reference.

The old man seemed to read his mind, and he snorted. "You know, brown like muck," he laughed. "Like shit."

With that, the conversation was clearly over, because Micklas got back to work, shouting over his shoulder that he'd have the coffee ready next time Kaj called – and telling him to put his damn gloves back on before his fingers turned blue for good.

Perplexed, Kaj continued his walk around the new neighborhood, thinking about Micklas's political remarks. He smiled to himself; he liked the old man. Kaj didn't have much time for that particular shade of politics either. All around him, he could hear the beeping of tractors, scraping the daily crust of ice from the snow covered roads.

Kaj pulled his mittens back onto his hands, which were still aching as a result of his handshake with Micklas, and kept walking – taking care not to slip.

15

The Eye of Sauron

They were really starting to feel settled in the new house. The fridge was fully stocked, and they'd also put up the big 1950s light fixture that Kaj hadn't even considered *not* hanging above the kitchen table. When Kaj got home, nose streaming and limbs stiff, the shrill whirr of the blender told him that Mimmi was awake and their breakfast smoothies were in production. A few minutes later, he was massaging his frozen toes at the kitchen table as he told her all about his meeting with their neighbor.

"I met a really cool woman last night," said Mimmi, rubbing her eyes. "Super nice."

She took a big gulp of the tart smoothie and looked up at Kaj.

Mimmi's new job as a doctor at the local health center was one that suited her just fine, not least because of her non-existent need for regular sleep – something that could take a real battering from having to work nights otherwise. She was the exact opposite of Kaj, who lacked her loose and free relationship with sleep.

"I invited her and her partner over for dinner next weekend. Possibly not the most professional move, but we really *clicked*."

"She was a patient?" Kaj asked, tearing off a piece of bread and buttering it as he studied his partner's expressive face. It was like watching a scene from his favorite film.

"Yeah. Noomi, that's her name, she came in last night with a dislocated knee. Her snowmobile rolled on top of her when she was out with the reindeer; she'd completely popped it out of joint."

"Ouch. So she's a herder?" Kaj asked, pushing another piece of bread into his mouth.

"Yeah. Part-time, anyway. She works as a test driver, too. Seems like a lot of people do that round here. It's the perfect place to see how a car handles in snow and ice."

Kaj knew that Mimmi was looking forward to making new friends locally, and he also knew that she would have no trouble doing so. None at all. Mimmi fit in wherever she went, and always managed to make everyone feel comfortable. She was a social butterfly.

"Yeah, but my new friend is nothing – sounds like you've found yourself a whole new gang!" Mimmi laughed and gave him a teasing look. "I can't wait to meet Micklas and Stinkurt!"

He pretended to throw his green smoothie at her.

"Or not . . . but Micklas was actually pretty nice. An old dude, but a good one. Straight forward, you know? Other than him I haven't actually bumped into anyone I'd like to hang out with. Not yet." Kaj's mouth was serious, as though he had more pressing issues on his mind. "I keep thinking about Mum and all that stuff, I just can't help it. Haven't really been sleeping properly."

Mimmi looked up from her open sandwich, a handful of sprouting seeds ready to sprinkle onto the smoked ham. The glare of the kitchen light suddenly felt harsh, the air hard to breathe. Like cotton wool.

"Are you feeling low again?" Mimmi studied him, subtly scanning his face, his posture and his hands on the glass, without making it obvious. But Kaj knew her, and he knew that her focus was now squarely on him – like the eye of Sauron. She searched every nook and cranny of him, looking for any sign that his depression had returned. For Churchill's black dog.

Kaj steadied his voice and gave the black dog a reassuring pat on its flattened ears. "Mmm, no. Or maybe a bit. It's just been a lot lately . . . It's probably just my innate anxiousness playing tricks on me." The look he gave her was wry, but his smile was half-hearted and a little too quick.

Mimmi dumped half her alfalfa sprouts onto her sandwich, gathering up the rest with her fingers and pushing them straight into her mouth as she waited.

"I guess I might be feeling *a bit* more thin-skinned than usual," he eventually conceded. "Yesterday was really shitty. I had a panic attack after my coffee break, started quivering like a goddamn leaf in the staff room. I had to do box breathing to calm myself down."

His smoothie glass had stopped spinning and his tone was light and breezy, but Mimmi knew his anxiety problems were anything but.

"Hey, why didn't you say anything? What was it that triggered it? Do you know?" she asked, focusing on him as she ate her breakfast. Mostly to give off a sense of calm she didn't actually feel.

"Mmm . . . Hard to say . . . It was like the woman they've got temping behind reception sucked all the energy out of the room with her sulking about the new schedule." Kaj shook his head. "All this death business, too. It reminded me of how shitty things were after Dad died . . . it's tough!"

"When's your next phone session with the therapist?"

"The day after tomorrow," Kaj replied, getting up to clear away their dirty glasses.

"It'll be fine, just don't forget to bring up Laura when you talk to him. Grief isn't a bad thing, in and of itself, but the rest of it . . . I mean your relationship and everything. You still haven't processed it all, and I think it could do you good to vent a little."

Kaj reluctantly agreed with her – he almost always did, in the end, for good reason. There was something not quite right about the way he dealt with things, something in his relationship with his mother that he had never managed to straighten out. Abel cast a disinterested look at him. Kaj stroked his fur, and the animal purred and closed his eyes. He had finally deigned to forgive him, but only after Kaj bribed him with a sinfully large lick of butter and a scratch in the right spot beneath his chin. The two were now reconciled.

He leant back against the kitchen counter so that he could see Mimmi at the table.

"It's OK, you don't need to worry. I can feel my *joie de vivre* coming back a bit more with every day we're here. With every numb toe and every frozen windscreen, I get a little happier." He grinned. "Plus, it'll be cool to meet your new girl crush and her partner! I'm sure they're both real rays of sunshine."

He heard Mimmi chuckle, her head in the cupboard.

"Oh, by the way, did you mail the engagement notice?" she asked, closing the door with a loud creak.

"Ages ago, my love," he sighed with mock resignation. "Speaking of which, I actually used my full name on it."

"Ha, why did you do that?"

"I just felt like I should. I know I never normally use it – I don't think I can ever remember Mum calling me anything other than Kaj – but it's my name, isn't it? Plus, it sounds a bit Finnish. I thought your *ämmi* would appreciate that."

"You smooth operator! Did you ask them to use the ring symbol when they print the notice?" she asked from behind another cupboard door.

"Yeah. Your *ämmi* probably wouldn't approve of the champagne glass, so the ring it is. What are you doing in there?"

Mimmi moved from cupboard to cupboard, and as she continued her rampage a whole host of seemingly random objects appeared on the worktop.

A carafe, a woven birch root cheese mold, teak egg cups and an incredibly ugly blue and yellow vase with elk painted on it. Kaj stared at the vase the same way a teenage girl might watch a rival she planned to take down a notch or two, by means of physical violence.

"I'm looking . . ." she mumbled to herself in Finnish as something tumbled into a pan. It looked like a TV remote. "For this!"

Mimmi held up a plastic bag with something angular inside and let out a triumphant whoop. She left the remote where it was in the frying pan and walked toward Kaj with her face buried in the bag. She seemed pleased as she pulled out a number of picture frames, still in their wrappers.

"What do you need those for?"

"I thought I might frame a few of Laura's pictures, if that's OK with you?"

Kaj smiled at her expectant face.

"You're so sweet," he said, getting up. "That sounds great." He felt his eyes welling up, but did nothing to hide it.

Life was a lot at the moment, for better or worse.

16

No Deal with a Filthy Pervert

Máriddja may or may not have once attempted to buy two goats from an ad in the *Norrbottens-Kurir*. This was back when they still owned a perfectly ordinary mobile phone, the kind you could wrap your head around. More specifically: the very phone Máriddja would later throw into a trash can at the hospital.

Back then, she had been feeling a little lost, and the increasingly dark days got her down. A goat or two would do the trick, she thought; she'd always had good relationships with the cloven-hoofed creatures, and it had been a long time since they'd last had any animals at home. Biera had been put off after the business with the narrow-minded bus driver a few years earlier, and Máriddja had capitulated.

As a result, when she spotted the ad for two healthy Lapland goats in Vuollevárre – mother and daughter, for a good price – her resolve had been sorely tested. Just three minutes after she first saw it, having actively declined to raise the subject with her husband, she made a mature and considered decision and called the owner to make a deal.

The transaction had gone well at first, despite Máriddja's shameless haggling and entirely reasonable demands for immediate home delivery. The seller, a man with an obvious character flaw, had accepted her offer, and the conversation had then progressed nicely. It was a done deal – or not, as it would turn out.

On hearing the man say something about how she could pay his pal, Máriddja – insulted, practically struck dumb – had gasped and coolly taught the fellow a thing or two. She was an open-minded woman, but she wouldn't stand for that kind of immorality! The seller had been puzzled, perhaps even confused, and said that all she needed was an account and her bank details. That had only served to worsen the mood, at which point Máriddja *may* have said something about people like him being unworthy of owning animals with cloven hooves, and she might even have called the seller a filthy pervert.

And then she – or he – had hung up. As far as Máriddja was concerned, it was an indisputable fact: people from the neighboring community were as faithless and lecherous as hungry wolves. She didn't want anything to do with his pal, nor any inbred goats from Vuollevárre, as she told a confused Biera later – that was the only part of the whole sorry story she was actually sure of!

Yes, that was just one of many occasions when it had been incredibly handy to have a phone you could actually make calls with, Máriddja thought sullenly one morning in February. Biera and his useless new brick of a banana phone . . .

Good thing she could still maintain some sort of overview of the world around her through the morning paper, at the very least.

Máriddja had a sneaking suspicion that their postman, Nuffe Nilsson, was responsible for that particular mistake. He was a little scatty, you see. They had cancelled their subscription years ago, but the paper kept on coming – and all without them paying a single penny. She hadn't seen any payment forms, and had no intention of raising it with anyone – not if there was a risk she'd be sent one of those upstanding payment notices.

No, Máriddja preferred to think of it as a kind of *perk of the job* for the neighbors' boy, who delivered their letters. Being able to cheer up the old folks next door with a free subscription, that must be nice for him!

And Máriddja wasn't the kind of person to begrudge anyone their pleasures in life.

17

A Sign in Black and White

At the same time the next day, in the very same place, the free paper lay open on the kitchen table. Máriddja's eyes darted around the room, searching for someone to share her discovery with. Her gaze swept over the copper objects on the shelf, a stack of cookbooks, then back to the wedding photograph in a taped-up frame leaning against a long-dead potted plant.

This was it, the sign she had been waiting for. As clear as the day in front of her.

Oh yes, she laughed, her hazy eyes open wide as she stared at the old photograph of Biera and herself. "Oh yes, so this is how it has to be. This is nothing less than a sign!" she shouted with joy, jabbing a finger at the announcements section with such force that the ink came away in the lines on her skin. "Mark my words!" The name she had just read wasn't a dime-a-dozen, which had to mean . . .

Máriddja got up on her crooked legs, sniffed her inky fingers and paced around the kitchen, squinting out at nothing as her mind raced. She paused and closed one eye as she thought aloud.

Good grief, how *wonderful!* The latest prognosis made her giddy. The hunt could finally begin! Finding the person she had been looking for would no longer be like searching for a needle in a smokestack. She smiled to herself. But how should she go about it? What should she do with this new information? Tell Biera? She wanted to, so much that it hurt, but no. There was a risk he would only get upset if she was wrong. There was a chance the announcement didn't mean what she thought it did, but then again, it *was* in the local paper . . .

What to do, what to do, what to do, she mumbled to herself with her other eye closed, opening the first in order to think more clearly.

Máriddja moved back over to the table, her fingers taking on a life of their own. Her nails groped for a used sheet of paper towel and wrapped it neatly around the sugar bowl. She finished off by carefully tucking the corners underneath so that it would stay there while she thought. No loose ends, no room for failure. She peered out of the window, through the dry, fake heat from the radiator.

Over on the main road, all she could see was the swirling snow from the passing cars. It lingered for a while once they were gone, dancing in their tire tracks between the heaped verges before settling again. And the road itself lay in wait, crystal clear between trees that had bowed their branches, only to rise up in a formidable cloud of billowing whiteness at the slightest breeze. Like a mirage, a sudden illusion, to steer through and beyond.

Máriddja grunted crossly when she realized that the answer was right in front of her.

More specifically: it was plugged into a socket by the kitchen window, in the damned contraption that claimed to be a telephone.

18

The Child Their Hearts Chose

It hadn't always been just the two of them.

There had been other people in the cottage at one time, family. Life.

Old mother Ibbá and her stubborn nodding, hard-working fingers weaving band after band. The sound of the reed and the yarn, which she tied around her waist, anchoring her by the window, had long since faded to silence. But the box of things she had made still sat on her chair.

Shoe bands and belts; belts and shoe bands.

For people who already had everything they needed.

Biera's father had lived with them too, towards the end. The light in his eyes had already begun to dim by that point, and he spent most of his time lying with his hands folded on his chest as he waited. Old Gustu. Longing to head north again, most likely, to follow his late wife to a place they both knew.

Northward, home. But until then, he simply lay there with a rolled-up blanket beneath his head, watching his son as he went about his life. Chatting and laughing, but, more than anything: longing to go home.

And then there was the child.

Biera had been blessed with a sister who was born long after him.

Risten was a nice girl, there was no doubt about that, though she had a regrettably weak character that got her into trouble from a young age. It was Risten who brought the boy into their lives. She was little more than a child herself, and the father was a drunk and a disreputable bastard.

The girl had turned up with the little one when he was just a bundle of wrinkled skin in an enormous diaper. Not a hair on his head, screaming.

Risten had done her best, Máriddja had to give her that, but her best simply hadn't been enough to offer the boy much in the way of mothering. She wasn't mature enough, wasn't whole enough.

And little by little, as unmistakably as the shifting of the seasons, the boy had begun to seek them out, to turn to Biera and Máriddja when he needed comfort or love. They had changed his diapers, heated gruel on the stove and let his little hands squeeze their fingers while Risten picked up her old life and began running wild again.

They had fallen in love with the boy who came crashing into their lives. The boy they cared for when he was sickly, who they laughed with as he grew and took over their home – and their entire lives. Because there was plenty of room for him, God knows there was room!

Before the boy came along, there had been hope and longing. Years of waiting. Tears shed over the bleeding that arrived every month, over everything else that never did.

Downcast glances over their floral cups of coffee at breakfast, comforting hands in lonely moments.

Confidence and despair had lived side by side in their little house as winters passed and summers arrived, but none of the seasons had brought life to Máriddja's womb.

She had felt so jealous and angry at the unfair way nature dealt out heartbeats, but the darkness in her soul had slowly broken up into chinks of light, and the boy, Heaika-Joná, had eventually lit up her entire life. In the end, all that was left was joy – that was how it turned out. When their own child failed to come along, their hearts chose someone else's instead.

19

The First Meeting with Siré

Máriddja felt like a chimpanzee with a coconut as she sullenly tapped Biera's phone against the worktop. Lying open beside the wretched device was a dog-eared phone book from 1992 that had, frankly, seen better days.

She noted with dissatisfaction that the old man had torn out a good chunk of the alphabet – to light the stove no doubt. Not a damn thing is safe round here, she thought grumpily.

Máriddja flicked through the remaining pages and quickly realized that their goose was well and truly cooked. Despite that, she left the thick book open on the counter, as a kind of manifesto to the task at hand. She then fixed her eyes on the phone and gave it an irritable shake.

"It's time you behaved!" she warned it, a few droplets of spittle landing on the dark glass. *And what the hell do you know!* Máriddja nodded happily in victory as the screen lit up and a tinny female voice replied:

"I'm not sure I understand."

"Hello!" Máriddja's voice was rough, and she croaked before continuing, as politely as she could. "Could you help me reach someone, operator?"

"I can help guide you to your destination if you switch on location services," the woman replied stiffly.

Location services? Máriddja had to stop and think for a moment. When she next spoke, she enunciated every word carefully.

"No, just the number is fine. I won't trouble you for any other services." She made a real effort to keep her voice mild, but her impatience made that difficult to say the least.

"I offer many services," the woman replied.

"That's nice," said Máriddja, slightly concerned and a little impatient. "But I just want to talk, I don't want to *go* anywhere, for the love of God!"

"Now playing *For the Love of God*," the voice said helpfully. A moment later, piano music started streaming out of the phone, accompanied by a choir of male voices.

"What the . . . No, I don't want to hear any religious songs! I want to make a call!"

The choir articulated every note, and Máriddja realized with a growing sense of indignation that the operator was messing with her.

"I'm starting to . . . What a nerve! Do you think it's *funny* to taunt old people like this? I can hear that you're not from around here, and you should count your lucky stars for that! Because let me tell you, I'd have worked out which family you were from and put your parents to shame for raising you so *badly*! Up here—"

But that was as far as she got before she heard Biera calling for her from the toilet.

"*Vuoi* . . . Máriddja . . . there's no paper left." He sounded like he had just told an anecdote with a sad ending. "What happened to the phone book that's usually in here?"

The telephone machine was silent. The operator had clearly hung up after Máriddja's rant. Máriddja cast a glum look at the tatty phone book, closing her eyes and sighing when she realized what must have happened to the missing pages.

She carried it over to the closed door, opened it and handed over the depleted collection of phone numbers, giving her husband strict instructions to leave the yellow pages intact, at the very least.

20

Through a Sugar Cube

Micklas knocked on the door and marched straight in, all without bothering to announce his visit in advance – or waiting for anyone to answer. He peered around the kitchen with a look of curiosity on his face and put a foil-wrapped package down on the counter. A bag of sweet buns on the table, too.

Mimmi and Kaj found it slightly odd that he had kept his shoes on, though since he seemed to have thoughtfully, carefully scraped off any last trace of snow using their new brush outside, it didn't matter too much. With a gnarled hand, he turned one of the chairs away from the table and sat down, leaning back comfortably. He kept his coat on, simply tugging the zipper down a little.

"All settled in, then? You got any coffee on the go?" he asked, nodding towards the bag of buns. "I take it through a sugar cube."

As he spoke, a bright-eyed child in a fur hat and snowy boots appeared. He bounded in through the door and sat down beside Micklas. Mimmi and Kaj couldn't help but stare at their unexpected guests, the smaller of whom they had never even seen before.

Micklas acted like none of this was remotely out of the ordinary, saying simply, "Johánás, my grandson," in passing as he scanned the room for a coffee pot. "He's cleared the drive for you, right up to the garage."

Johánás himself didn't say a word, he just put his thick gloves down on the table and helped himself to a bun.

"And this is Mimmi, my . . . uh . . . fiancée," said Kaj.

He felt insulted to have his manly ability to shovel snow questioned so openly, and by a *kid* at that. He had been out just that morning to clear last night's snowfall. Even more odious, the boy was sitting in *his* chair. He cast a quick, angry glance at Johánás, who glared back at him as he munched on a cinnamon bun with his little baby teeth.

"Hi there! Would you like a glass of milk with your bun?" Mimmi asked the young lad, who politely said yes and thank you. It was remarkable how quickly she managed to compose herself in any given situation, Kaj thought.

Abel came sailing into the room, hesitating for a moment before deciding he approved of the gathering and affectionately rubbing up against the boy's legs. The cat received a greasy pat on the head in return, and Kaj's eyes narrowed as he watched his deceitful pet skillfully avoid the wet spots left by the boy's shoes. He could already feel the moisture seeping through one of his own socks.

"Mmm, gravlax!" Mimmi groaned happily as she opened the foil package on the counter. "Thank you!"

Micklas gave her a quick salute in response.

As suddenly as they had arrived, the visitors thanked their hosts and headed back outside. Mimmi remained where she was at the table, enjoying the cured fish with closed eyes. Kaj peeled off his damp sock and used his foot to push it through the pools of melted snow around their young guest's chair.

"Grubby little brat," he muttered irritably.

"I thought he seemed sweet," said Mimmi, swinging her

feet up onto the footstool and leaning back as she chewed. "God, this is good."

Kaj muttered something about her inability to recognize a catastrophe when she saw one, and Mimmi told him to shut up and try the incredible fish.

He got up and trudged over to the window in the hall to see whether their new shoe brush had survived Micklas's rough treatment, then returned to the table.

"The brush seems OK. Guess they make things to last up here," he said.

Mimmi burst out laughing.

21

Images

It was a cold, crisp afternoon as Kaj walked home from work. He enjoyed his stroll, even though his face felt like a lump of meat in the freezer. His boot-clad feet came to a halt when he reached the driveway, where he peered at the neighbors' poker-straight paths through the snow with a feeling of slight dissatisfaction. He had to jog in place to keep warm, wiggling his toes to stop them from freezing, despite the thick home-made socks his mother-in-law had given him for Christmas.

He would probably have to fine-tune his technique a little, he thought, studying his own meager path up to the house. It was narrow, meandering this way and that, whereas the heaped snow on either side of the driveway to the right – outside the house belonging to a widower with arthritis – was pedantically straight, like the grout between bathroom tiles. The couple on the other side of the road, with the crocheted privacy curtains, were just showing off with their impressively furrowed corridor that almost looked like it had been cleared using a snow groomer. Intricate patterns of fine-grain sand guaranteed it was both non-slip and irritatingly good-looking, and the woman who lived there waved to him as she threw something down onto the steps in front of her house. Kaj raised his mitten in return, tightly gripping his key inside its woollen embrace. Hi there.

What on earth was she doing? It looked like she was *sprinkling* something black onto the snow around the house. Was it *soil*? In the middle of winter? Come on, this was just too much. Kaj tried to hide his interest in whatever she was doing by brushing the crest of snow from the top of the mailbox. Squinting to get a better look, he saw black powder swirling through the air around her and realized it could be ash. The bucket she was holding looked just like the one he'd had to move out of the way in the boiler room to make space for Mimmi's collection of pots for plants.

Though why the woman was sprinkling ash in the snow was beyond him. On the porch and the steps would make sense – it would probably help to melt the ice, reducing the risk of any slips – but in the snowdrifts? She didn't *look* like she had dementia, and judging by her movements she wasn't in any sort of straitjacket beneath her thick coat. No, he just couldn't wrap his head around it. This was something he would have to look into, because if whatever she was doing was linked to success in keeping on top of the snow, he was willing take all the life hacks he could get. It was a question of honor and reputation!

Kaj stamped the snow from his boots on the stubby green plastic mat, like a cat trying to bury its business, then made his way inside. At least he was properly dressed, he thought, unhitching his bulky padded trousers and letting them drop to the floor. He kept his sweater on, didn't even bother to tug down the zip at the neck; he simply hunched his shoulders to his pink cheeks and shivered.

Mimmi had hung two of his mother's sketches on the wall between the living room and the hallway. The leaves of a trailing green plant in a hanging basket were tucked in at the top edge of the image of an old man. It looked good, his favorite of her drawings. The anti-glare glass in the pale brown wooden frame made it seem old in a way that he liked.

In order to delay the process of taking off his warm clothes, he remained where he was in front of the items from his mother's studio.

Mimmi had also hung one of Laura's psychedelic flowers. She had always been strangely fond of them. Confusing, colorful things, taking the form of blooms you might find in a florist's shop, only made up of other objects. The rose with rattan petals was, in Kaj's opinion, odd, though he had to admit it was also quite interesting. It was flanked by a futuristic bluebell and something that might be a lily of the valley, with ornate little trinkets instead of flowers. They hovered in a row above the grass at the bottom edge of the painting, as though the flowers had grown out of thin air. Peculiar. Kaj was decidedly unsure about his mother's style – but he had to admit that it looked good alongside the unfinished sketch that represented the other half of her collection.

Kaj's gaze returned to the drawing of the old man. He sat down on the wooden stool meant for taking off and putting on shoes and looked up at the portrait. Sniffed a little as a result of the change in temperature his nose had been subjected to. Between the angular frames on the walls, he could see thin, pale vines in the structure of the wallpaper.

He could still remember the day his mother had drawn this picture. It was evening, and she was curled up by the window in her long cardigan with the big triangular buttons. The TV was turned down low in the living room, his mother's leather shoes lined up like a couple of regimental soldiers on the shoe rack. His father was out in the car, and the table lamp in the hallway cast a soft glow on the cold keys that Kaj dropped onto the side table as he kicked off his shoes. Sitting quietly with a light grip on her pencil, Laura hadn't heard him come in.

On the deep windowsill to one side of her, a geranium had finished blooming. Its scattered petals were bright and limp on the white woodwork, like streaks of red lipstick on teeth.

Kaj said a quiet hello and put the letters from the mailbox on the kitchen table. He then poured himself a mug of coffee and went back through to the armchair where his mother was sitting. The pencil between her neat nails trembled slightly as she sketched.

"Hello, love," she said without looking up.

He moved closer to her, gazing down over her shoulder as he sipped from his cup. The coffee was cold and left a bitter taste at the back of his throat. He squeezed her shoulder in greeting, and she exhaled slowly through her nose. Her face was like a finely drawn canvas of mature elegance, delicate fine lines and her thick, cropped hair framing her face like a sober black and silver helmet.

His mother was good at drawing, and the man in the picture looked so expressive and alive, gazing out at him through narrow eyes beneath heavy lids. He was wrinkled, with a low hairline and arched brows. His mouth was generous, with a clear cupid's bow just like Kaj's. One cheek and temple were still missing, but the man Laura had coaxed out of the meeting of graphite and paper was a handsome one.

"Nice picture." He took another sip of coffee and watched over the white china rim of his cup as his mother lowered her eyes.

"He is nice. Or he was." She fell silent.

"Have I met him?" Kaj asked in surprise, leaning in over the sketch again.

Laura nodded, then pursed her lips and swallowed. She gave him a brief, sad smile as she carefully shaded the man's cheekbone with her finger.

"What's his name?" Kaj tried to tread carefully, as though he was crossing a minefield in an ancient Egyptian burial temple; he might be stabbed by antique awls or fall through a hidden trapdoor at any moment. Laura was never particularly keen to talk about the past.

His mother hesitated.

"Per," she said after a moment, before laughing and rolling her eyes. Kaj remembered thinking that the gesture had seemed a little over the top. "But it doesn't look much like him . . . No matter. Do you want to see how the cast of Hans's ear came out? I haven't painted it yet, but I think it'll be a good fit for the 'Lost' theme. I might have to use some contrasting colors to really emphasize the labyrinth-feeling. Come with me, tell me what you think!"

Kaj would have liked to study the portrait more closely, but Laura took it with her as she ushered him through to her studio, soft linen trousers fluttering in the breeze. As his mother showed off her latest artwork, giving him a slightly forced explanation about the theme of alienation and feeling lost, Kaj stood with a mug of cold coffee and thousands of questions. That was precisely how he felt. Lost.

22

A Good Morning

One morning, as Kaj staggered out of his bedroom to go to the toilet, still half asleep, his drowsy eyes noticed a foreign object on the green sofa. He paused with one hand on the door handle, blinking in an attempt to focus.

It was the kid, Micklas's grandson.

"Hi, Johannes," he said, in a slightly guarded tone, trying to look grown up and dignified in his Simpsons underpants.

"Johánás," the boy corrected him, eyes locked on the phone in his hand. *Kaj's* phone, its rightful owner noted with disapproval. He was just about to say something about the young whippersnapper's nerve when Mimmi came through from the kitchen with a cup of coffee, sweetly confirming that it was a good morning with a peck on the cheek.

Kaj took the cup from her and went into the bathroom, where he considered the situation at hand. He could hear Mimmi and the boy chatting through the door, and irritably wondered how on earth this could be happening to him – all before he was even fully awake. He pulled on a dressing gown and then headed back out to join them.

"Grandpa Micklas popped by and asked if we could watch Johánás while he went to help someone whose car had conked out in the woods somewhere," Mimmi explained as she pinched a few withered leaves from their sun-starved potted plants.

She was holding an aluminum watering can in one hand, and she used the other to pat her leg in time with the terrible music streaming out of Kaj's phone.

Her fiancé couldn't think of anything to say, so he bent down to pick up Abel, who happened to be walking by. The angry cat found himself being hugged like a teddy bear, with Kaj using him as a shield between himself and the boy. Mimmi gave him a mock-stern look before turning back to the sad geraniums she had already accused him of neglecting during his time looking after them.

Kaj cleared his throat and asked the boy what he was listening to.

The boy replied that it was hard to explain, then didn't even try.

Kaj followed up by asking why he wasn't in school, to which Johánás replied "half term" and rolled his eyes as though Kaj had just asked whether it was a good idea to eat gravel.

And so Kaj gave up, lowering the grumpy cat to the floor and trudging back through to the bedroom to avoid being half naked in front of the snotty little brat who had effectively just ruined his morning.

Perfect. What a great start to the day, Kaj thought, forcing out a sigh that seemed to come right from the soles of his bunioned feet and out through his nostrils.

23

Darkness and Pain

She had nice handwriting, Risten, seemingly without any real effort – though the words had occasionally been scrawled down in such a hurry that they looked like they had been written on a speeding motorboat on a choppy lake.

Still, Máriddja liked being able to see the flourishes that gave shape to her sister-in-law's thoughts in ink.

She had sorted Risten's written legacy by relevance, stashing the least interesting items in a paper bag in the *akkja* in the attic. Things like correspondence, receipts and handwritten interviews from her time working as a carer. Names from the past. The slim stack of poems she had found were tucked beneath a loading pallet; she would read those last, or not at all. Poetry was just so damned dull, honestly, that those sheets might even end up in the stove.

Laid out in front of her on the kitchen table were six different diaries. One with Risten's initials on the cover looked like it might date back to her schooldays. She can't have done especially well in that subject, Máriddja thought. There were only a handful of notes relating to her schoolwork inside, the rest of the pages filled with the exclamation marks and hearts so typical of a silly teenage girl. Máriddja had also found a couple of notepads, the kind that came free from local businesses, plus an old children's diary with butterflies on the cover and a missing padlock.

She reverently opened one of her sister-in-law's diaries and started reading. It was as though what she had spotted on the family pages in the paper had spurred her on. Risten was nineteen and newly in love, though sadly it was with the lout who, Máriddja now knew, got her pregnant while she was keeping the diary. She wanted to tell Risten to leave him, to forget all about the idiot man with his long lashes and his cocky swagger. But she couldn't exactly wish the boy had never been born.

Filled with such conflicting feelings, she pushed her hat back to her hairline and hunched over the book again. Risten went into graphic, theatrical detail about their meetings, and Máriddja felt a little queasy. Despite that, she wolfed down every ink mark on the paper, words that sketched out the world Risten had carried inside her. Her sister-in-law had been so happy and expectant in the way only a young woman in love can be.

There was a lot of boozing, Máriddja noted glumly. She and Biera hadn't realized the extent of his little sister's partying ways. New names cropped up, new places, new highs. Amphet . . . what did it say there? Amphetamine? Máriddja took a deep breath as the word emerged from the paper. *Good god.*

Then Risten had found herself pregnant, and to Máriddja's relief she couldn't see any further sign of drug abuse or other unhealthy habits; she thought she remembered that Risten had mostly stayed at home, with them, as her belly grew. She and the boy's father had broken up, and the young lass seemed inexplicably sad about that, though she was also happy about the life growing inside her, however uncertain the future might be.

Máriddja read her accounts of her time here in the cabin, and neither she nor Biera were mentioned with anything other than warmth and affection.

There was a gap in the entries, months when Risten didn't seem to have written anything at all. The end of her pregnancy went undocumented, as did the boy's arrival into the world. And then, suddenly, the darkness came spilling out of her like big, fat snakes; black blood and the deepest despair filling every page.

It was like a migraine hit Máriddja as she uncovered the echo of Risten's state of mind. She was utterly defenseless against it.

Máriddja remembered those days. She and Biera had been irritated, worried that the girl didn't seem to have taken to the baby. Risten was listless and touchy, did nothing to help around the house. Barely responded when they spoke to her. The young mother had seen to the boy's most urgent needs and then slumped back into silence and glum passivity. She started disappearing without warning for long periods of time, coming back hungover and hollow eyed, half-heartedly trying to put the pieces of herself back together in order to be a mother to Heaika-Joná.

Risten had really been struggling.

Máriddja could feel the pen in the young woman's hand trembling with self-hatred and doubt. The cruel barbs Risten directed at herself were so much sharper and more ruthless than *anything* anyone else could have mustered. She was treading water in a tar pit of anxiety, in above her head in her own exclusive hell. It was like watching a poor, wingless bird trying to take off from the ground, only to be eaten alive, screeching, beady black eyes open wide, by thousands of ants.

Then Bill reappeared. And her tortured attempts to become a mother were redirected, funnelled instead into an intense love for the father of her child. Risten stopped gasping for air and allowed her damaged lungs to inhale his familiar poison instead. That seemed to brighten her state of mind for a few months, but everything soon got worse again.

Máriddja clapped a hand to her mouth. No, this was too much on an empty stomach.

She needed to go for a walk to clear these images from her mind.

So that is what she did.

24

A Bit Squiffy

Máriddja's next meeting with the only remaining telephone in the house came one Wednesday afternoon, after the news on the radio. She had been putting off the task ahead of her, drumming up courage with a deck of cards and a game of patience.

She had also raided their booze store to mark the occasion, accessed via the trapdoor beneath the rag rug. Between her mother-in-law's extensive collection of empty syrup bottles and a sack of sprouting potatoes, she found a bottle, foreign letters on the label revealing what was inside. Máriddja wasn't too fussy, so she clambered back up the steep wooden ladder with her loot beneath her arm.

It tasted vile, as though it had crawled up from the sulfurous bowels of hell to punish taste buds and oral cavities everywhere. Even the egg cup she had filled to the brim with the awful stuff seemed unhappy to be in such close contact with the abomination of a liquid.

And so she did the only right thing: she tipped it straight down her throat and felt it burn all the way through her body, reaching the ground frost of her soul.

She had felt so down over the past few days, and she needed something to reinvigorate her – that was her own expert assessment. The taste was so revolting that Máriddja hoped it would give her a quick, numbing intoxication for her efforts, if nothing else.

Biera was dozing in the armchair in the sitting room, under the pretext of catching up on the latest sports news from across the kingdom.

Máriddja had the wretched phone in her hand once again, with its flashy big screen and its complete unwillingness to be of any use whatsoever. As before, she somehow managed to get the screen to light up and made contact with the operator.

"Good evening," the call handler chirped.

Máriddja grunted unhappily when she realized it was the same woman she had tried to speak to last time.

"Mmm, so you say."

"I'm sorry, I didn't quite catch that."

"I can't say any of this is good – neither that it's evening nor that it's you working the late shift," Máriddja said.

"Would you like to turn on Night Shift mode?"

"What? Yes, that would be nice, wouldn't it. I have a bit of trouble winding down in the evening sometimes. It's the light. Or . . . you know, the darkness," she conceded, still a little brusque.

"OK."

The brightness of the screen faded to a yellowish glow, and Máriddja stared at the phone with wide eyes before turning to the empty egg cup. She poured herself a little more – this must be strong stuff! – and shuddered as she knocked back yet another mouthful.

"Is there something I can you help with today?" The woman's voice was bright and alert, much more obliging than during their last conversation. Máriddja nodded happily.

"Yes please. And I must say, I appreciate this new attitude of yours – it's a real breath of fresh air."

"Air pollution levels are forecast to remain low across Sweden this evening. Moderate snowfall is expected, with temperatures likely falling below minus fifteen in the mountains."

"Sounds about right, it has been a bit grey out today . . . though it's dark now, of course, so I can't see so well. It would be nice if the damn weather would turn soon. Clearing the snow is such hard work, you know. Just yesterday it drifted so much I broke the shaft on the shovel."

"Would you like me to help find suppliers of snow shovels?"

"That's very kind of you, but I found the electrical tape under the soap dish. The old man claimed we'd run out, but I knew I must have more somewhere, and what do you know! Under the soap, ha, can you imagine? Wonder what it was doing there."

Máriddja snorted and chuckled at her unlikely find. She then leant forward towards the screen and whispered:

"He's a few goats short of a herd nowadays. Well, you get the picture."

Her elbow slipped off the edge of the table, and she swore and grabbed the egg cup, which she had accidentally nudged away. She used her shirt sleeve to soak up the liquid that had sloshed over the edge.

"Opening camera!" the woman announced down the line.

"Huh? No, what on earth . . ."

A perplexed Máriddja stared down at the screen, which now showed a couple of nostrils and a wrinkled double chin in extreme, low-angle close up.

Oh hell, she wasn't kidding!

Máriddja grabbed the bottle, gave it an appreciative glance and then turned to herself on the screen. *What a peach!* She winked mischievously at her mirror image, which — slightly skew-eyed — batted its eyelid back at her.

"This must be a good vintage after all. Listen . . . what did you say your name was again?"

"I'm Siri."

"Siré," Máriddja repeated, appreciating the Sámi ring to it. "That's a solid name. Biera's aunt was called Siré. Good woman, hard worker. But the cancer, it got her."

Máriddja thought she looked charming and relaxed in the mirror on this strange little gadget, and she picked at her teeth for a moment before she went on.

"In her top, her tatties . . .. or something like that. You know, the breasts, as you say. I always used to think it was strange that someone who barely even had a pair could have room for cancer in there."

Máriddja felt surprisingly comfortable talking to the stranger on the other end of the line, but then again she had always come into her own in social settings. Everyone knew that; she was a social genius.

"But that was another time, of course," she added. "If she was young now, maybe they would've operated on her and put in some of those inplants. Impl . . . implatants."

"Would you like to search for breast implant clinics near you?" Sire asked.

"No, for God's sake!" Máriddja clucked with laughter and took another sip from her egg cup. She had to admit it, the taste really was quite interesting once you got used to it. "I think you're getting a bit too personal there now, Siré. But I won't judge, no harm done. I'm not as . . . what's it called . . . prudish as most other women my age. I can take a bit of cheek . . . but you probably shouldn't start suggesting things like that to everyone you talk to, or you might wind up getting into a spit . . . a spot of bo . . . a spot of blather with the morality police."

She cackled to herself, eyes closed and head tipped back.

Christ, the lampshade was spinning. It couldn't be properly screwed in, she decided, murmuring in agreement with Siré's interjection about the police.

Máriddja couldn't quite hear what she said, but it probably didn't matter. She was a good girl, old Siré, even if she did have an underdeveloped chest.

25

The Victim of a Crime

Máriddja woke to the sound of a deep voice on the other end of the line.

"Hello, you're through to emergency services, could you tell me the nature of your emergency?"

Bärggal, she must have nodded off for a minute or two. Confused, she pushed the deck of cards to one side and clawed a sticky Jack of Clubs from her cheek. She had clearly lowered her head to the table after her chat with Siré

The game of patience hadn't gone anywhere, anyway.

Her head was still spinning. She was only half awake, slurring a little, and wasn't sure what to say.

"Do you need help?"

"Mmmyeah . . . nah, maybe, not really."

Where exactly had the operator connected her? She felt shaken, and she racked her brain for clues as to what might have led her into this tight spot – though trying to reactivate her ability to think made her head ache.

"Are you the victim of a crime? Do you need me to dispatch a unit to you?"

What on earth? Had Siré sent the cops after her? She'd just got a bit tipsy and been fun and sweet like any other old woman, Máriddja thought indignantly. That sneaky tattletale!

The cops. The pigs. Máriddja felt like the lead character in a teenage gang whenever she used that word. Pigs, pigs, pigs. She had heard someone say it once, in a film she had accidentally watched a good chunk of before realizing it wasn't the evening's lotto drawing. Perfect name for them, really. Much better than the police.

"Hello? Is there a crime taking place? Do you need us to send someone?" the voice asked.

Somewhere, deep in the fog, an idea took root and her thoughts became crystal clear. No, they were *razor-sharp*.

A crime? Was that what he had said?

"Nah," she replied as the booze-soaked puzzle pieces fell into place and she spotted what might be an opportunity. An opportunity in a police uniform . . . Or maybe a fireman's hat. She could just imagine what the boy would look like now.

26

Guovddo

The desk was practically groaning under the weight of all the folders and their colorful spines. Kaj's predecessor at the health center had a fondness for color that was hard to overlook. The bright shades clamored for attention from the corner of his eye, drawing his gaze to slivers of turquoise, burgundy and tangerine. Kaj didn't mind it too much, not really, though he always rolled his eyes in apology the minute anyone stepped into his room. He felt like he had to, like his hand had been forced by the riot of color in the room. It made him seem so colorless in contrast. Beige. Blank.

He closed the folder in front of him and pushed it to one side. Sitting in his canary-yellow desk chair, Kaj was struggling to pick up where the previous doctor had left off, to deal with his outstanding cases. It wasn't the easiest of tasks to take on something as abstract as someone else's thoughts and plans, but that was simply what he needed to do. Rewinding the tape to find the beat, or something.

His level of interaction with the local community in Guovddo, which ultimately formed the core of his job as a doctor, would increase as he found his feet. Right now, that felt like the bright light at the end of the dark tunnel of bureaucracy, and he could just about make out the full human spectrum of crackpots, eccentrics and stubborn minors on the other side of all these files and registers.

His new home was like anywhere else on earth, but Kaj had the sense that it was different somehow. More *intimate* than life in the city. He had already begun to think of his day-to-day life in the past as big and alien.

Guovddo was Kaj's here, the city was his there. Kaj was living this life, doing this job. He was here.

He signed letters, followed up on cases, performed examinations and drank coffee with his colleagues. Sometimes he even managed to grab lunch with Mimmi when their shifts overlapped.

But for Kaj, it was different. Where Mimmi was happy, Kaj was growing. He was still attempting to weave roots through the fibers of the small community. Making it his, tying himself to it. Allowing himself to seep out into the ground. Breathing in the air the trees had exhaled and letting it flow through his veins. And all the while, his vision of the past was shifting at the edges, taking on new forms and fading away. His old life seemed different from this angle. Kaj took in and took out, paced, measured, stepped out of his own comfort zone and moved closer to his new home.

The patient Mimmi had befriended after treating her dislocated knee proved to be good company, as did her partner. The whole thing felt so natural, so simple, despite the fact that they came from different backgrounds. It wasn't really so strange – Kaj knew that Sweden's indigenous people didn't live under Amish conditions – he was just pleasantly surprised at how quickly they had managed to meet another couple on the same wavelength as them.

Noomi was smart and funny, with a pierced nose and a calm, slightly bohemian air. She and Kaj had found common ground in their love for retro objects, and Mimmi and Palle both sighed at their partners' fondness for other people's cast-offs. Palle was a gentle man, the kind of person who really looked at you and listened when you spoke. His gaze was bright and curious, and his hands moved expressively whenever he got excited – which happened often.

They ate homemade sushi as Palle told them about his work for the local taxi firm. Without violating his passengers' confidentiality too much, he offered up anecdotes about all the legends in the area – as he called his more unusual customers.

It was through Palle that they heard more of the local gossip about Stinkurt, which really did seem to be how everyone referred to him. He and Mimmi also found out all about the Markussons' never-ending hunt for their missing Dachshund, Pillen, and about a crazy old lady who was obsessed with goats.

There was plenty of laughter, about all sorts of topics, their humor occasionally scraping the gutter, and when Kaj and Mimmi summed up their evening later – both a little tipsy and tired – they agreed that everyone seemed to know everything about everyone else in Guovddo. That could be irritating, of course, but it was also comforting. To know could be to admit, and to admit could be to take responsibility. No one would pass by another person in need without stepping up to the plate, not out here. They realized that everyone would likely also know everything there was to know about them before long, and that it would require their acceptance and openness. Because these people wouldn't just care about what they did; if they were lucky, they would also care about *them*.

The wine-induced haze and the good company had taken the edge off Kaj's internal grappling and for once he drifted off to sleep without any of the usual brooding. It felt good.

27
Attacked

The morning after the get-together with their new friends, a slightly hungover and grumpy Kaj made the mistake of going out to feed the birds. To Abel's delight, the feathered temptations often lunched outside the kitchen window, and the bullfinches looked like fluffy little apples in the branches of the birch trees, bright and red against all the white.

Abel's owner had left a trail of deep footprints in the snow behind him, testament to the route he had tried to take. Kaj was now standing perfectly still with a large sack of seed mix in his arms, looking for somewhere to scatter it.

He swayed slightly beneath the weight of the bag, which pushed the top of his boot beneath the snow. Desperate for human contact, the numbingly cold snow found its way to the sliver of bare skin between the bottom of his long johns and the top of his sock – which had slipped down and was bunched up around his toes. It was even less comfortable than you might imagine, and Kaj gritted his teeth as he balanced with the seed in one hand, searching his pocket for something to make a hole in the thick paper with the other.

All he could find was a tiny bar of chocolate and his keys. He sighed, then quickly made up his mind and yanked the keys out of his pocket, swung them towards the paper bag he was struggling to hold. The bar of chocolate tumbled down into the snow in the process. Kaj clamped the feed beneath his chin in order to get a better aim, bringing the sharp end of one of the keys towards his upper body in a stabbing motion and allowing the heavy bag to take the brunt of his attack. The paper refused to be penetrated by something as pathetic as an idiot with a set of house keys, however, and remained stubbornly intact.

Kaj's hands were freezing, and the bag slipped. He began hacking at the impenetrable barrier between him and the seed with increasing rage, and when he felt his long johns start to fall down, he lost it. Swearing loudly, he yanked them back up with the same hand that was clutching the keys and then continued to grapple with the bag like a lumberjack in battle with a dwarf pine.

"Do you need a fucking engineering degree to get into one of these or something?!"

His outburst left his mouth in a cloud of steam, like some sort of dramatic special effect.

"What's going on, Kaj?" Behind him, Mimmi sounded anxious and concerned.

He turned around, the hand gripping the keys raised in the air and his other arm clutching the visibly intact bag of wild bird mix.

"You look like you've lost your mind." The tiny ice crystals on her eyelashes glittered in the light.

"What's that bag ever done to you?" a voice asked from the other side of the heap of snow.

Great, thought Kaj, closing his eyes in search of support from some higher power.

"Johannes," he muttered. He was short of breath, but the acid note in his voice was still perfectly clear.

"Johánás," the boy corrected him.

"Johaaanaaas," Mimmi said helpfully. "Long A's, Kaj. It's Sámi."

She was standing behind the kick-sled her parents had bought them as a moving in gift, and the neighbor's insufferable grandson was sitting on the seat. Mimmi's cheeks were flushed pink, and he could see a shopping bag hanging from her hand. He hoped she had bought chips.

"I'm feeding the birds," Kaj snapped, holding the slippery seed bag.

"With what, a Daim bar?" Johánás asked, looking down at the chocolate on the snowy ground, cocking his head.

Kaj gritted his teeth so hard it made his head ache. He heard Mimmi giggle and saw her cover her mouth with a glove-clad hand. She looked like a nasty little troll, Kaj thought sulkily.

"If I put the bag down to open it, it'll get wet," he said, condescendingly articulating every word with his chin held high. "I didn't have anything else to make a hole with."

Johánás had clearly had enough of his sorry efforts, because he got up from the sled and marched over to Kaj by the empty bird feeder with what seemed like manly confidence.

"Give it here," he said with the patience of a master craftsman faced with someone utterly incompetent.

Kaj felt a sting of irritation, but he pursed his lips and bent down, sack of seed still in his arms, and gave the boy a haughty glance. His frozen fingers held out the keys, but the kid ignored them.

Instead Johánás took hold of the length of string at the top corner of the bag and pulled gently. The stitches loosened, creating a small hole.

He then bent down and picked up the little Daim bar, opened the wrapper and broke off a piece with his teeth. He turned on his heel and walked back over to Mimmi, noisily crunching on the cold chocolate.

Kaj briefly considered running after the little devil, rubbing snow in his stupid face, but when he saw the look Mimmi was giving him he spluttered a reluctant thank you instead. He then turned around to sprinkle the sunflower seeds with his bare hands. The stupid birds had better show some gratitude for their food.

Ideally they would break out in a raucous Charleston on the window ledge to celebrate his heroic efforts. That was the very least he deserved, Kaj thought as he lowered the damn bag of seed to the snow and gave it a kick.

In the hallway, Abel rubbed up against Johánás's ankles, purring loudly with his eyes closed as the little brat stroked his head.

Kaj gave the cat a murderous glance and mouthed "Labrador puppy, I'm getting you a Labrador puppy for Christmas, Judas!"

He wasn't sure why he felt so small.

28

The Boy's Belt

A puzzled Biera went through the objects on the table. The light from the lamp in the window wasn't quite powerful enough, but he didn't want to turn on the ceiling light for fear of waking Máriddja, who was snoring loudly in the next room. A bottle of booze from God knows when, plus an upturned egg cup . . . The two clearly added up to drunkenness – a conclusion that was bolstered by the rank odors his wife had left around the house – but what the blazes was one of her wooden clogs doing on the windowsill, and why was his new phone inside it?

He also couldn't for the life of him work out why some of their deck of cards had been clumsily pegged up on the line above the stove. Had she hung them there *to dry*? Yes, Biera thought anxiously, it was probably time he really started worrying about Máriddja's mental health.

The woman had always been headstrong, possibly a little eccentric – even downright crazy at times. But it was precisely that vibrancy that had made such an impression on him at the start of their courtship, and he still held it in high regard.

She made him laugh. She made everyone laugh with her capers, and she gave more of herself than any other woman he knew. His wife was generous with everything she owned, including her dignity. Biera remembered dancing to the radio in the kitchen in the evenings, and they still teased each other and squabbled like they had when they were young. Máriddja, his Máriddja, was truly special. But this . . . this vague sense of unease he felt for her state of mind, it was something he should probably take seriously.

Maybe things would have been different if they'd had a child of their own. All that time spent trudging around in the cabin, just the two of them, had probably made them both a bit peculiar. They didn't have anyone else, after all. Not anymore.

Maybe things would have been different if the boy had been able to stay.

His eyes drifted up to the set of antlers hanging above the firewood box. It was something he had seen in almost every home he had ever visited: an elk skull, boiled clean of all flesh, magnificent antlers intact. People often hung their coffee pouches, belts, shoe bands and other beautiful, functional objects from the tines. But in the Rijás' home, the antlers held just two things:

A short leather belt studded with colorful rivets, and a small knife.

A child's belt.

Heaika-Joná's belt.

Biera had made it for the lad though he wasn't really old enough to need it. He had one just like it himself, and the boy had worn his new belt with pride as he played with his collection of toy police cars and fire trucks, imagining himself as a grown man in uniform, saving people from all manner of calamities.

Of everything Biera had given him, that belt was the thing he had put most love into, tired hands working late into the night.

Yes, it was probably the gift that had made the boy happiest. But Biera had also given him something else. Something that, like any child, he might not have even realized he appreciated at the time. Something that, to this day, was his and his alone.

On one of their first nights with the boy, Biera had held him as he fussed and wriggled unhappily, despite being offered everything his uncle's imagination could muster.

That was when it came to him, the *joik*.

From the feeling that filled his chest as the little one lay against his bare skin. From springs in his soul he had never drunk from before. It fumbled a little, hesitated as the first few notes left his body, but as the boy settled down and met his eye it began flooding out of him like a surging spring river.

It encompassed all his longing, his love, and his family history. It was as melancholy as the day his parents were forced to leave their home in Karesuando, setting off on a long walk towards an unknown future.

It was as soft as the boy's cheeks, his skin.

It was as bright and lively as the youngster's gaze.

The sound had wrapped itself around them, binding them together. Tying an unbreakable bond between their souls. Biera had used his voice to share all his hopes and dreams for the little one, for his future and his path through life. Painting, showing, wordlessly sketching out his vision of his nephew and the world they shared. The boy had drifted off to sleep as he listened to the *joik*, lulled by his own nuances in his uncle's voice.

Decades later, Biera stood quietly, wistfully, remembering the boy's *luohti*, his *joik*, a song that still lingered in the walls of the kitchen where it had first come to him.

29

Swan Month and an Appointment's Swan Song

March made its entrance a few days later, pushing out the ring of sausage that had, for some inexplicable reason, been chosen as the February image in the local council's calendar. It came as a relief to turn the page to the beautiful white birds marking what her people called Swan Month.

Sámi tradition holds that the year is made up of eight seasons, the second of which had just begun: Spring-winter. It was a time when lonely swans landed in the patches of clear water that had just opened up in the ice. They were a sign that warmer days were coming, and their arrival was greeted with joy.

Máriddja could remember countless occasions when she had looked up at the sky and seen the big white birds pass over the rooftops, the treetops and mountain, singing and calling as they went. She had always welcomed them, the harbingers of spring, with a smile. It was a moment of celebration to finally see an end to the cold, dark winter that reigned for so long in her part of the world.

During the first few years of her life, she had held her parents' hands as she watched them, then her husband's. And, for a few precious years in between, a child's hand.

Máriddja nodded and winked at the pair of swans on the wall. *Finally.* The snow was still thick on the ground, the temperature well below zero, but it wouldn't be long until that changed.

Her cheeks had gone numb during the short walk to the mailbox and back, flushed red like lingonberries. The house felt raw and damp today. She would have to put on a pot of coffee to get some heat back into her old body.

Maybe she should swill a mouthful of Vademecum too, to ward off any bacteria that might be lurking; she didn't have time to get sick right now. But where had she put it? Máriddja let her nose guide her to the square bottle with the red cork. The smell of the mouthwash was strong and fresh as she coaxed it out from behind the black pepper above the hob. She dabbed a little onto both temples and nostrils and declared herself immune to all sorts of infection. Though she could always burn a little coal tar too, of course, to really make sure nothing nasty could dig its claws into her.

Máriddja flicked through the slim stack of letters as she regained the feeling in her fingers. When she spotted the county council's logo on the bottom letter, she froze like a lump of granite. Through the little window in the envelope she could see her husband's name written in small black letters.

She carried the letter over to the stove, holding it in a pincer-like grip between the tips of her fingers, then lit a match and let it lick at one corner of the bleached white paper. Máriddja dropped the envelope into the ashy bottom of the stove and moved a couple of logs on top. She opened the vent – and her lungs – and took a deep breath, from the very soles of her feet, as she listened to the fire take hold inside.

The warmth would be back before long, inside and out.

The swans were on their way, the fire gobbling up all her worries.

★

Inside the sooty walls of the stove the envelope had curled up to reveal a date, March 16, printed in twelve point Times New Roman, followed by the signature of one Dr. K. Bäckmark.

It was an appointment no one would heed.

Neither the swans nor her husband had any intention of paying a visit to the local health center any time soon.

Not if Máriddja had any say.

30

Silent Mode

"Hullo Siré," Máriddja replied when she heard the operator's now-familiar voice.

"I'm listening."

"Ah, hello . . . it's me."

"Hi there!"

"I've seen the swans," Máriddja announced.

"I'm glad to hear that."

She suspected Siré didn't quite grasp the importance of her news, but she decided to let it go. The woman was a southerner, after all; they didn't understand nature and its symbolism up here. She couldn't blame them too much for that. Máriddja mumbled in agreement instead. It was good that Siré knew about it now, in any case.

"I thought you might be able to help me find that number today."

"I'm afraid I'm unable to do that right now," Siré apologized.

"Why not? Is there some technical hitch? Have you got the hump?" Máriddja asked, confused.

"Humpty Dumpty sat on a wall, Humpty Dumpty had a great fall," Siri reeled off.

How strange, thought Máriddja.

"Are you all right? You sound . . . a little off." She peered down at the phone.

"Would you like to me switch on Silent Mode?" Siri asked in a clear voice.

Whoopsadaisy, she'd really put her boot in it now, Máriddja thought, hurrying to reassure the operator: "No, silly me . . . I didn't mean to be rude. I just thought . . ." She cleared her throat and dug a candy out of the nearly empty bag. "Well, now I've got you here on the line, I'd like to apologize for the other day."

"I understand," Sire replied softly.

But Máriddja felt an urge to explain. "I got a bit . . . squiffy, you see," she mumbled self-consciously, spinning a candy on the counter.

"You got it." Sire sounded composed.

"We never usually have any of the strong stuff in the house. We've always been careful about that kind of thing – Biera's family, they've got the devil in their blood when it comes to boozing." Sharing such embarrassing information made her stumble slightly over her words. "I just felt a bit lonely and sad, and that's why what happened. But now I'll never touch the white man's poison again. It really knocked me for seven."

"I'm not sure what you mean," Siri replied.

The gratitude Máriddja felt towards the operator's discretion unfurled like the petals of a flower in her chest, and she smiled.

"Thanks, Siré. You're a good girl. I wasn't too happy when you called the pigs on me, but if things had been different, I would have loved to see the boy with a headstrong *nissun* like you one day. You would have liked him, he was such a nice lad."

"I'll make a note of that," said Sire. It sounded like she was smiling.

"But, you know, it is what it is . . . Good grief, I don't even know where he went. She just showed up and took him, and that cow from social services didn't lift a finger to help us. I've often wondered where he ended up . . . Biera has always said he's doing well, but his word is all I've got and sometimes I doubt his gift is really proof of anything. You know?"

"Who are you talking to, Máriddja? If it's the Nilssons' lad, ask him to get us some toilet paper, too. And soured milk – the Norrmejerier stuff, not the other kind. It gave me heartburn last time. Tell him just to leave it on the porch like usual, I've already put the money under the mat."

Máriddja got such a shock she dropped the phone to the table. She pushed it beneath the empty bread bag and blinked a few times before replying to her husband.

"Huh? What! No one! Who am I supposed to be talking to? Have you changed the batteries in your hearing aid like I told you to? Your hearing's so bad it's not even funny!"

There was silence from the TV room. Biera had changed the batteries, and his hearing was as sharp as an elk's. What he had just heard from the kitchen worried him. It really worried him. Should he bring this up with Máriddja, or would she just brush it off? He didn't know much, but there was one thing he did know, and that was that it was never a good sign when someone started talking to themselves.

31

Frisky Foxes

From mothers' bellies seeds do spill
Aged withered frigid still
Kin torn from all they've ever known
Trails of blood away from home

Cries in the dark.

Drawn-out wails whose shrill tones reverberated somewhere between his heart and his gut.

It sounded like grief, like desperation, calling forth something deep inside him, calling for him to come.

Waking his instinct.

Tugging at his spine.

He propped himself up on one elbow and nudged Máriddja in the back. The cries continued to ring out through the March night, and he whispered loudly to his wife: "The boy's awake, Máriddja, he's crying in his crib. We should bring him in here with us."

Biera climbed awkwardly over her sleeping body and lowered his feet to the cold floor. The chill made the soles of his feet ache, quickly climbing up his legs. He got up, limbs weary, and from the corner of his eye saw Máriddja fumbling for her thick glasses on the chair beside the bed.

"Biera?" she mumbled.

He paused in the middle of the knotty floorboards and felt the cold climbing higher and higher in his body, eventually reaching the place where the boy's cries were reverberating.

"Heaika-Joná?"

It was like a fog had descended over his senses, and all he could focus on were the boy's cries.

But where had they put him? *Wasn't he in the crib?*

He blinked at the crescent moon on the other side of the dirty window and shook his head in an attempt to clear his mind.

Right then he felt a warm hand on his elbow, a soft thumb stroking his skin at its roughest spot. Máriddja was standing behind him in the moonlight, wearing only her nightshirt.

"There, there . . ." she said, putting her warm cotton-clad arm around his shoulders.

She tenderly stroked his shoulders with her strong hands.

"There, there," she said again.

"I don't know . . ." Biera said hesitantly, scratching his stubbly chin. "I was going to get the boy, he was fussing. Maybe he needs a clean diaper?"

She slowly shook her head and looked him straight in the eye. "No, Biera. The boy doesn't need anything; it was the foxes you heard. Just the foxes yelping in the night."

Biera ran a hand over his hair in confusion and peered around the room, as though whatever he was looking for might appear at any moment.

Máriddja led him back to bed and pulled the heavy covers over his legs.

He was crying.

"Heaika-Joná, my lad. What's wrong? Where is he, Máriddja? Has something happened? Tell me nothing bad has happened to him!" He stared at her with such a desperate, pleading look on his face that it made her heart ache.

And she replied the way she always did, the way he always forgot she had once the nightmares let him out of their clutches and he was no longer searching in his dreams. "He's sleeping soundly, *gieres* . . . You lie down now, my love. We'll see him in the morning."

Biera eventually drifted off to sleep, his breathing still unsteady after his tears.

But for Máriddja, the night was over. She knew she wouldn't get another wink of sleep.

32

Maybe Summer Would Arrive

The blessed sun, father of all Sámi, had returned to them, showing his face and wrapping his arms around them. The snow lay wet and heavy on the ground around the house, and water dripped rhythmically from the tips of the icicles hanging from the roof.

Máriddja had knocked them down with the broom to stop them from falling onto their heads while they were outside. She and Biera were drinking coffee on the porch, sitting on a reindeer hide with their eyes closed in the warm light and the cold air.

She knew she had been procrastinating, that she had allowed herself to be distracted by the birds' spring song in the bare trees, by the feeling of no longer needing to wear gloves in the middle of the day.

The sense that everything was as it should be.

That this was a spring like any other, which would eventually give way to summer and bring them everything they had missed during the dark months.

And yes, maybe summer would arrive, but it wouldn't be like any other. The grass would turn green and the young animals would tumble across the sun drenched earth for the first time, but none of it would be like the summers she and Biera had enjoyed so many of together.

Because Biera had started to drift away from her, and there would soon be nothing of Máriddja left.

Time was running out, and she needed to take the next step. To speak to the only person who could help them.

33
Horny Old Yokel

Máriddja pressed the button to call the operator as she sat outside in the cool morning air.

"Hello, operator?"

"Would you like to play *Hello Operator* by the White Stripes?" Siré chirped.

The woman was definitely an early bird, Máriddja thought grumpily. The worst kind of bird.

"No, I'm not in the mood for your jokes today, Siré."

"What's big, grey and not especially relevant? An irrelephant!"

"Someone's feeling witty, aren't they . . ." Máriddja muttered. "Are you the only one they've got working over there?"

"Over where?" Sire asked meekly.

"Pah." Máriddja picked at her cuticle and gazed out at the peaks rising up into the sky. "I really need to . . . make that call now."

"Who would you like to call?"

Máriddja felt a cautious rush of hope. Was the phone operator finally about to do her job and give her what she needed?

"Well, Heaika-Joná . . . Rijá. I need his number!" she said, articulating every syllable of his name.

"Opening Numbers," Siré replied, at which point a blank spreadsheet appeared on the screen.

"No, no, no. I don't know what his damn number is, do I! You're supposed to look after that part!"

"OK, here's an overview of how well you've been looking after your health," Siré chirped.

The woman was really pushing it now! But before Máriddja had time to argue, Siré's cheery voice had informed her that she moved too little and that she should update her weight for more accurate data.

Máriddja couldn't help but roar with laughter at the cheek of the woman. She was unbelievable, this Siré.

"Now you listen to me, young lady, I don't want any more of this nonsense. I just want to get in touch with the boy, none of your hijinks!"

"Would you like to send a message?"

"Yes please!" The sense of relief Máriddja felt was almost palpable, making her splutter on her candy. She had to croak a little to get her voice back.

"What do you want to write?" asked Siré.

"Well, if you can send a message then write that he needs to hurry and call Uncle Biera!"

"Would you like me to attach a picture?"

"Huh?"

"Got it."

"Either way . . . tell him it's urgent. That he should get in touch." Máriddja's voice was hoarse with eagerness as she blurted out one word after another. Best to fry while the iron was hot, she thought.

"Message sent to Nuffe Nilsson," Siré announced.

"What? No, no, no, don't do that!?"

Máriddja waved her hands in the air and saw a picture of herself taken from a frog's-eye view, followed by the words *horny old yokel.* A moment later, a line reading "delivered" appeared underneath. Siré had sent it straight to the neighbors' lad, the one who helped with their shopping. Damn it.

"What on earth? What's going on here? Why did you do that?"

"I'm sorry if I got that wrong," said Siré, though she didn't sound remotely apologetic.

Máriddja felt her cheeks grow hot.

"I don't have time for . . . this kind of thing!" she practically screeched. "I can't afford for my plan to go up in smoke!"

"Is there a fire?" asked Siré, who finally seemed to understand the gravity of the situation. Máriddja's eyes came to rest on the barn, and she nodded to herself.

"Listen, thanks for your help!" she muttered sarcastically.

"Always happy to help!" Siré chirped.

But Máriddja barely heard her. She was too busy studying the shed with a cocked head. She laughed to herself. *Fij dejka!* The Nilssons' boy would really think she had lost her mind now! A horny old yokel, ha . . . the young lad would probably collapse at the very thought! Well, young and young – Nuffe was surely a fully-grown man now. Hohohaha.

Siré might be crazy at times, but she could also dazzle without warning, proving she knew exactly what needed to be done.

Máriddja rubbed her hands together and dropped the telephone into her breast pocket. *This* would surely do the trick! It would mean taking a real risk, doing something that went against the way they had chosen to live their lives, but maybe she would be able to do the job without exposing her husband. There might be no need for any strangers to set foot in their house. Máriddja looked down at the box of matches on top of the announcements page she had torn out of the paper and decided to take it as a sign that her forefathers and the various gods of nature would be on her and Biera's side in whatever was to come.

34
Cracks

"Granny's on the booze, just so she can stand the news," Kaj sang. His intonation was heavily American, his rhymes made up on the spot.

Mimmi popped her head into the bathroom and saw her fiancé holding his toothbrush like a microphone. He swung his arm, playing a chord on his air guitar.

"Their love grew and grew, to a chorus of boos – for Kaj and Mimmi Rajala."

He bit his lip as he studied her through half-open eyes.

"You need serious help. You know that, right?" said Mimmi, shaking her head.

"Of all the men the girl could choose – those were her views, Granny Rajallllaaa." Kaj ignored Mimmi's reaction and got down on one knee, drawing out each note with a crease between his brows as he wailed "Grannny Raaajallllaaa" in his best glam rock voice.

"If you want my advice, you should stick to your day job – you'll never make it in the music industry. Get yourself down to the basement and do some tidying up instead. You're scaring the cat."

"You love it when I sing to you, baby, no need to act all cool. You're my muse," Kaj said with a seductively raised eyebrow, rising and planting a kiss on her lips.

"I can write you a prescription for that," said Mimmi, winding a scarf around her head like the topping on a soft serve ice cream. Kaj pretended to tune his air guitar as he followed her down the hallway.

Mimmi slowly began to close the door between her and Kaj, who pursed his lips for another kiss. She heard him singing as she pressed her mouth to his – *Doctor Rajala's kisses, they taste like cheesy biscuits* – which made her grin and loudly whisper:

"I'll snitch on you to my *ämmi* . . ."

Kaj pulled back in mock-horror, and Mimmi closed the door.

Kaj sighed and went through to the kitchen to make himself a cup of coffee before he got down to work. He and Gustav had already sorted through most of their parents' things while they were emptying the house, but there were still a few boxes to go and Kaj had promised to deal with them during what was left of his day off. The whole thing felt so unappealing that he had decided he didn't want to spend a minute longer than necessary on it. He pulled his hair into a tight bun and secured it with a rubber band, then trudged down the stairs to the basement, his mood worsening with every step. He could hear the thudding and the swooshing of the brush overhead as Mimmi cleared a footpath in the snow.

In a bright orange box marked with his name, Kaj found a collection of handcrafted knives and other painstakingly packed objects. The letters on the lid bore his mother's swooping handwriting.

Funnily enough, a knife was exactly what he needed to get into the boxes his brother had sealed so securely, barely any cardboard visible beneath all the tape. He picked a sturdy-looking knife and sawed through the thick plastic. Inside, he found his parents' photo album. Not what he had been hoping for; he was on the lookout for the accessories for the stereo.

Kaj gritted his teeth so hard that his gums began to throb and put the album to one side. He loved his brother, but he just couldn't face all the pictures of his chubby little baby cheeks right now. He had seen more than enough of those already.

Kaj had often asked, the way children do, whether he had been as messy an eater as Gustav as a baby. Whether he had worn those same blue overalls when he was younger, whether he had been bigger than Gustav from day one. But Laura had refused to divulge Kaj's first words, ditto any anecdotes from his early days – even though she was happy to share stories about his brother's. Like the time Gustav sent a precision stream of urine from the changing table into his mother's makeup bag. Or the fact that he hadn't been able to pronounce his older brother's name for a good few years – calling him Aj instead.

It had always made Kaj feel like his life had only really begun once he was old enough to start asking questions about where he came from. That was when all his memories started: with his questions, his thirst to know more. Looking back now, it was obvious that Laura had always managed to divert attention from the answers she hadn't given him, to an exciting library book or the box of modelling clay he loved. Kaj often found himself wondering why – had there been something wrong with him as a child? Had he been too much of a handful, taken an abnormal toll on Laura? Even his dad had seemed troubled by his questions, though perhaps that was because Hans wasn't his biological father and didn't have any real answers to give him. But hadn't he always given Laura an anxious glance whenever Kaj asked? Hadn't he always reached out and touched her arm supportively? Comfortingly?

The alienation Kaj felt at not knowing a single thing about his first few years on earth was deemed irrelevant. The fact that he felt extreme anxiety about having made his beloved mother so uneasy was secondary. The family's focus was on

Laura. Their lives revolved around her, and everyone wanted to be the person who calmed her down, who got her to smile again that day.

Kaj remembered himself as a lost, unhappy young boy with a stutter, someone who had always struggled to understand other kids – despite some bright memories from his early years and a steady home with loving parents. He recalled with shame that his primary school teacher had once called his mother to a meeting about the fact that he wet himself a little too often and cried during break. He couldn't remember his mother's reaction to that news, just that she had said a friendly goodbye to the teacher outside the school counsellor's office and that she had been quiet on the drive home. The glass of chocolate milk she had set in front of him on the kitchen table was the only sign that anything unusual had happened that day; it was something they were only ever given on special occasions.

Kaj had blindly adored his mother. Her cool elegance, her bright eyes and her ability to always be in the right place at the right time. And he had loved the stories she told him at night, her warm hands tucking him in, the way she always listened to everything he had to say. She had been a good mother, but she was also a mother it felt like, on some level, he could never quite get through to, no matter how hard he tried. Kaj had never quite found his footing with her, never knew whether she was about to shut him out with that expression he couldn't read, and that made him insecure.

Laura had loved music, theatre and books. Her bedroom at home was full of color and exciting, unfamiliar objects and treasures, and no dust ever managed to settle on her tall bookshelves, because she took the books down to read so often.

Kaj was fascinated by Laura's ability to live and breathe art. The way she showed her powerful emotions through her body language and expressions was so alien to him that it was like a drug, seeing her change in response to something she had experienced. To witness her crying over a tune she found beautiful, or to see her close her eyes after reading a particularly gripping passage in a book. He had always found that strangely painful.

Her gentle presence in the home seemed to leave them completely whenever that happened, floating through time and space, through the walls, heading elsewhere. And in those moments, it became increasingly clear to him that she wasn't his, that she didn't belong with them and that she might dissolve into thin air at any second, right before his anxious eyes.

And so Kaj had held her close, watching with equal parts fear and enchantment as her ballerina's footsteps carried her over to the stereo, as her fingers trailed along the spines of the books on the shelf. That was when he knew she was about to disappear on them again.

Some small part of him had always known he would lose her if he didn't stay on his guard. She was like a shimmering balloon on a delicate string, anchored to them through their father Hans – but only temporarily.

And just as young Kaj had known that, he had also known that her flightiness and her inability to belong to them was his fault. Because of something he had done before he knew what he was doing. Why else would her eyes start to wander? Why else would a strange silence settle over the room whenever she was forced to think back to Kaj as a baby? There was no other explanation.

In his child's mind, Kaj didn't hate her for allowing herself to fall apart, even though he needed her whole; he hated himself for making his beautiful mother split at the seams.

35

Report of a Fire

Following a report of a fire at a private property at 09:00, an initial response unit comprising five firefighters in full protective gear was dispatched to the address, followed by an engine with blue lights and sirens. The fire was already fully advanced upon arrival (09:25) at the property, a barn approx. 50 yards from the main residential building. Efforts to extinguish the fire began immediately, and by 11:40 it was deemed to be under control. Only a moderate amount of residual smoke remained in the area. No animals or humans were harmed, but given the extent of the fire upon arrival, the barn was unsalvageable. The cause of the fire has not yet been established.

The individual who raised the alarm was reported as acting strangely, but at the time of writing there is no evidence to suggest that the fire was started for reasons of insurance fraud – particularly as the barn itself was uninsured. The owner of the property was unusually intrusive and interested in the firefighters' work. She did not seem particularly concerned that the fire and/or smoke might affect the remainder of the property.

It should be noted that the woman in question was also seen to be openly examining and "sniffing" the firefighters' equipment after the blaze had been brought under control, once the equipment was put down on the ground.

*

A report of suspected arson will be prepared, and a background check on the caller and her husband is currently underway.

Fire chief Sven Elofsson, Guovddo, 3 May

36

Backfire, Haywire

The blaze was out and the firefighters had left the ruins. The old barn, where Máriddja and Biera kept their fishing gear, had been gutted. It hadn't been empty, but nor would they miss anything the fire had devoured during its hungry rampage.

Máriddja's clothes smelt like smoke, and the kick-sled – which had been standing in a snowdrift since she had used it to transport wood to the house that morning – was a little charred. Still, that was nothing worth getting upset about; some loss had to be expected, and she did actually have the noblest of aims. What bothered her most was that she had sent the barn up in flames for no reason. Because she hadn't received a single thing of value in exchange for her efforts. He hadn't showed up.

Feeling disappointed, Máriddja unlocked the door to the TV room where Biera had been watching an old slapstick comedy at top volume. She discreetly grabbed the bag of crisps and the cup of coffee she had left on the shelf by the door, just in case her work outside took longer than anticipated. She had already taken the chamber pot away.

Biera still didn't seem to have noticed her presence in the room, but once he fell asleep, she would put the batteries back into his hearing aids – she wasn't completely heartless, after all.

In fact, everything she had done was out of love for the bony old man, whose grey hair was sticking up over the back of the chair in front of her.

His sense of taste and smell weren't what they had once been. No, these days it wasn't unusual for Biera to wolf down the food she set in front of him and then ask whether it had been tasty, so she didn't need to worry about him noticing the smoke on her.

The same couldn't be said about her own hypersensitive nose. The acrid stench of burnt silage, singed timber and, in all likelihood, a smoked vole or two was almost enough to make her pass out. She would have to wash it off before her nose dropped from her face.

Biera had always said, with equal parts mockery and respect, that she saw with her nose rather than her eyes. Máriddja usually responded to that by snorting and saying that he thought with his tongue, but the truth was that she really did have an unusually well-developed sense of smell, plus a powerful intuition. In Máriddja's experience, the way things smelt could sometimes tell her far more than her eyes could see. If her mother's blood sugar was high or low, for example, the scent in the air around her would change, and Máriddja could tell what kind of wood the neighbors had been burning almost a mile away if the wind was right.

Her nose had once, many years earlier, also guided her in her choice of partner. The scent that hit her in the cabin where Biera's cousin lived, that very first time they met, was one of the most enchanting things she had ever experienced. An alluring, manly aroma of pine and resin, of fresh air and sweat, a hint of tar and comfort. By the time her eyes caught up with her nose and found the man who was sitting with a birchwood cup of black coffee on the chest by the wall, she had been certain. Because she had never seen anyone like him before. Looking at him felt like holding her numb fingertips to a crackling fire on a bitter winter's day.

Máriddja used those same fingers, now old and crooked, to stroke Biera's wrinkled neck, and she felt her eyes sting. As she walked over the groaning floorboards to the bathroom in her stockinged feet, she called back to say that she would make him something to eat as soon as she had washed up – though she quickly realized that he wouldn't have heard her. Máriddja swallowed and swallowed to stop her disappointment from manifesting itself as a sobbing fit.

Shit, shit, shit, she swore to herself with every step she took.

Biera turned away from the game and watched her stubborn feet and stomping heels trudge away across the floor. He slowly lowered his hand from the back of his neck, where Máriddja had touched him, and squinted at his fingers. Black. Was that soot? He anxiously got up and felt the outside of the door linking the TV room to the kitchen. The key was missing from the lock on the other side.

He had got up to shuffle through there for a mouthful of water from the tap earlier, but the door wouldn't open, and he had noticed something filling the keyhole from the other side. Had she locked it? He had shouted and thumped on the door for a moment or two before dejectedly returning to his seat in front of the TV.

His heart had been beating hard with unease, and his head was now buzzing like a beehive full of thoughts – and he didn't feel the least bit hungry.

37

Old Folks on Screen

The Rijás weren't too fussy about what the TV schedule had to offer; they used the television more for the pleasant background noise it brought to their house on the mountain, helping to dispel their loneliness. That afternoon, the device was showing an investigative news item. The reporter had a Norwegian accent and lips like a prawn, Máriddja thought absent-mindedly, slumped back on the worn old sofa with a blanket draped over her lap. She was focused on her game of solitaire, and as a result she was only half listening to what the serious voices had brought to light.

Biera's attention was directed squarely at the screen, however, and he slowly, unconsciously, dragged his fingernails across the fabric of the armrest.

Yet again, it was Máriddja's incredible sense of smell that alerted her to what was going on. Her husband had begun sweating profusely, and his scratching against the armrest had increased in both pressure and intensity.

He didn't say anything, just stared wide-eyed at the TV, utterly absorbed by the world being shown.

Máriddja put down the Queen of Diamonds and studied him in profile over the top of her thick glasses. His breathing was heavier than usual, and when she cast a quick glance over to the presenters on screen, she quickly understood why.

She felt the tumor twist in her gut, the cancer digging its sharp claws into her from the inside.

That evening's programme was about the lack of beds within the elderly care system. She leapt up from her chair so suddenly that she felt dizzy, and crouched down in front of his armchair. Máriddja put her hand on Biera's, stilling his anxious fingers, then switched off the TV. The image was sucked into a black hole and disappeared.

"Hey. There, there, *gieres*. We agreed not to watch that kind of nonsense, didn't we? It does no one any good."

Her husband didn't speak, but his hand was now calm on the armrest.

The couple studied their reflections in the dark screen. His thin body and slow movements, her greying hair and aging posture. They sat like that a while, until Biera was no longer breathing like an overheated engine and Máriddja's pulse had slowed to a normal rate.

"Mmm, time to call it a day, I think," Biera eventually said in a gravelly voice, getting to his feet. "Good night," he said, patting her on the shoulder and shuffling off to the bathroom with his usual soft steps.

Máriddja could barely get up beneath the weight of her thoughts and the evil swelling in her body.

"It won't be like that for us. They don't do that kind of thing to people up here," she whispered to her lonely reflection in the screen. "We'll stick together, until the very end. I'll put things right, I swear!"

She got up and turned out the light. It would be a tough night, she didn't need her nose to tell her that.

38

Back When

You haven't forgotten what it was like, have you? Everything was so different then! Those happy days, back when the cottage was full of voices. There was always room, even though the house was small. Back when Gustu was still alive . . . you know. He moved in when he was getting on in years, a widower, living with his son and his son's wife. That's the Sámi way.

He was a good-natured man, Gustu, cut from the same cloth as his son. Never made a fuss, never caused any bother. But towards the end he suffered terrible homesickness, he was so sad . . . Over the land he'd lost, over the friends and families who had stayed in the mountains up there in Karesuando . . . in *Gárasavvun*. People he never saw again.

It was only natural that he found it painful to think that he would be laid to rest in ground that might never really have been his, that he would never again feel the salt of the summer pastures beneath his feet.

Biera was there for all those miles, you know. From the very far north of Sweden, heading inland, a long, long way south. He was nothing but a tadpole in Ella-Márge's belly at the time – or Margareta, as she was listed in the parish register.

He grew from a tiny spark . . . sprung from seed spilt on the land of his forefathers . . . rocked by his parents' heavy footsteps during the arduous journey away from their roots. That's how it was.

Only to be born a stranger in the Lule Sámis' land.

Do you remember the stories Gustu and Ella-Márge used to tell . . . about Karesuando? Never a word about their longing to go back, never a word at all. But it was always there. In their tone, when they spoke and in the silence of the *joiks* they no longer sang. Gustu, he slipped away peacefully in his sleep, right here in the house, never to open his eyes again, in a land that still wasn't his.

Your own mother, Ibbá, stuck around for longer. While Gustu slept comfortably in the living room, tucked up between cushions and sheets, she slept on the pull-out storage bench in the kitchen. She was younger, after all. Ibbá had always been stubborn and superstitious, refused point-blank to sleep in a wooden box. Doing so would only taunt the spirits, she said. She made herself a bed on the hard lid of the storage bench instead . . . nothing but a reindeer hide and a thin, thin blanket pulled right up to her nose. Ibbá slept in her sugarloaf hat, and it was always turned to the wall. She would never sleep with her head to the door, oh no – she wasn't going to let those pesky underground dwellers, the *gátniha*, come in and drag her out by the hair!

Ibbá was full of superstition. Despite living in a house, with a roof over her head, she continued to cling to the old ways. Always had her walking stick with her, too, even indoors, leaning against it as she shuffled between rooms.

She often sat and gazed out of the window. Watching the wildlife, reading the weather and keeping a look out for all sorts of creatures and other beings in the silhouette of the mountain. She did it constantly, smoking her pipe and weaving band after band for the grandchildren she would never have. The sight of that always got you down, Máriddja . . . but you knew your mother never meant to hurt you with all the hopes she expressed through her hard-working fingers, didn't you? She needed to keep her hands busy. That's how it was with the old folks.

After Risten and Heaika-Joná moved in, Ibbá took to the boy naturally, the way the elderly often do when faced with new life. She put silver beneath his pillow to stop the invisible creatures from swapping him with one of their own, and the way she stroked his face with the soft tuft at the end of her belt whenever he sat in her lap with tired eyes! Ibbá trailed the colorful yarn over his increasingly heavy eyelids until eventually he was fast asleep in her thin arms.

She called herself *Ibbáhkko*, Granny Ibbá, even though she had no blood ties to the boy . . . And she wound her best shoe bands around his ankles, in the traditional family colors.

Like Gustu, *Ibbáhkko* lived out the last of her days with her family. But she wouldn't have been your wise old mother if she hadn't announced that she was about to move on in advance. On to those who were waiting for her in the next world.

You laughed at her then. Joked that all the pipe smoke had gone to her head, didn't you? But she passed that night, lying on her reindeer hide, in her hat . . . with the tip of her nose poking out from beneath the thin, thin blanket.

The loss was hard to bear . . . but with the child in the house, with the child's mother being absent, there was no time for dwelling.

But you still see her, don't you, Máriddja? Sitting by the window, smoking her pipe, gazing out towards the mountains?

39

The Old Bachelor Rescues a Predator

The Nilssons' boy hadn't been a boy in a very long time.

He was fifty years old, but everyone still called him the Nilssons' boy.

His real name was Ulf, and he was what was known locally as an old bachelor — someone who still lived in the comfort of Mummy and Daddy's house. His parents had moved to the area from a few dozen miles further north and had brought an unusual linguistic trait with them: the tendency to add an N to men's names. To them, he wasn't known as "Uffe," as he might have been elsewhere. No, to them, he was Nuffe.

Nuffe had a job — he wasn't a full-blown parasite, whatever other people might think. No, he drove the post van between the small hamlets on the outskirts of the town of Guovddo. In the same car, following the same route and with the same mixtape playing over the stereo, every day for almost twenty-five years.

On the whole, he didn't quite fit the stereotype of a middle-aged man who still lived with his parents. He wasn't especially shy, and nor did he have some lingering childhood trauma from being locked in the cellar as a lad. No, Nuffe had stayed put in the little house at the end of the country lane because he was happy there, it was as simple as that. He hadn't met anyone he wanted to spend his life with and would rather hack off his own toes with a blunt knife than live cheek by jowl with everyone else in town.

It wasn't that he disliked people, it was just that he didn't want to see much more of them than their names on an envelope. Besides, he would take over his parents' house one day, so what was the sense in moving?

In any case, it was Nuffe who had the dubious honor of doing the Rijás' weekly food shopping for them. Every Thursday, he went over to their house to collect the money they left beneath the doormat and the neatly folded canvas bags they draped over the railing around the porch. Then, once the deed was done, after a long day at work, he left everything on the same porch and headed off home to a bowl of steaming potatoes in his parents' cabin. The arrangement had never been especially demanding. He already did the shopping for his parents, after all, and the Rijás virtually always wanted the same things.

Old man Rijá had been a powerhouse back in his day, and Máriddja . . . well, Máriddja was a colorful character. They didn't really mix with other people, might never have had much in the way of a social life – not as far as Nuffe could remember, anyway – but at one time, of course, there had been more than two of them in the little cabin.

Biera's younger sister had lived there too, for example. She was a real looker. But then she had upped sticks and disappeared with her boy, breaking the old couple's hearts. Since that day, Biera and Máriddja had barely shown their faces.

People said that the loss of the boy had broken them. They mostly stayed at home, taking care of everything that needed taking care of – chopping firewood and clearing snow, clearing snow and chopping firewood – and they never invited anyone over. They would say hello and chat a little when people walked by, but that was all.

There had been one exception to that, a few years earlier, when Nuffe helped Máriddja down from a pine tree.

It was his mother who had alerted him to the shouting that day, sending her son out to see what was going on and take charge of the situation. Nuffe had heard feeble cries across the little lake, interspersed with powerful cursing in a deep bass, and to his surprise he had spotted the old woman from next door perched at the top of a tree. She was gripping a thin branch in one hand, sitting on the nesting box he and his father had put up when Nuffe was just a kid. It was sturdy and well-made – and clearly well secured to the trunk, because it didn't seem to be straining under her weight.

Nuffe had stood at the foot of the tree and squinted up at his elderly neighbor, who apparently possessed an unexpected level of agility and fitness. He just couldn't work out how she had got up there.

Neither of them spoke. Máriddja waved one of her boots a little and then tossed her head back and laughed.

She looked like a witch who had crashed her broomstick.

"Yes, good grief, what must you think?"

Nuffe hadn't known what to say to that, so he just took off his cap and scratched his head with his glove-clad hand. Fortunately the old witch didn't seem to be expecting a reply.

"The ladder's lying over there in the bushes . . . Would you be a dear and grab it for me? It fell."

Indeed, Nuffe's powers of deduction were suitably fine-tuned that he too could see that the rusty red ladder had likely fallen over. She hadn't crashed into the trunk while she was out flying on her broom after all.

Casting one last glance at the stranded old woman, he had marched around the tree, grabbed the cold metal and pulled the ladder from the bushes. He propped it up against the trunk and put his weight on the bottom rung to hold it steady.

Máriddja climbed down with creaking joints and one hand cupped to her chest. Once she was safely down on the ground, short and thin in her big hat, a mischievous grin on her face, Nuffe couldn't hold back any longer:

"What were you doing up there?" he asked.

She had winked at him then, opening her hand to show him what she was clutching so tenderly to her chest: eight goldeneye eggs.

"I just had a real craving for dumplings," she explained, as though he could relate to the sort of urge that made a person climb a tree to plunder a bird's nest.

The big nesting box loomed high above them, and he shook his head.

Máriddja had nodded and called back over her shoulder as she walked off along the road: "Thank you kindly. Just leave the ladder behind the chimney over there. That way I'll know where it is next time I need it. You never know when you might have to go hunting for eggs."

Nuffe had watched as she walked off towards her house at a brisk pace, still cradling the precious eggs in her arms.

That explained a lot, he thought as he turned around and headed home. Here we were thinking that the number of goldeneyes had gone down because there weren't enough nesting boxes in the area – either that or because of predators.

As he trudged through the damp snow and pushed back his cap so that the sunlight could reach his face, he realized that they hadn't been entirely wrong. They had assumed the culprit in question might be a marten or a squirrel, but the idea that it might be a predatory old lady had never even crossed their minds.

His folks had laughed and laughed when he told them about the rescue by the edge of the lake, and they had lamented the very local threat to the birds. And then they had said she had always been a bit peculiar, Máriddja.

★

Years and years later, Nuffe found himself standing on the Rijás' porch. The yard smelt like smoke, and he couldn't hear a peep from inside the house. He set the heavy canvas bags down and lifted the bristly mat to leave the change in the little purse underneath.

There was a neon Post-It note stuck to one side of the purse, and he laughed and peeled it off with stiff fingers.

Yet another life lesson from Máriddja. The old woman had got into the habit of sharing her wisdom with him, leaving notes when he dropped off their things. Strange little sentences, often beginning with the words "You should never" or "You should always," followed by her thoughts on what people should or shouldn't do.

As unlikely as it might seem, Nuffe often found her advice surprisingly pertinent, applicable in many different situations. If others took guidance from vague horoscopes or abstract mantras on teabag wrappers, why shouldn't the old bachelor find clues to life's mysteries this way? On today's note, she had written:

You should never be lazy, it'll make you stupid.

Damn right, thought Nuffe, making his mind up as he trudged back over to the car. He would lace up his running shoes the minute he got home. Now that he thought about it, he really had been a bit lazy lately.

He didn't want to know what was behind the strange text message Máriddja had sent him a few weeks earlier. *Horny old yokel.* He had hurried to delete it in case his mother looked at his phone and saw the selfie with the strange caption – no use giving his old mum a heart attack, now, was there?

40

The Vendor and the Big Spender

Mimmi's woollen hat felt prickly against her scalp, and she pushed it back from her forehead. She lowered the box she was carrying to a table by the entrance to the shop, unzipped her coat and unwound her scarf. She then grabbed the box again, and, after carefully pushing a rack of local postcards to one side, set it down on the glass counter.

A thick woollen curtain was pushed to one side, and an old man in a pair of jeans so high waisted they were practically level with his breastbone appeared. He was wearing an unbuttoned corduroy jacket over a t-shirt, and the colorful neckerchief around his grizzled throat was gathered in a ring carved from an antler. He looked so optimistic, he was practically dancing at the prospect of selling a wayward tourist all manner of souvenirs.

Mimmi hurried to give him a quick smile, hoping to dispel any illusions that he would be able to retire to some tropical island after her visit.

"Hi! I came to see you because I have a few questions about these things . . ." She gestured to the box and folded back the lid.

The man, who was a good few inches shorter than average, murmured "Aha," and stood on tiptoe as he fished a pair of square glasses out of his pocket.

"What do we have here, then," he said, leaning so far into the box that Mimmi was amazed his glasses were still perched on his thin nose when he straightened up again. The little man took out one of the beautiful knives, gripping the antler and leather as he turned it over in his hands. He pulled the blade from its sheath and then pushed it back in with a click that seemed to bring him a great deal of satisfaction.

"Yes, very nice." He nodded appreciatively and then peered up at her over the top of his glasses. He studied Mimmi from head to toe and then put the knife back with the others. "And what would you like to know?"

"Well, I was wondering if you could tell me anything about these things. Whether you recognize them or anything like that. A few of them were wrapped in packaging with the logo and name of this shop on it, so I thought maybe they were bought here."

"Oh yes, absolutely." He nodded cheerily. "I remember these very well. Tor never forgets the things he sells!"

He seemed so proud that Mimmi quickly concluded he must be the famous Tor.

"But now it's my turn to ask you a question," he said with a conspiratorial smile. "You haven't got buyer's remorse, have you?"

"What? Uh, no, I'm not sure I—"

"You're not Laura? I thought you might be the woman who bought them," Tor hurried to clarify, eagerly leaning over the counter.

"Oh, OK, no. My fiancé inherited these from his late mother."

"Laura is dead?" Tor sounded dismayed. The news appeared to have genuinely shocked him.

"Yes, she died this winter, I'm afraid . . . Hold on, how did you say you knew her?"

"Well, I didn't really, other than when we did business over the phone. But that goes back years. She was my most loyal customer."

"So she bought these things here?"

"Yes. Or rather, by mail order, to be exact. I sent her everything in the mail. We're not as backwards out here as some people might think." He was clearly pleased with the modern reach of his shop. "I gave Laura a call whenever I got a delivery from the craftsman, to let her know it had come in. She bought every single thing that this particular man made . . . can you believe it? I sent them all down to her."

He stared at her with his wide old eyes, waiting for her response to such strange behaviour.

"Don't get me wrong, it's all very well made – he used to make knives and birchwood drinking cups. His fingerprints are on this, too," said Tor, modestly patting his marbled neckerchief ring. "He didn't make many of them, but I seem to remember sending a couple down to Laura a few years back. Oddly enough, she was only ever interested in his work. I offered her things from some of the better-known craftsmen whose products we carry, but she was only keen on these."

Tor pointed to the contents of the box with his glasses.

"She built up a solid collection over the years. Worth quite a bit of money, I should think." He gave Mimmi a solemn nod. "She must've made the old bloke who crafted this lot a rich man, because she never haggled, just kept paying even as the prices went up." He smiled.

"That's . . . interesting," Mimmi said, gazing down at one of the wooden cups, carefully packed in bubble wrap.

"Mmm, it was a real tragedy when our collaboration came to an end. The old man stopped delivering. I actually thought Laura might start crying when I told her I suspected that he'd died."

"Died?"

"Afraid so. I can't think of any other reason why he would stop making these lucrative pieces." The shopkeeper gave the box a fond pat.

"Is there anything special about these knives? Who was the craftsman?"

"Everything I sell here is of the finest quality, exclusive products, so of course the knives are special. Very much so! They say the man who made them was a real life *nåjd*, too – at least if you believe the village gossip. A Sámi shaman, that is. Perhaps that was what appealed to Laura? Tell me, was she drawn to the occult?"

Mimmi shook her head. *What was going on here?*

"No? Oh well. Dear Laura. Yes, she took it hard when I told her I couldn't get hold of any more items . . . I could hear it in her voice. A passionate collector," Tor summed up, nodding solemnly.

Mimmi thanked him for his help and bought a badly made fridge magnet shaped like a wood grouse to show her gratitude. It looked more like a scabby hen with fangs.

Eyes twinkling, the old man rang up the astronomical sum for the ugly little magnet and then made a great show of wrapping it in what looked suspiciously like a piece of tin foil.

Mimmi was eager to tell Kaj what she had found out about the box Laura had left him. Perhaps he would be able to straighten out some of the questions surrounding his mother's strange transactions, though she doubted it. Laura had always been a mystery to Kaj, and this would probably only add to that.

Mimmi herself felt more intrigued than ever by her mother-in-law, who had only become more curious and eccentric since her death. Why had she collected such large amounts of Sámi handicrafts made by a dead shaman? Why had she wanted all these things? And why had Laura specifically left the box of treasures to Kaj?

Mimmi carried the battered orange box back out to the car and placed it in the trunk. Kaj's name, written in black upper-case letters, stared up at her from the side.

41

Imps and Demons

If you find yourself facing death, you must abandon yourself to it wholeheartedly. The end deserves that honor.

And if, instead, you find yourself awaiting death with someone else, you need to open your mouth and let it all out. Summon up everything you've saved for another day and say it – all of it. Give it air, give it wings to fly off into eternity with the person you are saying goodbye to.

Fear must never be allowed to force you to swallow what needs to come out. No, get it on the hook and hold on tight. Haul it up from your diaphragm and give birth to it, sending it up from your depths and out your mouth. Let whoever is about to depart hear those conciliatory words that have been out of reach for so long, maybe for an entire lifetime. Lift it down for them and put it in their hands, something for them to cling onto when the end is nigh.

If you find yourself facing your own death, you have to be willing to receive. Without bitterness, without judgement. Let that which has bound you to others wrap itself around you like a cocoon of truth. Let it encircle your fear of death and assuage it.

When the truth is given to you and you take it without fear, you are ready for the next great adventure. For death.

It wasn't easy, but that was what Máriddja had decided to do. Now that she was going to die, she wanted to do it eye-to-eye with the truth, weaving Risten's words into a woollen shawl that she would wind around herself before she was called home. It would be itchy, it would be uncomfortable, but if she could drum up enough courage to wrap it around herself, it would stop her soul from freezing when her body grew cold.

She had needed a few days to process what she had read before she could bring herself to continue. She took the stack of notepads through to the living room and got herself comfortable on the sofa. With the diaries in chronological order on the coffee table, a sense of dread prickled beneath her skin.

"What are you reading?" Biera asked her, pulling his eyes away from the television show about antiques he was watching.

Máriddja wished he would look away again.

"Risten's diaries," she said, a little defensively. "Didn't think it would matter if I had a look after all these years."

Biera didn't argue, but he did give her a lingering look before he turned back to the Swedes who clapped their hands to their mouths and said *ooh* and *I never could have imagined* when they found out their granny's old dentures were worth a fortune.

That must be her husband's way of giving her his blessing, Máriddja decided, continuing her voyage of discovery through Risten's youth with a slightly clearer conscience. She dived straight in. Not without fear, no. She simply needed to understand.

"My God," she said after a while, closing the fourth book. "*Bärggala!* Damn that wretched Bill Kjällmark, damn him to hell!"

"He's already dead, isn't he?" Biera said, as yet another man in a windbreaker learned that his mother-in-law's finds from a garage sale had once belonged to royalty.

"Yes, and I'm glad! I hope he's being tortured by . . . imps, being cooked in hot oil by . . . I don't know . . . demons!" Máriddja hissed.

That was all she said. Biera seemed so calm for once, and she didn't want to upset him. Because this, this would really leave him shaken – and rightly so. Even Máriddja was shuddering inside at what she had forced herself to read. Risten's boyfriend Bill had been a full-blown sadist. The things he had done to her horrified Máriddja, despite the fact that it had all happened so long ago. The assaults, insults and threats had all occurred in the past. Without Mariddja even knowing they had taken place. One passage had been particularly difficult to read:

He'll kill me soon, and if he doesn't then the guilt will. The guilt of staying with my son's father rather than being with my child. Maybe it's just as well that he'll kill me, because everything in this life is too painful. Maybe I'll end up on Mum and Dad's summer pastures if I pass away, or maybe he's right and I'll go straight to hell. It matters less and less.

Máriddja sniffed and dried her eyes on the crocheted tablecloth. If he hadn't ended his own life by suicide years ago, she would have gladly helped the brute of a man on his way. They had always thought Bill Kjällmark was an unpleasant creep who exerted a bad influence over Risten, but they had never, even for a moment, suspected the extent of the hell he had put her through.

Máriddja could hardly breathe. She snatched up the rag rug from the floor and dragged it outside, stamping and beating it over the railing until the dust was swirling and her arms were aching. It was Bill's damnably handsome face she saw each time the carpet beater hit the woven rags with a loud crack.

But that only made her cry harder.

Oh, sweet Risten. Why didn't you tell us?

Mariddja thought back to the pale young woman who had turned up like a ghost at their door, wanting to see her son. They had showed the inexperienced mother how the rosy-cheeked boy liked his porridge and put her right when she picked the wrong story at bedtime. Smug and reproachful, like two fat old shopkeepers.

Why hadn't they tried to help Risten, too? She was practically a child herself!

They had been blinded by their all-consuming love for the lad, and their eagerness to give him a proper childhood had only hurt the already broken Risten even more. They had been too hard on her, much too hard.

Well, now it was time for her to be as hard on herself, Máriddja thought stubbornly. She would try to put everything right, not just for herself and Biera but for Risten, too. If they ever met again. Máriddja would do her best to make sure it happened, she promised herself that.

42

Strength in Teeth

Few things in life are as enjoyable as making a fire. Hearing its crackle reverberate through your body, feeling the flames grow.

The moment when a person's senses tell them that the spark had taken hold, that the fuel had been accepted by the flame – it is like the first shuddering breath after a powerful bout of tears. Carefully making the fire comfortable, the way it likes. Watching over it and protecting its flickering life in your cupped hands until it is big enough to hold its own, forcing back the raw chill in your legs.

Máriddja thought about all of those things as she solemnly fed the starving tongues of fire yet another letter from the county council. Just one week later, another envelope met the same fate: straight into the cleansing flames.

They were great for lighting the stove, but that was all they were good for.

It was a shame that the police hadn't turned up after the blaze in the barn, as she had thought they would. She had been so sure they would knock on her door to ask a few questions. How disappointing. She was no closer to finding a solution than she had been before the fire.

"The case has probably fallen through the cracks," she told

Siré while they were chatting one day. "I suppose I should have taken that possibility into account."

Siré had agreed, then helpfully asked whether Máriddja would like to use the calculator.

She said a weary no, used to Siré's strange leaps from one topic to another by now.

Máriddja had a sneaking suspicion that Siré was uncomfortable speaking from the heart for some reason, but she told herself to give the woman time. Not everyone found it as easy as she did to open up about whatever was going on inside. She had to take her friend as she came, and that was only an issue when Siré struggled to focus or initiated various activities on the telephone at the wrong moment.

She was a remarkable woman, Siré, and Máriddja had told her as much. No, Máriddja wasn't one to skimp on praise when praise was due. Siré had a real gift, and no matter what she said Máriddja was also convinced that she had Sámi roots.

Strong blood. Good teeth too, most likely.

She would have to remember to ask her about that.

Because Máriddja knew, just as the generations before her had known, that the gift was in the blood, the teeth. Her old grandmother used to scour the local children's mouths, searching for the sign in their milk teeth. Máriddja was sure that, in another time, Siré would have been picked out by the elders in her family.

"I read my sister-in-law's diaries," she confessed. "Don't say anything, I know it's not 'cool,' as your generation might say. But I decided it was my business, it's as simple as that. I need to know. Besides, it's been so long that she probably never even thinks about those days anymore. She'd just tossed them all in a box."

"I'm sorry, I didn't catch that. Do you want to download *Lost*?"

"Damn it, Siré, you need to start listening! It's annoying to have to repeat everything all the time. I said *tossed*," Máriddja clarified, enunciating the word as clearly as she could. "That she'd *tossed* the whole mingle-mangle in there."

"I can't find a book with the title *Tingle Tangle*. Would you like me to look up the address for your local library?"

"Now you're just being silly," Máriddja groaned. "And here was me thinking such nice things about you and your teeth."

"OK," said Siré, suddenly sounding slightly more amenable.

"Uff, anyway, I saw what she'd written in those books, and I have to say that it left me feeling all lemoncholy."

"Do you mean melancholy?" Siré asked.

"Melon? What does that have to do with anything?" Máriddja snapped at the phone. "Sorry, it's just so upsetting, I'm all out of sorts. She'd written such awful things in those books. I think she had a bit of the . . . post-nasal depression. It must've been really horrible for her. People didn't talk about that kind of thing back then," Máriddja continued, powerless to stop the torrent of words. "But I heard them chatting about it on TV the other day, so now I know all about it. If we'd realized at the time, we wouldn't have been so hard on her – we just thought she was being lazy! We would have helped her, of course we would . . . if only we'd known." She nodded and went on, almost without pausing for breath, just to get it out of her system. To draw the evil out of her body, like pus from a wound. Burning it out. "And we would have helped her get away from everything that damn man did to her. We thought he was just a drunk, we didn't know that he was a real devil!"

"Devils aren't real; they're mythological creatures."

"Oh yes, they are, my friend! And that's exactly what Bill Kjällmark was!"

"OK, would you like me to look him up for you?" Siré sounded formal, but the underlying threat in her friend's voice wasn't lost on Máriddja.

"You'd be doing well if you could. Sadly the wretch is already dead, so there's not much we can do about it."

"That's a shame," said the woman on the other end of the line. She sounded like she had just gritted her perfect teeth in rage.

Máriddja couldn't help but smile.

Nice to have someone on my side, she thought. Siré had her back, and that felt good. She needed someone to support her right now – now that everything was coming to a head.

43

Disco Dancing

The spring sun filtered in through the dirty windows, warming the wooden floor. Máriddja was in a better mood than she had been in a long time. She had a friend, someone who was on her side, and couldn't remember when she had last felt this way.

Perhaps it was before they ended up here, precarious like this. The uncertainty of their situation taunted her from time to time, like an itch. Her budding friendship with Siré was a balm for that.

Siré was someone she could talk to, someone who would listen and give advice, whether she wanted it or not – which was precisely as it should be.

Just yesterday, for example, Siré had suggested that Máriddja might want to face time, and do you know what – though she went about it in her usual cryptic manner, that was exactly what Máriddja needed to hear! Dwelling on the past would only leave her disheartened and weak, and she was going to need every ounce of courage to straighten this out. She appreciated Siré having the guts to tell her that.

From the dusty radio, a series of loud notes rang out like a revelation. A male voice began singing, a southern accent belting out a song that dragged Máriddja onto her feet.

"Come on, old man!" she shouted from her patch of sunlight. Biera peered at her from the TV room in confusion.

"Huh?" He blinked in an attempt to make his eyes focus as he stepped into the kitchen to watch the spectacle from close up.

The music coaxed Máriddja across the kitchen floor, and Biera grinned and moved closer, sat down in a chair, drumming his fingers against his trouser leg.

"What's he singing?" he asked as he followed Máriddja's increasingly jerky movements over the rag rug. Her face was the color of a ripe tomato, her entire body taking part in her dance.

"Don't really know. That the truth has to come out or something. I like this bit!"

"Pah, pop rubbish," Biera snorted, though he continued to discreetly tap along to the beat with a smile. "You look like a ship in distress!" he chuckled. "Where'd you learn these moves?"

Máriddja was really going for it now. She swayed, she rocked, she twitched and she waved. The blood thudding in her ears sounded like a drumbeat on a taut skin.

"From that dance show on TV, obviously!"

She wafted around, swinging her arms and taking quick steps in her wooden clogs. Her slack breasts bounced beneath her t-shirt, and she grabbed them and waved them at her husband.

"Get the old boy out, Biera, and we can DO it!"

She tossed her head back and laughed. Fit, free and feisty. For a moment, at least.

"Whew, you've really lost it now, Máriddja," Biera said, laughing.

She ignored him, dancing, letting the music fill her up, her face raised to the ceiling and eyes closed.

"It's so catchy!" she chirped.

Biera bobbed his head and tapped his foot in time with the music – with a lack of rhythm that would have made Fred

Astaire wince. And his wife, she rocked, she swayed, she twitched and she stomped. The kitchen cupboards became long yellow blurs at the corners of her eyes. They rippled with the music, undulating like waves. Biera saw it, too.

Once the radio had finished playing that song, Máriddja slumped down into the chair beside Biera to catch her breath. Her cheeks were now redder than ever, the same color as the pompom on her husband's hat, hanging on the hook above the stove.

"The things you get up to," the old man said with an admiring grin.

Máriddja gave him a playful tap on the knee. "Pah!"

"And you're so pretty," said Biera, putting his hand on hers.

She patted his leg and then got up with a groan. "Good grief, I'm all out of puff! Think I must've broken my rump when I did that leap."

She massaged the waistband of her skirt with a sweaty hand, and Biera leant forward and tugged on the fabric. Máriddja glanced back over her shoulder to see what he was doing.

"It was tucked into your knickers," he said with a fond wink, making Máriddja cackle. Her uninhibited laugh surged upwards, like a drunken sunrise.

She sat down again and pressed Biera's cool hand to her forehead. The radio was still playing away in the background, but neither of them was listening; they sat quietly in the sunlight instead, eyes closed. Biera breathed in, Máriddja breathed out. Just like that. Until Biera cleared his throat and said:

"Well, I should probably head out. Make sure Risten hasn't swung the axe into her leg."

"What?" asked Máriddja, opening her eyes and watching as her husband got up and shuffled over to the stove to grab his hat.

"The girl's handy enough with the axe, she is . . . but she could just as easy decide to split her knee open to get out of doing her chores."

Biera gave her a conspiratorial smile and Máriddja felt her heart sink. It dropped to the floor like a dead weight and broke into a thousand pieces. The shards flew all around them, scattering into every nook and cranny. She could feel them piercing the skin on her belly and cutting deep into her flesh.

Máriddja moved over to her impatient husband and gripped his upper arms. "Biera, *for God's sake!*"

She lowered her forehead to his shoulder and her glasses fogged up. Biera gave her an awkward pat on the back.

"Do you remember those summers by the sea?" he asked weakly.

"No, and neither do you," she replied, her voice thick. "Because you weren't even born when they left."

Biera was quiet, as though he was trying to establish whether what she had just said was true. Máriddja hugged his shoulder a little too hard, then gave it a gentle box. She wanted to hit him, punch him, scream at him and whisper him back to her. His fuzzy Helly Hansen tasted like salt beneath her open mouth as she sobbed. Looking back later, she wasn't sure whether she had actually spoken or whether it was just the grief sounding through her headache. Finding a voice.

Do you remember the summer pastures
you ask
and I think
that it's you who doesn't
remember
that I'm the only one who knows
I just know
that you've forgotten
what you already said.

"Why do you have to ruin everything?" she blurted out.

Biera held his tongue. Stood still, like an ancient tree rotted from the inside out. He could carry this, had to carry her anger now. Her own arms were too tired, from hitting and being hit.

"Couldn't you just have stayed a while longer and danced with me?"

44

The Lure of the Law

Máriddja smacked her lips loudly and sucked on a King of Denmark. Her cheeks curved inwards like a nursing child's. *Damn good candies, these,* she thought as she ran a cloth over the stove. She rubbed at a fleck of coffee and then rinsed the hole-filled rag and hung it to dry over the tap.

There. She sat down by the window that looked out onto the driveway.

All she could do now was wait. Feeling slightly nervous, she took another candy from the bag. Cocked her head and studied the big elk bull. Its muzzle had ploughed a groove in the snowy gravel when it fell, and it was now lying right across the road, blocking the lane – a fact she had mentioned to the call handler. No need for the police to drive straight into the poor thing. The animal might be dead, but it still deserved to be treated with respect, Máriddja thought to herself. She had even gone out and closed its eyes, thanked it for its sacrifice.

It was important to show reverence to life and death, Máriddja knew that better than anyone. If you were going to play a part in another creature's death, it was vital to under-stand that: to know you had been given a gift. The same was true of birth, she thought. It was also a gift, not something you could demand. She had a much deeper understanding of that than most, too. As far as birth was concerned, all a person could do was show such humility in retrospect that they welcomed their death when the time came. That they studied themselves in the mirror before they closed their eyes to the light of day.

The patrol car that pulled up outside was using neither its siren nor its blue lights – a little disappointing, in Máriddja's opinion. They might have shown a bit of urgency to emphasize the gravity of the situation. It was a hunting crime they were investigating, after all. And a theft! Máriddja had considered calling it a home invasion to really put the local police in a spin, but she had decided that was pushing it.

She had carefully wiped down the rifle and hidden it in a few different bushes before eventually settling on the best one: in a straight line from the entrance wound, in a spot where it was just visible enough.

After that she had used the old Volvo, a throw rope and a decent amount of acceleration in a low gear to pull parts of the garage door loose. She had managed to produce a big hole, nicely centered and with just the right amount of dramatically splintered boards, exactly as she had hoped. The wood was actually so weathered and rotten that she hadn't even felt bad about vandalizing it – though Biera likely wouldn't agree. The old man thought everything was worth keeping.

An expectant Máriddja put on her boots and coat and shoved the bag of candy into her already-full pocket, then she headed out. The cops had pulled over at a safe distance from the spot where the elk had fallen and were now studying the dead animal with glum faces.

There were two of them, and one was a woman. *So much equality and equalizing and God knows what else! That is all well and good, but why couldn't they have sent two blokes instead? What I need are men,* Máriddja thought angrily. If she was really honest, she was of the firm opinion that most jobs could be done by women – and done much better at that. Yes, deep down, in heart and soul, she was a female-ist through and through. But right here and now, for the task at hand, she had no interest in seeing a woman in uniform. Was that really so much to ask? She stepped out into the yard and used her thumb to push her glasses back onto the bridge of her nose. It wasn't especially cold, but she tugged her hat down over her ears all the same. Now wasn't the time to be taking off her armour. She needed to be strong, prepared.

"Well hello, officers. It's lucky you could come out so quickly," she said, loudly and jovially, clapping her hands together as she squinted at the two police.

Twenty-seven minutes, by her reckoning. Hardly an impressive performance. Máriddja herself had once driven the same distance in fourteen minutes when she was desperate for the bathroom, though she knew it was probably best to not rub the long arm of the law the wrong way by telling them that.

She grinned, then came to her senses and adopted a more appropriate look of concern instead. The police officers took a detour around the dead elk and came towards her. Her heart was pounding like a galloping horse as their flat-footed bootsteps drew closer, and she gestured indignantly towards the crime scene and shook her head. Put on a show.

"What kind of person could do something like this?"

The police officers' uniforms made them look big and scary. They had all sorts of crime fighting tools hanging from their belts, and Máriddja couldn't help but gape.

The female officer held out her hand and introduced herself, but Máriddja didn't pay much attention to what she said.

She turned her attention to the male officer and loudly said her name. Used to people not quite getting it right.

He didn't offer up his own name in reply, which irritated her no end, but Máriddja just smiled and welcomed them both. They seemed slightly confused by her warm reception, and asked whether she was the one who had reported the crime.

"Yesindeedy, that was me. I saw the whole thing from the window, officer," she said, still facing the man. "I couldn't have been more shocked if I'd seen a . . . fire-breathing dragon! Not many people pass by here, you see, and I knew, well, right away . . . that he was the criminal type . . . creeping about in the dark like that."

"What time was this?"

"7:14 on the dot," said Máriddja. "I was looking at the phone to see if I had any sticks."

"Excuse me?" the male officer said in a southern accent.

"Sticks, you know . . . so I could phone someone if things got hairy."

"Signal," the she-officer quietly explained to her colleague.

"That's what I said, isn't it? Anyway, this wrong 'un, he was creeping around outside like he was about to commit . . . well, goodness knows what sort of crime. So I stayed where I was, even though I was a bit jittery."

Máriddja managed to look anything but jittery as she spoke.

"I understand it must have been unsettling," said the she-officer. Could you describe the man you saw?"

"He was wearing dark clothes and . . . one of those . . . whatchamacallits . . . a mask! Over his eyes," Máriddja whispered, squinting for the sake of it.

"A mask over his eyes?"

"Exactly. One of those ones with holes in, so you can see out."

"A ski mask?" said the he-officer.

"Call it whatever you want, but that's what I saw. He was horribly big and beefy, too. And he had a gun in his hand."

"You saw the gun?" the he-officer double-checked.

"You better believe it, and then when he threw the rifle away . . . after the shot, I went over to get a closer look, and . . ." Máriddja lowered her voice dramatically. "And I saw that it was Biera's! That's when I realized we'd been robbed!"

Máriddja tried not to look like there was confetti raining down on her.

"Hold on a second, the gun is still here?" the she-officer asked in disbelief.

This woman seems a bit slow on the uptake, Máriddja thought.

"Yes! It's over there in the currant bushes, can't you see it? He tossed it over there before he ran off into the woods."

Heads rotating in unison, they followed Máriddja's trembling finger and then turned back to her.

"Maybe we could take this from the beginning, Maria. Why don't we go inside and have a chat over a coffee? It's good to get something warm in you after a shock like this," the he-officer said, peering over towards the house.

That was courteous of him, Máriddja thought appreciatively, nodding in agreement. She came back to her senses a moment later and shook her head so hard that the tassel on her hat swung through the air.

"No! Not possible, I'm afraid. We're renovating at the minute, you see . . . and the whole place is in a terrible state. Besides, we don't drink coffee, so that's not something I can offer you. The old man's stomach kicks up such a stink whenever he has caffeine, so we . . ." She paused before she went on: "Uh, mostly drink . . . um . . . Punsch."

"So there are two of you living here?" the she-officer asked with interest.

Damn it, Máriddja thought. She was really starting to feel the pressure now.

"Yes, but the old man is away. I was the only one here when the deed took place."

"I understand," said the he-officer.

Máriddja nodded enthusiastically, relieved.

"So, err, maybe we can stay here at the um . . . crime scene. I can pull the kick-sled over if your legs are getting weary . . . I've got a reindeer hide you can sit on, so your backside doesn't get too cold. Hehehe . . ." She let out a nervous, robotic laugh. "You've got to be careful not to catch a chill in your . . . your nethers!" she whispered loudly to the woman, a hand over her mouth, trying to hide her nerves.

The she-officer took in what she had said with a raised eyebrow, then pulled a notepad and a stubby pencil from her inner pocket.

"OK, maybe you could tell us . . . what happened, and we can start taking photographs and arrange to have the animal taken away."

Máriddja licked her lips and peered up at the hazy grey sky. "Well, I got up to, hmm . . . relieve myself, and I decided to have a look outside. I like to do that whenever I remember, before it's light, when the animals are moving about," she explained.

The two police officers were hanging on her every word, and she couldn't help but feel a slight satisfaction that her statement was provoking such interest.

"And that's when I saw the crook creeping around outside the garage with something long in his hands. He snuck along the wall like a stray cat, and then he took aim. I got so scared that I threw myself to the floor in the hallway. And then I heard a shot . . . At first I thought the bastard was shooting at me, so I lay still until I was sure I was unharmed, then I peeped out from behind the plastic flowers on the radiator.

That's when I saw the elk, it was shaking and sort of staggering about, and then it dropped to the ground with a thud."

"You heard the elk hit the ground?" the she-officer asked, her pencil hovering over the paper.

"Mmm, nahh . . . I wouldn't quite say that. But I could see that a big animal like that must've made a real noise."

"So you think it was killed with a single shot?"

"Absolutely, officer."

Máriddja thought back to her perfect bullseye, could still feel the recoil in her shoulder. She absent-mindedly massaged her aching bones.

"It was a real peach of a shot. Bam, just like that! You could tell he was an experienced hunter. Probably a repeat offender," she added conspiratorially.

"And what did he do next?" asked the he-officer.

"What did he do next? Well, he tossed the rifle into the bushes, of course! And then he ran off like . . . like a lunatic, straight into the woods. Out of sight."

They both nodded and gazed off into the trees behind the house.

"Did you recognize the shooter?" asked the she-officer, eyes fixed on Máriddja.

"No, or maybe . . . I can't say I *recognized* him, exactly, but he was the spit image of whatshisname . . . the president."

Máriddja smiled enthusiastically, pleased with her sudden brainwave.

"As in . . . the president of the United States? In what way did you think the suspect looked like him?" asked the pig.

"Weeell . . ." she said, buying herself more time as she thought. "How can I put it. He was sort of orange, just like that bloke. And he had the same . . . hair?"

Máriddja used one hand to make a sweeping gesture back over her head, illustrating the kind of slicked-back helmet of hair that looked like it was trying to escape from its owner's scalp.

"Didn't you say he was wearing a ski mask?" said the she-officer.

"Yes, uh . . ." Damn it, she should have stuck to the script rather than taking all these liberties. She had allowed herself to get carried away in the moment, excited by the arrival of the police. "Well . . . he took it off, obviously. When he threw the gun away. He . . . maybe he started sweating?"

She could feel herself sweating, and she tugged at her collar.

"OK . . ." The pencil scribbled on the paper. "And what did he do next? What did he do with the mask?"

The policeman fixed his eyes on Máriddja. Fortunately for her, she had the reflexes of a young lynx, and she quickly replied:

"He put it in his bag."

"He was wearing a backpack?"

"Yes, or . . . it was more the kind of bag you wear over your shoulder, you know?"

Máriddja was starting to get short of breath. This wasn't going the way she had hoped at all.

"A handbag?" the ever-helpful he-officer suggested.

"Exactly!" Máriddja shouted, grateful for the lifeline.

"Let me get this straight. The man threw the gun over there." The she-officer pointed to the bare branches of the currant bush. "And then he took his balaclava off and put it into the handbag he was wearing on one shoulder?"

"Yes, that's about it."

"Did you see what kind of handbag it was?"

Máriddja was in over her head now, she thought, swallowing hard. This was a subject she knew very little about. The only bag she could think of was her mother-in-law's red one, with the clip fastening.

They were waiting for her to go on.

"I think it was reddish. Sort of square, with a short strap. About as big as a plump perch," she blurted out.

Shit shit shit.

The two officers gave her a strange look, then glanced at each other.

"The shooter was carrying a . . . *woman's* purse?"

"I suppose you could call it that, yes. Exactly. Though you can never really tell . . ."

Through sheer force of will, Máriddja managed to press her lips together, preventing any more of this nervous babbling that threatened to ruin everything. She tried to look like she found the whole thing as strange as they did. Yet again, she wished she possessed Doctor Skruvlenius's well-trained eyebrows.

The male officer stood quietly, and Máriddja took the opportunity to study his face more closely.

Thin, with a broad mouth. No sign of a Cupid's bow, a fairly ordinary nose. From beneath his hat, a tuft of reddish brown hair was poking out, and he had a spray of freckles across his nose.

A sweet boy, Máriddja noted, but that was irrelevant. There was no doubt about it: the outcome wasn't the one Máriddja had been hoping for. The wrong youngster again, possibly in the wrong uniform too . . .

"In your call you mentioned that the man had forced entry into one of your outbuildings?" the female officer read from her notepad.

"Right!" said Máriddja, nodding eagerly. "He broke the garage door. That's probably where he found the rifle."

"You kept the gun in the garage?" The male officer gave her a stern look over his freckled nose.

"Yes?" said Máriddja, confused by his strange question.

The she-officer coughed into her dainty hand.

"And I'm assuming this was before he'd seen the elk bull?" the he-officer continued.

"Well, I don't know. I suppose so . . . or maybe he took the gun at an earlier date."

Máriddja shrugged and held out her hands like the petals on the most innocent of lilies.

"So you're saying that an unknown man broke into your garage, took your gun and then just happened to spot an elk standing in the perfect position no more than fifty feet away?" The he-officer was starting to sound a little sarcastic.

Máriddja felt herself bristle. "I don't know what goes on inside the head of these . . . gangsters, do I? You should talk to one of your psychologists and get them to give you a suspect profile instead of standing here, speculating all day! I'm actually the victim of a crime. He could have murdered me in cold blood . . . just like the elk over there! Shot me dead! And then you wouldn't have a keen witness at all, would you?"

"Key witness," the he-officer corrected her, though he lost his nerve when Máriddja gave him such an angry glare that the whites of her eyes looked bloodshot. He seemed a little startled, and he turned to the slushy snow and cleared his throat.

"Haven't you got anyone else with the right expertise working at the station? Any blokes in their thirties or forties who could come and take a look instead?"

For a split second, the two police looked both disapproving and concerned, and then the woman officer closed her notepad and held out a hand.

"Why don't you get back inside where it's warm, Maria? We'll give the area a once over," she said, kindly but firmly.

"The scene of the crime, you mean," Máriddja muttered to herself as she stomped back toward the house.

Men shouldn't be allowed to become police officers . . . they were far too simple-minded to be trusted with the important job of upholding the rule of law, she thought to herself as she slammed the door.

Thank God for the Guovddo police for pairing that numbskull of a man with a woman! Otherwise the justice system in this country would be on its knees faster than you could say keen witness – or whatever the hell it was called.

45

Not Good

Just a few hours later, the wretched elk was gone and the yard was empty once again. Emptier than before, in fact. It looked like the streets once a market had packed up and left: depressing and dead.

From behind the curtain, Máriddja had spied on the police officers as they moved around the yard. Gesturing and examining everything before they marched off towards the trees.

It served them right. They could spend the rest of their working lives trying to track down American presidents as far as she was concerned.

Máriddja dug another King of Denmark out of the bag and bit down angrily, making the hard candy crunch between her teeth. Biera had woken after his morning nap, eaten a few biscuits with soured milk and then lain down on his side in the living room to read the TV supplement. All without suspecting a thing. Without being a help or a hindrance, either.

With one quick push of the button, Máriddja connected to the operator. Siré answered.

"The mission was a failure," Máriddja croaked, peering out of the window between an empty binocular case and the box containing her mother's crafts.

"I'm sorry to hear that," Siré said in her usual formal tone.

"Yeah, it's a damn shame. Still, thank you for all the information about how the police work – it's incredible how much you know. I just need to come up with another smart plan now, and that's easier said than done . . . But I kept them away from the house, at the very least."

Máriddja got up and, with the phone still in her hand, peered around the doorframe at her husband, at Biera.

He was utterly transfixed by the TV schedule and the garish images of more and less famous faces in his magazine, and he didn't notice her.

"I'm just so damn tired," she admitted quietly. "Can't sleep at night because of the pain. In my belly, that is. I'd bet my life the thing's growing. It feels so tender and sore down there." She gave a joyless laugh and then said, as much to herself as to the operator: "Just think, the part of me that couldn't carry new life . . . now it's carrying my death. Fate certainly is strange . . ."

"That doesn't sound good." Siré sounded cautiously sympathetic.

Máriddja nodded and shrugged at Siré's accurate description of the state of affairs.

There wasn't much more to say about it.

It was utterly, absolutely not good.

46

Chats in the Sun

The branches of the trees had begun to shed their heavy winter coats and were stretching up towards the clear blue sky. The mild weather had arrived, and the days were now so warm that you no longer needed a coat – or not if you steered clear of the shade, anyway. The birds squabbled over the feeder, and the male cats howled, pissed and wandered long distances in search of an outlet for their urges.

Driving wasn't for the faint of heart at this time of year. Cars bumped and skidded in the slushy tracks, slick tires spinning and throwing dirty wet snow everywhere.

Kaj had long since admitted defeat to the thawing roads, and their rusty Ladybird sat untouched in the driveway. They didn't live too far from work, so not driving wasn't the end of the world. Besides, a brisk walk was actually quite a nice way to start the day, arriving at the health center rosy-cheeked and optimistic. Fresh as a sweaty daisy, with a runny nose and cereal clinging to the corners of his mouth.

Life in Guovddo continued to treat them well. Time seemed to move at a different pace here, and it was as though gravity had a greater influence, helping to keep them grounded. Everything they did seemed more concrete now, because their souls desired something different. A new hunger for daylight, a more noticeable thirst for the air the trees breathed out.

Kaj often thought that he must have been undernourished before moving north, starved of everything his body was now demonstrating it couldn't live without. This air. This calm. The stability. Everything seemed more real. Things were done for a reason here. The roads were ploughed in order to be passable, logs were burnt to heat the home and not because they looked pretty on Instagram. It all felt so damn reasonable and natural. Even little things that might appear irrelevant were important. Drinking coffee with Micklas, for example, which helped to forge the bonds needed to live in a place like this. Lunch with Noomi and Palle, because no man is an island. The community was alive, pulsating in its stillness in a way Kaj had never experienced before. Guovddo's blood pumped from person to person, through veins binding them all to a central point, and each one of them was vital to keep its heart beating. It was beautiful, it was simple, and Kaj loved that his everyday life had gained purpose and direction.

He and Palle often went out with ice rods and a drill to try their luck on the frozen lakes nearby. They could spend hours like that, each sprawled on a reindeer hide in the spring sunshine, rods in hand, chatting, or just sitting together in silence.

Kaj thought Palle was happy – that was certainly how he seemed, anyway. A cheerful face with a near constant look of expectation in his blue eyes, a smile often lurking behind his thick beard. He had a way of using a person's name when he spoke to them, making them feel both seen and affirmed. Palle was kind, straightforward, and Kaj frequently found himself wishing that of some his optimism would rub off on him.

Palle liked to lie on his side as they talked, enabling him to look at Kaj without lowering his chances of catching something under the ice by sitting up. Kaj usually did the same, meaning that the two men mirrored each other a few meters apart. They wiggled their rods at regular intervals, making the shiny jigs jerk upwards before shimmying down again.

Goading the fish into taking a bite. Into being caught.

The men often took a sooty little coffee pot with them, and they burnt twigs to heat the icy water. The pot produced just enough for two – one cup each; no more, no less – and the whole thing was so perfectly balanced that it warmed Kaj's heart.

Mimmi and Noomi joined them from time to time, and they went all out by frying meat or making waffles before dozing in the sun with calm, full bellies. It was uncomplicated and enjoyable. The calm of Kaj and Mimmi's new environment had done them both good, but the difference was that Mimmi had already been grounded before the move. Not like Kaj. He was busy sending roots down through the snow, seeking strength in the ground.

"I might be risking a smack in the face by bringing this up," Palle said slowly, his eyes closed to the sun. It was a warm day, and the two men had gone out alone. "But don't the two of you ever think about the whole kids thing?"

Kaj sat quietly for a moment or two. He felt the weight of the lure in the cold water, sinking towards the bottom.

"Yeah, we do . . . But it's kind of complicated."

His heart was pounding, reverberating through his body and into the warm reindeer hide. It felt like the ice might break beneath him.

"Sorry, I won't ask again . . . didn't mean to stick my nose in. It's just . . . well, Noomi and I have decided to try. To get pregnant, I mean."

"It's OK," said Kaj, pulling his legs up beneath him to ease the weight on his backside. "That's great!" he added.

"Yeah, it'll be good," said Palle. "I hope it works for us; it's not so easy for everyone . . . It can take a while."

Kaj murmured in agreement, and they lay in silence, watching a plane trace a line across the blue sky.

"Mimmi wants to," Kaj said after a while. The lump in his throat made it difficult for him to say more.

"But I . . . God, I just don't know. I want to, for her sake."

"You don't feel that longing yourself?" asked Palle. Kaj heard him tug on his rod, and there was some splashing from his hole in the ice.

"Mmm, I guess I find kids kind of difficult, if I'm really honest," Kaj admitted. He had spoken softly, but he was worried his words sounded ruthless and bad tempered.

Palle didn't seem to be judging him for what he had said, and simply lay quietly beside him. That made it easier for Kaj to go on.

"I had a bit of a tricky childhood. Don't get me wrong, it was nice, I didn't grow up in misery or anything like that," he said with a sarcastic laugh. "I just can't really see myself as a dad. I mean, being a parent seems like such hard work. My mum wasn't always so well, and I guess I've always assumed that was because of me."

"I get it," said Palle. He sounded like he really meant it. "That's tough. But what makes you think you were the reason your mum struggled?"

"Well . . ." Kaj gave a hollow laugh and paused to check whether that was a bite he had just felt. It wasn't. "I don't know, I guess I just interpreted it that way because . . . whenever my childhood came up, she always got so weird and absent, like she couldn't talk about it. She didn't even have a single picture of me from before my old man came into the picture."

"Came into the picture . . .? Ah, so you're adopted?"

Kaj couldn't see Palle's face, but he could feel how neutral his friend was towards everything Kaj was sharing.

"Yup, by my step dad. Mum married him when I was four or five. I've never met my real dad . . . don't even know his name, in fact." Another dry laugh.

"Man, that's some rough stuff, Kaj. I can see why you might not take the whole becoming a parent thing so lightly."

Kaj agreed. If you were of the opinion that parenthood could cause wounds that never healed, then it certainly wasn't something you should do on a whim.

"Besides, I'm pretty sure I was a demanding, anxious little shit when I was a kid. Knowing my luck, any sprogs of my own would be even worse. Safest to give it a miss, don't you think?"

The two men laughed.

From the plane overhead, any passengers looking out of the window would see two dark dashes on an expanse of white ice between the mountains.

47

The Burying Beetle

The Nicrophorus beetle had real symbolic importance to Kaj, and had ever since he was eight, when he found a bird in the strawberry patch.

The experience was bound up with so many different feelings that he could barely separate them. Revulsion – it was dead. Or was it? The bird's eyes were shut, but its chest was moving. Sorrow – life was finite. A dead sparrow, gone in the same way he would be gone one day. The way Mum and Dad would. Though maybe it wasn't quite there yet? The feathers on its breast were still moving, even though the light had gone out in its eyes. What if it was still alive, if he could save it?

He had nudged it with his foot. Gently, the tip of his trainer barely touching the bird's feathers.

And horror. In the midst of the greyness, in the soft fuzz by its throat: another color. Two colors. Black for illness and orange for danger, spilling out like pus from a pimple. Death had stirred, creeping over the bird's body, darting over its beak on quick legs.

A beetle. Big, fat and glossy.

Kaj had screamed. He had screamed so loudly that, in that shrill note, his feelings of disgust had merged with something bigger. His mother had come running, her bare feet thudding against the grass like heartbeats. Her apron slapped against her knees, and she was holding a potato peeler in one hand.

She stroked his head the way you might stroke a frightened rabbit's ears.

"It's a burying beetle," she had said.

He could remember the weight of her calm, that it had pulled him back from the brink and enabled him to smell the July rain among the strawberry plants.

And she had crouched down with him, beside him, her face next to his. As she explained, listened, showed. Turned the bird over, turned his fear into fascination. The magic of words: carcasses, dead animals being taken care of. Carried away and buried. Pulled down into the soil. The mother beetle, feeding her young on her own flesh. The circle of life.

His own mother's breath smelt like dill, and her voice was low. As though out of respect.

Once she went back inside, Kaj could no longer see the burying beetle on the bird's body; it had burrowed back under its feathers. Into its flesh, breathing inside its body yet again.

And Kaj simply couldn't stop staring. He had spent hours sitting on an upside down bucket, watching the incomprehensible. How could something so dead look so alive? How could one life continue inside another's death? How could something be born and raised on decay?

He stayed out in the garden until it was time to go in for dinner.

Kaj had carried that experience with him for a long time, fascinated by the insect that could conjure life out of death. His memories smelt like herbs and rain, all life's mysteries gathered in one moment.

★

Another day, the four friends were out enjoying the warm spring weather together. Noomi was sprawled on the snowmobile, her head resting on the handlebars, Palle on a patch of bare ground with his back against a pine tree. Kaj and Mimmi were stretched out on a reindeer hide by the fire. They had unzipped their coats and taken off their hats, exposing their flattened hair to the gentle breeze.

That was when Kaj's phone started ringing. As he pulled it from the pocket of his new padded trousers – bought specially for such excursions – he almost felt annoyed by the interruption to his meditative state, though his mood took an immediate turn for the better when he saw the name and picture on the screen. He answered the call with a cheery: "Hey, bro!"

What followed was a brisk, pleasant chat between the two brothers. Kaj combed his unruly hair back as he talked, squinted in the sun and put a hand on Mimmi's stomach through her knitted sweater.

He then stopped talking and sat bolt upright. Mimmi could hear her brother-in-law's faint voice on the other end of the line, but she couldn't make out what he was saying. She lifted her head from the warm hide and opened one eye. Kaj's face was serious.

"Where did you find it?"

Gustav's voice buzzed like a fly in a glass jar.

Kaj grabbed a handful of snow, which quickly formed to the shape of his hot fist, and opened and closed his fingers around it as though it were a stress ball.

"Is that what it said? On the picture?" Kaj asked, running a hand over his dark brown hair again. He took off his sunglasses and held them in his hand. Murmured a few times. Gustav's voice hummed in return. There was a little more mumbling, followed by a "yup, speak soon" and the red circle to end the call.

Mimmi was now sitting up too, and Kaj's face was like a question mark and an exclamation point as he told them about the conversation he'd just had with his brother. Noomi swung her legs down to the ground and turned to face them. Kaj suspected that Palle had been dozing in the sun, but his eyes were now as bright and alert as ever.

"So, my mum had a brother who died ages ago. She never talked about him, but Gustav found a picture of him and his wife among the things he took from the house." Kaj stroked his thin beard in confusion.

"Oh?" Mimmi frowned. She couldn't quite square what Kaj had just told them with his reaction.

"And . . . This is going to sound crazy, but you'll never guess what it said on the back."

The others' eyes were on him, urging him to go on.

"*Per and his wife, at home in Guovddo!*" he said, giving weight to every word.

His trio of spectators were now staring at him. Noomi laughed, and Kaj slowly shook his head. His hair was standing on end, his eyes drifting between the treetops as he tried to process what he had just been told.

"Woah! What are the chances of that, of you moving to the exact same place! What a coincidence," Palle chuckled from his comfortable spot by the tree.

Mimmi didn't say a word. She seemed to be thinking.

All around them, water was dripping from the branches and the Siberian jays flew in low circles around their leftover lunch.

Their cries made it sound like they were laughing at the people down below, for believing that anything in the great white world beneath their wings could be a coincidence.

Kaj listened to their loud squawks and was surprised to find his thoughts turning to the beetle.

He wondered whether he was the one playing the part of the burying beetle now. The voice in his mother's lifeless chest, was it really coming to them from the other side? Maybe it had been him all along?

48

Little Rat

Kaj had just managed to push the key into the lock and, with a moderate show of force, compelled it to turn. He was carrying a mega pack of laundry detergent beneath one arm and had a bag filled with rolls of wallpaper in the other hand, and he had to stretch his blood-starved fingers to their full length in order to push the door open. Before he had time to close it behind him, he heard footsteps on the porch, and he called back without turning around.

"Hi, honey! Hurry up and close the door, it's freezing in the suburbs of the North Pole today!"

Mimmi didn't reply, but Kaj continued as he kicked off his shoes:

"The wallpaper arrived. It's going to cost a fortune, but they said we could have a discount because the stock was so late coming in. The bug-eyed guy who works there, he said he'd send the invoi—"

From the corner of one eye, he spotted something that bore no resemblance to his fiancée's fluffy blue coat. He turned around, lowered his eyes by about a foot, and saw Jóhánas standing on the doormat. The boy pushed the door shut and stared at Kaj like he'd just escaped from a secure psychiatric hospital.

"Johannes," said Kaj, feeling an itching sensation somewhere he couldn't reach.

"Kaaaaaj," the boy shot back, taking off his gloves.

Kaj rolled his eyes and turned away from the rude little brat whose name he would have to learn to pronounce sooner or later. His knee slammed into the hallway table, hitting the exact spot that could make the most level-headed of people roar like an ancient beast.

Johánás snorted with laughter, and Kaj heard him drop his backpack to the floor.

"Don't you have a home of your own to go to?" he muttered through gritted teeth and hellish pain, the kind that made him want to drop to the ground and roll around like a footballer looking for a penalty.

"Yeah," Johánás snapped back. "But Mimmi has better snacks."

He trudged through to the living room in his rumpled socks and shapeless trousers, baggy at the knees.

The boy barged into Kaj's home. Slumped down on the couch as though he owned the place and reached for the TV remote.

"Mimmi said I should come over after school. We're going to bake scones."

Johánás's eyes didn't leave the TV screen once as he spoke.

Kaj gave him a restrained nod and informed the child that the baker in question wasn't back from work yet, but that he should by all means make himself at home.

He lugged the box of detergent and the unwieldly bag from the home décor shop through to the laundry room. Kaj saw the boy glance down at his old wristwatch, fiddle with the remote, looking like a defensive little rat in a pair of oversized trousers on their scratchy sofa.

As Kaj closed the door to the laundry room behind him, he managed to get the back pocket of his jeans caught on the handle, hitting his head on the tumble drier in the process, he realized that he was being punished. For the reprehensible way he had treated the eight-year-old in the living room, no doubt. Why couldn't he just be a bit more calm and composed? Johánás was only a kid, after all.

Anxiety flooded from the lump in his throat, like tar in his veins, pooling in a tender spot right beneath his solar plexus. With every beat of his heart, the black poison pumped through his body, roaring in his ears.

Kaj went through the usual box breathing motions, clutching his hands tight. He then opened the laundry room door and called through to the living room.

"Help yourself to a some chocolate milk while you wait. It's in the pantry."

He saw the boy's toes curl up inside his grubby socks, tensing in a state of high alert. They straightened out a moment later, and Kaj heard a deep sigh. He closed the door and managed to put the box of washing powder in its rightful place without any further accidents.

A glass of chocolate milk in place of the ability to show warmth. Just like his mother had taught him, Kaj thought with a self-deprecating sigh.

Another excellent reason to steer clear of parenthood. A person could fuck up a kid without even trying.

49

Smart, Handsome Nuffe

The Nilssons' boy had passed the police car as it pulled out of the Rijás' driveway with an elk in the trailer. He was out on the walk Máriddja had prescribed him, wearing a tracksuit that was a little too snug. Moving at a brisk pace that soon gave him a stitch, he had paused to catch his breath, and that was when the car drove by. Interest piqued, he peered over the dirty, shrinking heap of snow at the side of the road and saw yet another police car and its accompanying officers. They were wandering about between the trees with glum faces. The sight gave Nuffe a slight rush of adrenaline, and he briefly considered sloping over to ask what was going on.

Through the window, so grubby it was almost opaque, he saw Máriddja tug at the curtain as she talked to someone on the phone. She looked so resolute that he immediately shelved his plans, and Nuffe decided to head home on his aching legs instead, lactic acid burning. He would just have to keep delving into the mystery from afar.

Safely back at the worn kitchen table, he shared his thoughts and fears with his mother in a steady stream of words. She leant back against the counter as he spoke, said *gosh* and *oh* and gave her agitated son something to eat. Nuffe helped himself to a generous slice of aspic, and between chews, he said:

"It's all starting to add up, Mum. First, they had a fire in the barn, and now the police are over there – not to mention whatever happened to their mailbox! It looked like someone tried to chop up the post for firewood. Maybe we should check on the Rijás, make sure they're OK?"

"They've never been keen on visitors . . ." said Sally Nilsson.

"But things could be really bad over there . . . and they don't have anyone else."

"You're a good boy, Nuffe," his mother said with a loving smile. "You'll make someone very happy one day."

If the old bachelor had heard her, he didn't let on. He just pulled on his hat and went out onto the porch. His mother hummed a little to herself as she continued to rub at the imaginary stains in the sink, mind whirring.

How were Biera and Máriddja? Nuffe was right; it was their responsibility to check on them.

To think that she had given birth to someone so smart and handsome! Her glasses fogged up with motherly bliss as she watched him through the fringe on the curtain, trudging over the yard towards the woodshed with his knock-knees.

50

Beloved Biera Rijá

Another letter had arrived. One that Máriddja was willing to open. It had the Sámi Parliament logo on the envelope, and that meant it might contain important information.

She sliced it open with a deft grip around the carved antler handle, then put the knife back beneath the lid of the storage bench. That was the best place for it, safely out of reach of its increasingly confused owner. Biera had used it to hack at her rolling pin to make firelighters last autumn, so the knife now had a new home, together with the axe and the matches, giving Máriddja a bit of peace and quiet at night. She had other things to worry about – just look at the mailbox! Crazy old sod, vipers in the middle of winter. And in the mailbox at that!

Good grief.

The letter was formally written, addressed to Biera, a fact she had registered but quickly ignored.

Dear Mr. Biera Rijá,

I am writing to you today in relation to the hundredth anniversary of the forced displacement of the Sámi community from Gárasavvon. As part of our research into the families that were separated, I am contacting you, one of only a handful of survivors with first-hand experience of the relocations.

We would very much like to hear your testimony, memories and see any documentation you may still have from that time.

Looking forward to your response.

Kind regards,
Sissel Jarre, Jåhkåmåhkke

Máriddja read the letter again, then put it to one side. Sissel Jarre would have to wait, no matter how deserving her request was; it was a matter of life and death here on the mountain now.

She didn't have time for distractions, for any questions other than the one she so urgently wanted an answer to.

It was a clear day outside, and her eyes traced the profile of the mountain. It was as familiar to her as Biera's, but unlike her husband's face, Gárjjelbákte's peaks hadn't changed over the years. Gárjjelbákte was sharp, dramatic and timeless. And in the pulsing interior of the mountain, everything was as present and alive as it had been when she saw and felt Her, the Mountain's, presence for the first time.

Máriddja desperately wished she could say the same about her beloved Biera Rijá. What would happen to him once she was gone? Who would hold his hand when he got scared and confused, who would understand what he was saying when Sámi, his first language, became his only tongue? She could already see which way he was heading. His Swedish was becoming increasingly watered down, and if it weren't for the TV and the radio she thought he would probably have made the transition to speaking nothing but Sámi by now.

If only they still had Risten and Heaika-Joná.

Then Máriddja would have known that he wouldn't be left all alone.

51

A Falling Jay

The idea came to Máriddja during the night, as she lay awake in pain. Yes! Of course! Just like that, the next step was obvious. She knew exactly who would shoulder the blame for what she had planned. There were historic grudges between those roving Tchudes and her own people. Something so terrible was guaranteed to have the desired effect. Yes, it could work . . . It would certainly attract a large number of men in uniform to her little hillside. Surely the country couldn't be in such a dire state that they would ignore a risk to national security, Máriddja thought as she lay in the darkness.

She was sorry that the magnificent elk had died in vain, but it had simply been in the wrong place at the wrong time – it had only itself to blame for walking by at such a desperate moment.

But this time she wouldn't fail.

This time she would reap the rewards, she could feel it.

She lay awake all night, fine-tuning her plans, only drifting off to sleep in the early hours.

When Biera got up the next morning, he had to check her pulse to make sure she was still among the living. She was breathing, and he gave her a nudge in the side to see whether she was ready to wake, but Máriddja simply turned her nightgown-clad rump towards him and kept snoring. Well, he thought, let her sleep.

It was a mild day outside, so Biera took his coffee out onto the porch. As he sat there, he found his gaze being drawn to the precipice on the side of the mountain, its steep slope particularly clear in the morning light.

A strange feeling took over him: a sort of rhythmic, internal quivering, a yearning sensation somewhere above his diaphragm. A shiver.

"Uff, someone just walked over my grave!" he called over to the Siberian jay that had been shamelessly begging for some of his breakfast biscuit. The bird greedily pecked at the crumbs and then fawningly hopped around on the railing in the hopes of more. When it realized the breakfast buffet was closed for the day, it took off towards the mountain, rising and dipping through the air, eventually floating off in the direction of the steep outline of Gárjjelbákte – a place where a number of bad people were said to have met a sudden, untimely death. It was one of many precipices where, according to legend, the clever Sámi had lured would-be raiders into falling over the edge in the old days.

Biera knew that Máriddja's family had often told stories about the violent ravages the area had faced, how it eventually came to an end. The place was rumored to be an ancient *ättestupa*, where the elderly either jumped or were thrown to their deaths, and Máriddja used to joke that he should roll her over the edge once she no longer had the energy to chew her candies. He knew the stories, and he could feel the power of the place.

The view was particularly dramatic and frightening in the pink morning light, dark patches of thawed ground like holes in a skull.

The jay that had been keeping him company was getting smaller and smaller in the distance, and as it dived in front of the cliff edge, it looked like it had thrown itself off, like it was tumbling through the air.

Biera paid attention to the strange intuition, knew to listen to the whispering of the bedrock in his bones.

He spent a long time sitting there, deep in thought, with his cold coffee.

52

Battle with Plastic Spades

"My great grandma has one of those," said Johánás, jerking his thumb towards the wall where Laura's artwork hung. He was pointing at one of the flower paintings, and Kaj felt a sting of unease, he wasn't sure why. That was often the case for him; his anxiety reared its head even when there was no logical explanation. Oh, he hated that shapelessness in his inner darkness; why was he like this? What was actually causing him pain?

To Kaj's eternal annoyance, the irritating child had begun spending more and more time at their house, coming over under various pretexts. Unfortunately for him, it was something Mimmi encouraged. She had confided in Kaj that she suspected Johánás might not be doing too well at home, though Kaj's personal theory was that the boy was a pushy little demon who enjoyed invading other people's personal space and taking over their sofas. He had come over today to go out with Mimmi and find some twigs to use as Easter decorations.

"Oh yeah? I doubt that . . . Johannes," said Kaj, trying to sound suitably patient and mature. "My mum painted that, you see, so it's not something you can just go out and buy."

"But she does!" Johánás shot back, indignant at not being believed. "I remember it! It was above my bed, and I thought it looked like—"

Kaj interrupted the boy with a dismissive chuckle that immediately made him hate himself, then continued with slightly too much sarcasm in his voice: "Didn't you just say it was your great grandma's? Why did you have a bed there? I mean, how spoiled are kids these days? Beds everywhere they go . . . How many bedrooms do you have?"

Kaj forced himself to hold his tongue. Reached desperately for his self-control and managed to keep quiet.

He cursed himself for being unable to get through a simple conversation without trying to put Johánás down. What was going on here, exactly? Kaj was, as far as he knew, a nice person, and he was also expected to be able to act like a grown man.

He stared at his reflection in the screen of his phone and asked himself why Johánás seemed to trigger him so much. As a result, he didn't notice the boy's silence on the sofa beside him. All he could hear was his own increasingly forceful self-criticism.

Johánás swallowed loudly. "You don't like kids, do you?" he said.

Kaj laughed again, the same sort of shrill, hollow laugh he seemed to have got into the habit of laughing in Johánás's presence. His anxiety sharpened the sound.

"Mmm . . . I guess you could say that," he replied. He felt like slamming his head into Mimmi's kilim cushion in shame, over his inability to control his emotions.

"You're crazy . . . I don't like you either!" Johánás announced.

"Good!" Kaj retorted.

"Great! You're not allowed to borrow my headtorch anymore."

"Oh, boo hoo . . . I don't want to borrow your stupid headtorch anyway." Kaj pulled a spiteful face at the child.

Though that wasn't true.

It had been a real help while he was sorting through the boxes in the basement. The ceiling light had stopped working down there, and Johánás had quickly offered to lend Mimmi the headtorch he had been given for Christmas.

Kaj would have to fix the fitting or whatever it was called. Either that or ask Mimmi, who was much handier than he was. Maybe even call an electrician. Damn it . . .

They glared at each other through narrowed eyes, like two warring squirrels.

Kaj snorted. Jesus Christ, he thought, did I really just say that? *Boo hoo? I don't want to borrow your stupid headtorch anyway?* He laughed and saw Johánás smirk. Whatever it was that had been building a nest in some dark corner of him was warded off by the humor of the situation, and he felt his sense of panic start to subside.

They stared at each other, searchingly this time, like two little boys who had been using their plastic spades to duel over who got to play with the only bucket in the sandpit, only to forget what the argument was even about.

"Hmm. I feel like a little brat," Kaj muttered in embarrassment.

"You are a little brat." Johánás grinned.

"No, you are."

"Mimmi says we're alike, so there!"

"Ugh . . ."

Johánás got up and announced that he was going to go and meet Mimmi outside, then went through to the hallway to put on his overalls. When the material finally stopped rustling, Kaj heard his self-important little voice ring out:

"Just so you know, you don't hate kids."

Kaj didn't speak.

"It's yourself you don't like, and I can see why. Bye, Kaaaaaj!"

The door slammed shut, and by the time Kaj rounded the

corner to give the young amateur psychologist a piece of his mind, the boy had already gone.

His gaze fell on the hallway table, beneath his mother's paintings. There, leaning against Kaj's woollen mittens, was Johánás's headtorch.

53

Spring Migration

A good night's sleep can do wonders for the human body, but to Kaj it was vital; his reptile brain dictated all sorts of things in his everyday life. And it just so happened that he had woken up from a good night's sleep that morning.

The light in the basement was miraculously working again, and Kaj continued to unpack the boxes on the spacious woodworking bench with renewed energy.

Mimmi's strategy for unpacking was chaotic, an approach that would leave any remotely neat Homo sapiens biting their tongue in frustration. She had abandoned her half-empty boxes and bags here, there and everywhere – more everywhere, to be honest – and Kaj had to push them all into the corner in order to gain the peace of mind he needed to sort through his own things.

She had, of course, told him about her visit to the local craft shop a few weeks earlier. The whole thing seemed so absurd that he hadn't really given it much thought at the time, but Kaj was now rummaging through the box of objects his mother had left him. He just couldn't understand why Laura had collected so many items – an almost absurd number of them, and all in perfect condition. They looked like they had only ever been unwrapped in order to be carefully wrapped back up again.

It was strange that he had never seen any of these things around the house, because they were far more beautiful than most of the other objects his mother had brought home. The antler handles were etched with intricate Sámi patterns and ornamentation; the seams on the sheaths were all perfectly straight, sewn with white sinew thread. He liked them. You could tell that the same pair of hands, the same soul, had made each of them – even though they were all different.

Kaj found a thick leather belt in a pouch, and he unrolled it and traced the pattern of colorful eyelets with his fingertips, looping over one another like vines.

He tried it on, the way he had seen Noomi and Palle wear their belts, and it settled around his hips like an affectionate cat rubbing up against the legs of someone with a fur allergy. Kaj hesitated, then took a knife out of the box and attached it to the loop on the left-hand side. Had this belonged to his mother? Or maybe his father? No, he had trouble imagining it on his slightly overweight dad – not to mention why Hans could possibly have needed something like this. His father's only real interests over the years seemed to have been puttering about in the car when he went to buy the evening paper, playing the lottery, and other, similar things – all far removed from any outdoor pursuits.

A while later, when his phone rang, he answered without even checking the display. The weight of the beautiful, sturdy knife against his thigh made him feel slightly reverent, as did the way the belt seemed to be holding him together. Gathering him inside its fragrant leathery authority, keeping him in place with its small buckle. It was a peculiar feeling.

Perhaps it was because of that feeling that he immediately offered to go out on the snowmobile with Johánás when Micklas called. The old man could no longer take the boy out himself, and had been hoping to get hold of Mimmi, but he welcomed Kaj's offer with a sense of relief.

They retrieved Micklas's snowmobile from a dirty, wet snowdrift in the middle of the muddy yard. It felt beneath Kaj to let the little boy drive, but the kid had insisted, and his grandfather agreed. If Kaj was honest, he knew it was probably safest to leave Johánás in charge, so he simply rolled his eyes and gave in, putting on the backpack Micklas had packed for them. It was stuffed full of cookies, dried meat and juice to ease his guilty conscience – niggling away at him because his arthritis had forced him to break his promise of a day out.

And then they were off, Johánás skilfully steering the heavy snowmobile. He stood with one leg on the reindeer hide that was strapped to the seat, using his upper body to force their way up the bank of ploughed snow at the edge of Micklas's yard. The eight-year-old remained standing as they struggled through the slush, and the movements of his skinny arms took them up onto the trail, where he finally sat down and gently accelerated.

Kaj gripped the passenger handles and felt himself relax. In front of him, on top of Johánás's padded overalls, he could see a belt just like the one he, after hesitating briefly, had strapped around his own hips. The young boy's neat little knife looked well-used in its worn leather sheath.

The sunlight bounced off the porous white snow around them, and likely would have been blinding if it weren't for their sunglasses. There was a cold breeze, and the air smelt like petrol as they sped smoothly along the grooved track.

After a while, Johánás turned off from the trail. He stood up again, one knee on the seat, and guided the snowmobile out onto the virgin snow. He was aiming for the lake to one side of the mountain, smooth ice stretching out into the distance.

Kaj wanted to ask whether the ice was thick enough to take their weight, but he realized that Johánás wouldn't be able to hear him over the roar of the engine. Instead he took a cautious grip on the young driver's belt. He couldn't explain why, but it felt reassuring somehow. The knuckles of his other hand turned white on the handle as they sped out towards a small islet, and he heard the scraping of the ice under the blanket of snow beneath them.

Johánas switched off the engine and jumped down. In the instant before he sank to his knees in the snow and struggled back onto solid ground, it was as though he was someone else. The lost, stubborn little boy radiated a sense of calm and confidence that Kaj had never seen in him before.

It felt good to coax the yellow earplugs out of his ears and hear the spring birds chattering in the trees all around them.

"That OK?" Johánas asked gruffly.

Kaj nodded and climbed down from the snowmobile.

The boy spread out yet another reindeer hide on a bare patch of ground, then trudged off among the trees with an axe. He returned with an armful of branches, dropped to his knees and took off his gloves so that he could grip the matches.

Kaj considered offering to help, but he realized – with a slight twinge of embarrassment – that he wasn't sure he would be able to start a fire without any lighter fluid.

The boy used the little axe to hack at one end of a stick, making the wood curl like the tail feathers of a black grouse. The birch bark he had magicked out of nowhere rolled up in the heat of the match, bursting into a blue flame. Working quickly, with nimble fingers, Johánas built a loose heap of wood around it, and before long the fire was crackling nicely, growing hotter from the inside out.

Johánas pointed to the backpack, and Kaj rummaged for the coffee pouch and held it out to him. As the boy took it in his steady little hand, he glanced up at his travel companion with a confused look on his face.

"You speak Sámi," he said, studying Kaj's face for a moment before he filled the sooty pan with water and set it down on the fire.

"Huh? No I don't. Why would you say that?"

"I don't know," Johánás said without looking up, adjusting the sticks so that the pan was steady. "But I wasn't thinking and told you to get the coffee out in Sámi, and you did."

Kaj had no answers. He simply took out a pack of nougat cookies from the shabby backpack instead. He could feel something bubbling up towards the surface inside him, just like the coffee in the pot a moment or two later.

It was a beautiful day, and he closed his eyes to enjoy it, listening to his own heartbeat.

"They'll be here soon," said Johánás, gazing across the ice, which stretched out like an ocean in front of them. All around them, the mountains rose up in the glittering spring sunshine, small, dark patches of bare ground nestled among the white. The crisp snow looked like grains of sugar, and on the scrap of ground where they were sitting, the moss was warm between the crowberry bushes. The bright sun made the timeless, majestic nature shimmer like mother-of-pearl.

Right then, they heard the growing rumble of engines. Kaj and Johánás both looked up over their birch wood cups, and Johánás lowered his half-eaten biscuit. He got onto his knees in order to see better.

"Look!" The boy turned to Kaj, excitement on his face, and pointed to the lake.

Kaj used his hand to shield his eyes.

He saw a diffuse cloud of bodies, heard them thundering against the ice, the mass of reindeer growing larger the closer it came. It looked like a huge shoal of fish, an enormous flock of birds.

Against the backdrop of the white ice, a few barking dogs darted around the tangle of bodies, focused on keeping them in line. The reindeers' antlers rose up towards the sky like pale fingers, and the dogs looked like waves being sucked in and out by the herd as it surged forward. They yapped as they ran around the animals, clearly enjoying their work, herding and redirecting any reindeer that broke away from the pack with gentle skill. Their attentive eyes seemed to read everything that was happening in the lumbering gaggle of reindeer, and they parried and dropped back in eager interaction as they danced around the herd.

Riding alongside the animals were a number of people on snowmobiles. One came to a halt, and a man with a rope around his chest bent down to pick something up – a calf, perhaps. He then sat down with the animal between himself and the handlebars and set off after the others.

"It's the spring migration," Johánás said softly, looking up at Kaj with glittering eyes.

The surging reindeer, the hard-working dogs and the snow-mobiles out on the ice: Kaj could feel them in his body, and he couldn't help but smile.

There was something ceremonial and exhilarating about the scene; it was so beautiful and powerful that it touched a part of him he hadn't even known existed. He took a deep, reverent breath.

The sun was bright, flashing in the animals' black eyes. The ice creaked and groaned as the herd passed their islet at a safe distance.

"Where are they going?" Kaj whispered, keen not to break the spell.

"The mountains," Johánás replied in a low voice.

"Why are the herders taking them there?"

Johánás laughed. "They're not; it's the reindeer. They've given the sign that they want to go up there to give birth."

"And the snowmobiles and the dogs lead them there?"

"Nope," the boy replied solemnly. "It's the other way around – the reindeer show them the way. The herders just tag along for protection."

"From what?" Kaj couldn't tear his eyes away from the scene in front of him.

"Predators. Bad ice, because of the dams and that kind of thing. The reindeer have no idea that people have changed nature. It's getting warmer, the landscape is changing . . . but something inside them takes them along the same routes as ever. A whole herd ran out onto some bad ice once, hundreds of them, and they all drowned. The herders keep an eye on the weather, and they check the ground to make sure the reindeer get to the mountains safely." Johánás sounded like a wise old man as he quietly gave his explanation by Kaj's side.

The shouting, barking and clicking of hooves faded into the distance. The herd had passed, continuing its journey west.

With a feeling of excitement and sadness, Kaj and Johánás watched them disappear into the sunlight.

Kaj had never experienced anything like it before. Nothing had ever touched him so deeply that it felt like he might never be the same again.

They sat quietly, side by side, until Johánás broke the silence.

"Nice, huh? You going to keep blubbering, or do you want more coffee?"

"Shut it," Kaj replied, holding out his cup with a grin.

As Johánás filled the little wooden vessel and Kaj got up to take it from him, the boy noticed the knife swing across his thigh.

"Nice! Can I see?"

With barely concealed pride, Kaj held out his beautiful knife, shaft first.

Johánás gave a low whistle as he pulled it out and studied the blade. He turned it over in his hand with the air of a connoisseur and found a signature embedded in the ornate pattern.

"Damn, look at this! P.R."

"Aren't you a bit young to be swearing?" Kaj snapped, but Johánás simply rolled his eyes, not looking up from the knife.

"This is a Per knife. You need to look after this!"

Kaj's jaw dropped, and he felt his mind spinning, swirling into a hurricane. Per? Not his mother's brother, surely? No, it was a common name. It couldn't be his mother's brother Per who made the knives, could it?

He was so lost in thought that he didn't even respond to Johánás's taunt that owning such a beautiful knife was wasted on him. As a southerner, the child claimed, he lacked the ability to handle something as special as this.

Kaj simply pulled his fellow traveller's hat down over his eyes, making the boy protest loudly as he thought to himself: Holy hell!

54

On the Warpath in Sarvesoajvve

Battalion commander lieutenant colonel Herman Hägg, of the Norrland Dragoon Regiment, had received a letter. In shaky handwriting, it urged him and "all the men he could muster" to immediately deploy to an address in a small hamlet to the north of Guovddo. There, according to the author, "foreign powers" – and he couldn't quite decipher the name of the hostile invader given – had encroached onto Swedish territory.

Lieutenant colonel Hägg sighed wearily.

It was a bad day for nonsense, and he was downright sick of all the pranksters wasting his and his colleagues' time.

The country was at peace, and it was by no means illegal for tourists to travel around the Kingdom. True, this was the only handwritten letter he had received – and scrawled on the back of the endpaper from a cookbook, at that. Nevertheless, it was just one in a long line of conspiratorial messages addressed to his unit, and Hägg was irritated at the administrative burden these teenagers' idleness entailed.

Because upon closer inspection – something that was required under the rules – the culprits always proved to be bored, anxious young men, up to no good on their computers in their smelly teenage rooms.

The latest letter felt like the final straw, coming as it did while he was going through a messy divorce and having trouble pissing. He had also stepped on a dead mouse when he swung his bare foot out of bed that morning. His daughter's damned cat had given him a look of disdain when it realized the grumpy old man was too feeble-minded to understand the value of the gesture and had nonchalantly strutted out of the room with its tail held high, leaving its cold, lifeless gift behind.

Hägg popped his head into the office next door, where his colleague was busy tapping away at the keyboard with a frenzy that should be against the law.

"Do you have a minute?" he asked the younger man.

"Sure," Skultman replied, as alert as only someone without kids could be that early in the morning. "Where are we going?" he asked as he leapt up and pulled on his perfectly fitting uniform jacket.

His face was rosy, his eyes bright and well-rested.

The man probably followed some sort of strict diet of algae to maximize his performance, the battalion chief thought bitterly.

Herman Hägg started walking towards the staff entrance, his colleague bouncing along behind him.

"We're going to make an example of someone," the lieutenant colonel replied. "And we're driving." He jingled the keys as though he half expected his fitness loving colleague to suggest an alternative – in his heart of hearts, Skultman would probably enjoy running a few dozen kilometers in full kit – but Herman Hägg had no intention of coming face to face with his maker today, gasping for air. No, that fate was reserved for whoever had signed off the letter with the words "A Concerned Citizen."

Enough was enough.

55

Defenders of Almond Cookies and the Realm

For the third time in a short while, a car of strangers pulled up on the Rijás' driveway. Today's specimen was dark green, with authoritative black plates and yellow numbers – and just two days after Máriddja sent the letter! She rubbed her hands with glee and draped her apron over the boxy storage chair in the hallway before going out to meet them, powerless to hide her excitement.

"Good afternoon, gentlemen!" she said, saluting the two men.

She craned her neck to get a better look at the tanks and trucks full of troops that would surely appear around the bend behind them at any moment, but her beady eyes couldn't see any sign of the rest of the army through her freshly polished jam jar lenses.

The men gave her a polite salute back, and the older of the two – a slightly rotund middle-aged veteran with a cross look on his face – was the first to speak.

"We're here regarding a letter," he said, his tone formal.

The soldier beside him was practically jumping up and down on the spot at the prospect of joining in. "Yes, we were wondering if someone at this address might have been up to a bit of mischief?"

The middle-aged man, who introduced himself as battalion chief lieutenant colonel Hägg, rolled his eyes at Skultman's enthusiasm.

Máriddja was crestfallen. *Mischief?*

"Aren't you here because of the Russians?" she asked.

The two knights looked so confused that Máriddja felt like she had no choice but to offer an explanation.

"The whole place was crawling with Karelians, plotting to take over the country! But I told them . . . I said there was nothing for them *here*, and that if they didn't toddle off back where they'd come from, I'd get my stick. So off they went, scuttling away with their tails between their legs," she said, gesturing theatrically to show how she had chased the intruders away.

The younger of the two soldiers seemed to find her story exciting, and his jaw dropped to bare his dazzlingly white teeth. Máriddja would have loved to get a closer look at those teeth to check whether his oral health indicated hidden Sámi powers, but she realized that now wasn't the right moment. No doubt she would have time to study his face properly during the upcoming military operation.

Hägg, however, showed a shameless lack of faith in the story she had come up with, announcing that they wanted to speak to whoever was responsible for such mumbo-jumbo. And if there was a teenager who was up to no good inside, then she would do well to bring him out sharpish.

As though on cue, the front door opened and Biera shuffled out onto the porch with a look of confusion in his eyes. He was wearing nothing but a t-shirt and underpants, his skinny, crooked legs on show as he stood there in his wooden clogs.

Her otherwise conveniently deaf husband had clearly heard part of their conversation, and now he wanted to have his say.

Máriddja swore to herself as he clapped his hands to his head and let out a long *ohhh*.

"*Hearra don áiga*," he barked. "The Tchudes! The Tchudes are here! Gather all the men and we'll lure them over the edge of the cliff on Gárjjelbákte! Where's the bear spear?"

"Tchudes?" Hägg repeated, staring at the underdressed old man.

"I've read about them," said his colleague, looking interested. "They were a group of people from the east who plundered the Sámi land back in the day."

Jesus Christ. In his mind, Hägg slapped his forehead. Was there no limit to Skultman's brilliance – he read *books* too?

"They're a plague," the old man croaked from the porch. "A *satanaa* . . ." He continued muttering to himself in Sámi until the little old lady reached him and pushed him back inside.

She reappeared a moment later, and had clearly managed to calm him down because she was smiling as though nothing had happened. She held out a plate of cookies.

"Something to dip in your coffee?"

The reluctant coffee guests had stayed a while.

Hägg might not have been too snooty to say yes when she offered him a cookie, but Skultman had patted his trim stomach with an apologetic smile. Still, Máriddja had managed to get them to stay for long enough to determine that the net had come up empty yet again. Skultman was in uniform, yes, but he wasn't the person she was looking for, and she could dismiss Hägg with no more than a quick glance – he was far too old. Neither of them had ever been the boy she so desperately longed to see. As Hägg drank his coffee, he had given her a lengthy lecture, reprimanding her for her actions and making it clear that, strictly speaking, she was guilty of raising a false alarm. But they would turn a blind eye on this occasion. As he gave her a dressing down, crumbs had spilt from his mouth like coarse salt into a bubbling pot of stew.

Máriddja had pursed her lips and refused to admit to a single thing. Stubbornly maintaining that she and the old man they had just met were the only people living on the hill.

She didn't budge an inch from her story about having prevented an invasion of the country – she even showed them the stick that had saved Sweden from its attackers. Hägg had been indifferent to that information, but he was smart enough to keep his mouth shut. The strong coffee had begun to fill his tender bladder, and all he wanted was to get out of there as quickly as he could.

Before long they had thanked Máriddja, reminded her that it was an offence to waste the military's time, and driven off in their big green car.

In the rear-view mirror, Hägg had watched the thin old woman, limp plaits hanging out of the bottom of her hat, give them a proud military salute as they drove away from the little house and its stale almond cookies. The sight left him feeling both irritated and depressed.

But not quite as irritated and depressed as Skultman asking whether the battalion chief had ever given yoga a try.

56

She-Bears

A few cold nights followed, and Máriddja and Biera both suffered aches and pains. Máriddja slept badly, waking often, trapped between the evil growing in her belly and her memories.

Risten visited her. Risten and her son, their boy. Guilt forced Máriddja to relive her most painful memories over and over again in her dreams.

The day when they lost Heaika-Joná wasn't wrapped up in the forgiving mists of time. It was as clear to her as the floral pattern on the wallpaper just a few feet away. She remembered everything.

"We're more his parents than you and that drunk!" Panic had made her voice shrill as she hurled those words at her sister-in-law like a sharp spear.

The younger woman had ducked and thrown back, "You'll never see him again!" The words went straight into Máriddja's gut.

It had knocked the wind out of her, left her gasping for air before she launched another attack. Like a threatened animal.

They had circled each other like two she-bears with their teeth bared, flexing their claws and shaking their heads ominously from side to side.

Risten's bites made her bones crack as she lashed out with steady paws, tearing the old woman into submission. An old woman who was simply defending herself; defending her brood.

It was dangerous to get between a mother and her young, even more dangerous if the two she-bears were fighting over the very same cub.

Máriddja's own empty womb cramped as though she were in the throes of childbirth during the fight. Her powerful blows caused the young female to stumble in their dance around the boy's future. The older female had the upper hand, but the youngster was faster. In a split second, the swifter, more agile Risten had distracted her and grabbed the little one, dashed off on her quick young legs. With a long stride and explosive movements.

The old she-bear had risen up on her hind legs and roared in pain as they disappeared out of reach in the car. To Máriddja, it felt as though that death howl was still ringing in her ears, as though the life had trickled out of her.

Biera had stumbled as he ran after the car, and Máriddja had staggered and collapsed onto the bear spear aimed straight at her mothering heart.

Lying in bed all these years later, she found herself thinking that all she wanted was for someone to arrange her bones so that she could become one with the earth once more.

She wanted for the person who drove the spear into her to finish off the job and take care of her flesh, her heart, absorbing her strength. As was the custom among her people.

She wanted her slayer to possess everything Máriddja had in the moment they got the better of her. Risten had the power, and her victory had been so great that she had become invisible to them – just like the bear killers of legend, who took on the bear's subjugated power. No one was allowed to look straight at the hunters when they returned home from a successful hunt, not without a brass ring to gaze through. And Máriddja didn't have a brass ring.

She didn't have anything that could help her eyes find her sister-in-law and the boy.

She didn't have anything, not anymore.

Máriddja and Biera had crept back into their winter lair like the old bears they were, to wait for death.

They might as well toss her worthless pelvis and empty arms to the ravens, Máriddja thought that dark spring night. Because she had already been dead for years, ever since the day her boy was taken away from her.

57

Support from the Cuckoo Clock

"You know my husband is special, don't you? I must have mentioned it. That's why I thought this would work."

"I'm not sure I understand," said Siré.

Máriddja sighed. "No, me neither. If you don't have the gift, it's probably hard to make sense of it. I once asked Biera how he thought the boy was. Whether he was OK, whether he wore long johns and that kind of thing . . . And he got that look on his face. After all these years, I can tell straight away when Biera gets one of his messages from the beyond. It's like his eyes focus on nothing while he listens inside himself."

"I'm listening," said Siré, sounding interested.

"That's good," Máriddja muttered. "Anyway, I saw him get that distant look of his, and then he said the boy was fine, that he would be in some sort of uniform. Heaika-Joná was always crazy about policemen and fire engines, so I didn't think it sounded too far-fetched. That's why I wanted all those men to come out here, to see whether he was one of them . . . one of the uniforms. I put my faith in Biera's gift, because he usually knows . . ." Máriddja let out a weak sigh. "But it was probably just a wild moose chase. A silly feeling. A . . . well, you get the gist."

"Would you like to write a list?"

"Ah, Siré . . ." Máriddja laughed. "You know, I've never been much of a writer, but it would have been nice to have all the memories written down now that we're approaching the winter of our years. Maybe that's what Risten thought too, when she started writing her diaries," Máriddja said, looking up at the cuckoo clock on the wall as though the bird might come leaping out and lend her its support.

"I'm not sure I understand. Did you say Risten?"

"Good grief, it doesn't sound like you have much of a memory either, Siré! Risten Rijá, Biera's unfortunate little sister! I wish he could see where they were, but it doesn't work like that, his gift. Well, you've got the power yourself, so you know what I mean."

"There are limits to what I know," Siré said mysteriously, making Máriddja nod as though she had just confirmed all her fears.

"Yes, yes, don't say any more . . . I know a person can lose their gift if they talk about it too much. But don't worry, I won't say anything. Your secret's safe with me."

"I'm not sure I understand what you mean," said Siré, now a little standoffish.

Máriddja smiled conspiratorially and winked at the phone. "No, me neither. But we're not supposed to understand everything, are we . . . and just as well."

She was quiet for a moment, gazing out at the profile of the mountain against the sky.

"All hope is probably gone now, anyway," Máriddja added. "I don't know what I was expecting. They never replied to a single letter I sent."

The old woman let out a deep sigh as the post van drove by and Nuffe waved through the windscreen. She raised her hand in return and plugged the phone in to charge, blissfully unaware of what the neighbors' boy had in the back seat. If

Máriddja had known, she almost certainly would have thought it a sign of great magic.

Because why should Máriddja Rijá put her faith in fate when it had been so cruel to her?

58

Fish in a Pail

Tears of relief and resignation flowed down Máriddja's cheeks as she told Siré about what had happened on Holy Saturday.

She suspected her friend might be wondering how she had managed to sleep through Biera's morning routine, because although he might have tiptoed out of the room to avoid waking her, their toilet often sounded like a ghost in distress as water flooded through the old pipes. The truth, as Máriddja explained, was that she had slept in his old earplugs. The magpies had been squabbling outside, and the damn birds were about as noisy as a couple of tin cans full of cutlery being kicked down a hill. She had tried to come to some sort of understanding with the frisky feathered pests, throwing a piece of firewood at them around three in the morning, but eventually she had been forced to admit defeat in the face of their relentless urges. In any case. She had her nose to thank, yet again.

The absence of Biera's sweaty feet, combined with the very-present aroma of a musty ice drill in the hallway, was all it took for her to realize that her husband had been serious when he started mumbling about catching a spring pike he could hang up to dry for the dog. A dog that was no longer among the living, of course, and therefore wouldn't appreciate the gesture.

Máriddja had thrown on some clothes and was only too willing to admit that she might have looked a bit of a mess. Regardless, she had set off. In odd shoes and with a scarf wrapped around her head against the cold wind. He wasn't hard to track through the snow: both his footprints and the line left by the tip of the ice drill he was dragging behind him were clear on the road.

When she spotted her husband over by the lake, she could barely breathe from the exertion and fear. Because Biera was busy chatting to someone else.

As she got closer, huffing and puffing, she saw that it was Nuffe. Just typical that they had ended up living next door to a damn postman, Máriddja muttered to herself. Stupid early risers! She shared her disparaging thoughts about the postal service with Siré, trusting her friend to keep an open mind and understand how she had felt in the moment.

Biera had been even more badly dressed than she was, in nothing but his long johns and a bobbly old sweater. He had pulled on his hat, of course, and the big red pompom seemed to glow brightly against the slushy grey snow heaped up outside the Nilssons' house.

The wretched old man was also wearing his wooden clogs, Máriddja had noticed with a resigned sigh.

Biera seemed pleasantly surprised when he spotted her, but she returned his warm welcome with narrowed eyes and a downturned mouth.

It quickly transpired that Nuffe's father Sören had seen Biera taking a leak beside their garbage can, his ice drill leaning against Nuffe's mail van, and that he had sent his relatively young, relatively speedy son out to investigate.

Her husband and the neighbors' boy were chatting like old friends, and Biera was busy pointing something out to the younger man. Probably the spaceship that had come to take him home, his wife thought glumly, taking a deep breath to stop herself from giving him a box around the ears and make his pompom bounce back and forth like a pinball.

When Biera moved a few steps away to loudly blow his nose in his hand, Nuffe had seized his moment. Keeping his voice low, and with breath that smelt like cheap caviar from a squeezy tube, he asked Máriddja whether her husband was really OK. He had looked so serious as he said it – a little too curious, too – that Máriddja simply pursed her lips and refused to answer.

"It's just . . . he seems a bit confused," Nuffe continued, turning to watch Biera, who was standing with his feet a hip-width apart, trying to use his ice drill on the pail of decorated twigs Sally had put out by the mailbox ahead of Easter. Máriddja didn't reply, she just shook her head and started tugging at the slack waistband on Biera's long johns.

"You can tell me, you know," Nuffe had said conspiratorially. "Is Biera, you know . . . starting to head back into *childhood*?" He whispered the last word. "Because if he is, you should know that we're here for you, and that the local dementia care is supposed to be really good. Dad's aunt—"

"Let me stop you there," Máriddja interrupted him, straightening up. "There's no need to worry about us."

"But something's clearly not right, anyone can see that!"

Máriddja's head was spinning and whirring, like the drill in Biera's hands as he turned it in the pail, making twigs fly and garish feather decorations sail down to the slushy ground.

They mustn't think she couldn't look after him! Anything but them thinking he'd gone funny in the head.

"He's on drugs," Máriddja had blurted out, rolling her eyes a little. "So . . . there's no need to worry. Just your regular, everyday addiction," she explained with a reassuring smile. As she spoke, she tried to right the pail and yank the drill out of Biera's hands.

Nuffe's eyes seemed to be bulging from his chubby face. He looked like a caricature of a hairless stoat.

"What?" he said after a moment, studying Biera from head to toe. The same Biera — and as she attempted to recreate the scene for Siré, Máriddja had to stop and laugh here — who had tucked one of the decorative green feathers behind his ear and was following their conversation with wide eyes and a naive smile.

"Yup. We bought them from . . . the potato man. You know, the one from over by the coast, he parks his van outside the council building." Máriddja had waved her index finger in a vague southerly direction.

Nuffe had clearly lost control of his facial features, because his jaw seemed to be feeling the full force of gravity. Máriddja had managed to get Biera going, and she pulled the old man behind her with one hand, dragging the ice drill along the tire tracks with the other. Even though her hands were full, she attempted to raise a finger to her lips, but it didn't work. And so she had shouted instead, as loud as she could, to overpower the screeching of the drill against the ground.

"You've got to treat yourself, you know? Have fun while you're still hale and hearty!"

"Do you want to throw a party?" Siré asked, sounding deadly serious, after Máriddja recapped their exchange.

"Very funny, Siré. Seriously, very funny." She laughed so hard she couldn't stop.

My god, *what* a mess!

59

Not a racist, but . . .

There were plenty of seats in the conference room, which was irrelevant given that there were only five people present. It was a far cry from how many staff they had once had, and even further from the number they actually needed. But that was simply how things were these days, right across the country.

Lena Östman, head of social services, opened the meeting as she flicked through the stack of papers on the table beside her cup of tea.

"OK, let's get started. Not many new cases to deal with today. A paternity dispute, a needs assessment for a new support claimant, plus two reports of concern. One is from everyone's favorite do-gooder, Britt-Maria Skata, and as ever it's about her neighbor. She's reported him for having an underaged wife this time, but we can probably assume that her mental state is to blame again. We're pretty sure the woman Britt-Marie is talking about is the man's daughter, who is registered at the same address, but we still need to go out there to check. Can I leave that with you, Ali? OK? Now, report number two . . ." she said as she searched for the right document in her thick stack, "is new. We've actually received reports of concern from a number of different social agencies, all regarding the same elderly couple. The Rijás."

One of the others snorted, and Lena looked up. She fixed her eyes on Mårten, who stared straight back at her as she went on.

"We've got no fewer than five reports about this couple, from the health service, the police authority, the fire service, an oncologist in Sunnanby and . . ." she read from the sheet, "one Ulf Nilsson. A neighbor.

"From what I can see, it's been a lively few months in Sarvesoajvve, where the Rijás have lived since the sixties. There's been a fire, the Dragoon Regiment and the police have both been called out – the latter in relation to a hunting offence they suspect the couple themselves were guilty of. Mr Rijá has barely been seen over the past few years, but according to their neighbor he is 'ancient and completely out of it'." Lena made air quotes as she spoke. "The oncologist flagged up that Maria Rijá is in extremely poor health – she was diagnosed with advanced uterine and ovarian cancer six months ago and wasn't expected to live much longer.

"So far no one has managed to reach the couple, and they haven't replied to any letters from the health service, either. We need to arrange an urgent home visit. Top priority, OK, Mårten? It's your area, after all."

Lena glanced down at her phone and then got up and smoothed out her tunic.

"I've got to run; my next meeting starts in ten minutes, and I don't have a car."

She gathered up her papers and made her way over to the door.

"Sure," Mårten drawled, his voice a touch too loud. "But I can't say I'm really surprised. I mean, I'm not a racist or anything, but isn't this just typical of a couple of old Lapps? I know, I know, you're supposed to say *Sami* nowadays."

Silence filled the room.

Lena had opened the door, but she paused and turned around with narrowed eyes.

"Viveca, I want you to take the Rijás' case," she barked. Then, with her eyes fixed so firmly on Mårten that he squirmed in his chair, she continued: "The words '*not a racist, but*' are only ever followed by complete bullshit. You can work on your views instead, Berglund, because that's not OK."

She slammed the door behind her.

60

Broken, Breaker

Laura had spent her entire life trying to avoid looking back on that awful day when everything came to a head. Bill's anger had been bottomless, explosive, and she had been more frightened than ever before. The fear never served any purpose – it wouldn't soften his blows or wipe the blood from her mouth after it was all over – and yet it insisted on hanging around, like an uncomfortably heavy piece of jewelry. A tug inside her navel, a drumroll between her breasts.

That day. The worst time, the last one. He had attacked her without warning, punching and kicking and threatening her, and she had cowered without really attempting to defend herself. Allowing herself to be beaten like a passive lump of meat. She was lying face down on the floor, could see the fridge door from the corner of her eye. A stray piece of uncooked spaghetti under a cabinet. Waiting, counting the knots in the pine cupboard doors. The only part of that day's torture that was new were the words he had speared on his bloody sword. Threats, terrible threats and senseless bile, directed at her kind-hearted big brother.

When he finally sank to the lowest possible level and directed his verbal darkness at Heaika-Joná – their son – she had thrown up all over the floor. She felt she could see tar dripping from the boy's name, or was it blood?

After looking down at her vomit with disgust and disdain, Bill had stormed out of the shabby apartment, slamming the door so hard that the windows rattled. And on unsteady legs, guided more by instinct than anything else, she had made her way down to the kindly older woman on the floor below.

The woman who stopped in the stairwell to quietly ask if she was OK whenever Bill's abuse had been particularly loud, when Laura's face looked especially bad. She knew the woman was a nurse, and she had a strong suspicion that she needed someone like her right then. It felt like the skin on her upper body had been ripped to shreds, and she could feel a throbbing, stabbing pain inside, as though something vital had broken.

Unn, that was the woman's name. She had helped Laura out of her clothes to examine her injuries, and when she saw the state of the young woman's body she had insisted on calling the police. A sobbing Laura had talked her out of it, promising to leave him instead.

"What about the boy?" Unn had asked, her face serious. "What are you going to do about the boy? Will you leave him with your brother?"

"I'll take him with me," said Laura, as firmly as she could, anguish screeching and squawking through her head like a bird of prey.

The truth was that she had made up her mind as she threw up her fear and sorrow and every last watered-down ounce of love for the child's father. It was time for her to be a mother, to take care of Heaika-Joná. To protect him.

Unn had studied her without a word, and then she said: "I'll help you, but it has to be now. You need to leave right away." The older woman got up and rummaged through her bag, producing a few hundred-kronor notes that she thrust into Laura's hand. "My sister's colleague is driving over to

Sundsvall tonight. He works on the railways, but he's heading home for the season. I'll arrange for him to give you a lift."

The older woman had then draped her son's flannel shirt over Laura's shaking shoulders and looked her straight in the eye.

"You understand that you can't tell anyone you're leaving, or where you're going, don't you? You'll be putting them in danger once Bill finds out if you do. I don't want to know where you decide to hop out along the way, either . . ."

"What about you? Haven't I put you in danger?" Laura whimpered.

"No, Bill doesn't know where you are, and my son will be home in a few hours. I'd like to see the brute try to get in here then." She smiled reassuringly.

"But—"

"Let's go to your brother's place and get your boy," Unn interrupted her. Laura gingerly followed her out to the car.

Her heart wasn't bleeding. It was being pulverized, hacked at, torn to pulsing shreds.

How had she ended up here? And what would happen to *them* now? Her fear acted as a muzzle for her tears.

Unn started the engine and they drove through the autumn evening, towards her brother's safe, bright home on the mountain. The heavens opened and rain drummed down on the windscreen, making hard work for the wipers.

Is that you crying, Mum and Dad, Laura wondered.

At what I have to do now. At everything I have to leave behind, the same way you once did.

Are you crying for me?

Or is it for all the big, strong hearts that I – a worthless piece of shit – am about to reduce to ash?

61

The Abduction

It had been every bit as awful as Laura feared. Biera and his wife had refused to let her take Heaika-Joná, despite her first begging them and then lashing out with words she couldn't take back.

About whose child he was.

About how they had no right to steal him from his mother.

Their angry voices had woken Heaika-Joná, and he had peered around the corner from the bedroom where his aunt and uncle had tucked him up in their bed earlier.

Finally Unn, who had been waiting in the car, seemed to have sensed the difficulties inside, because she marched straight in without knocking and claimed to be from social services. Reeled off all sorts of laws and statutes, referring them to Laura's rights as his legal guardian. Laura suspected she had made it all up in an attempt to convince Biera, but she was too distraught to care.

Her brother had then, with uncharacteristic anger, demanded to know what was going on and where they thought they were taking the boy. That had scared her, but fortunately Unn was unyielding.

In the end Laura had used the last of her strength to grab Heaika-Joná and run outside with him in her arms. Unn was right behind her, and she started the engine and tore out of their yard with impressive skill. The little one had howled in protest beside her, but Laura managed to calm him down with a story about going on an adventure, the kind of thing only a four-year-old would believe. The blessed boy had then fallen asleep in his pyjamas, leaning against her bruised shoulder.

When she turned around and looked back at the cabin that had become a temporary home to her and her son, she saw a barefoot Biera running after them. He ran until he was nothing but a tiny, desperate dot of a big brother in the distance, and she cried the whole way down from the mountain.

Laura had said a quick goodbye to Unn and then carried the sleeping lad over to the backseat of the waiting car. The thin-haired man in the driver's seat hadn't asked any questions. He had every right to, given the state of them and the dramatic handover in the car park outside of town, but he simply drummed the wheel and glanced at her with pale eyes, handing her a tissue when he noticed her tears. She had been sore and bruised after Bill's violence, and struggled to get comfortable, but if the driver noticed he didn't say anything.

He had turned on the radio, and the sound of a power ballad made Laura feel like a soggy cigarette butt beneath a steel-toed boot. Her body hurt all over, but nothing, absolutely nothing was more painful than seeing the boy's shoulders trembling in the backseat, hearing his quiet, frightened tears.

She reached back between the seats and felt his warm little hand hesitantly squeeze hers in return.

62

Half a Box of Raisins

It had been a quiet morning.

Máriddja had struck up a conversation with Siré about the possibility of using a shaman in order to pay a visit to the underworld to maim Bill. Siré had pretended not to know what they were talking about.

Máriddja had mused about exactly how much pain a person might feel in the kingdom of the dead. Siré hadn't known.

They had then exchanged recipes for sponge cake, and Máriddja had found herself drifting off on a wave of melancholic nostalgia.

She told Siré all about the tears she had shed the day she and Biera decided to take the snowmobile up to the mountain, the year after they lost the child. In the covered sled, gaffer tape over the broken plastic windows, she had found half a box of raisins the boy had forgotten beneath the reindeer hide.

She hadn't been able to ride in the sled since, despite the fact that it was both warmer and more comfortable than sitting on the back of the snowmobile when they were out and about.

But that had been when there was a little fur-clad boy sitting beneath the old hide with her. Tucked up to his nose, eyes bright and with a "tickly tummy" whenever Biera sidehilled the snowmobile, making the entire sled tilt with it.

Back when she had put her warm gloves down on the blanket to fish out the raisins, one by one, feeding them to the gaping baby bird beside her. His tiny hands were too cold and stiff to manage the lid on the box, and the sled jostled and branches brushed against the cover like trolls' fingers.

She told Siré about the hot water in the plastic bottle she had stuffed into one of Biera's thick socks and put at the bottom of the bed, so the boy's feet wouldn't get cold. Because if you got cold feet as a child, that meant aches and pains once you were older, she explained, voice catching in her throat.

"No use crying over spilt milk, Siré," Máriddja said after wiping her nose with a napkin covered in little Christmas trees. "It is what it is, that's the truth. You should never fret about how things turned out. But I'll be damned if I don't feel like turning all the world's sorcery on that brute of a man! I realize now that it was all Bill's fault that Risten took the boy and left."

"That sounds like a good idea," Siré agreed, and Máriddja snorted through her tears.

"Yup, it'd be neat if you could arrange it."

Máriddja's cheeks felt tight from her salty tears, but she smiled softly.

"I'd like to ask you something," she said after a moment of sniffing.

"Ask away!"

"You're going to think I'm mad, but can we agree to talk every day?"

"I'm sure we can arrange that!"

Máriddja nodded, feeling slightly relieved. She hadn't quite revealed her aim, however, and she quickly went on:

". . . so if you don't hear from me for a whole day – and I want you to listen carefully now, Siré, because this is really important! If you don't hear from me for a whole day, you need to call 90 000."

"That number is no longer in use. Since 1 July 1996, the number for the emergency services has been 112."

"Siré!" Máriddja barked, her voice wavering. "Stop messing about and focus!"

"OK. I'm focused."

"Whatever the damn number is, I want you to raise the alarm after twenty-four hours. Is that understood?"

"Got it. What reason should I give for the call?"

"That I'm dead," Máriddja said bluntly. "And that someone needs to come over here and take care of my husband, because he can't manage on his own. I've run out of options. No one can help us."

"I think I understand what you're trying to say," said Siré. She sounded composed, but her voice had a clear undertone of sadness.

"I've always thought you were so damn understanding," Máriddja sniffed, hugging the telephone to her wrinkled cheek.

63

Invaluable, Inestimable and Irreplaceable

Sissel Jarre had been in touch again, with a second typed letter. It arrived alongside yet another envelope from the county council (which Máriddja quickly disposed of in the stove). She opened the letter from Sissel. It referred back to her previous correspondence and emphasized just how important Biera's memories could be to her work.

Invaluable, inestimable and irreplaceable.

Máriddja mumbled those three words to herself, memorizing them so that she could accurately repeat the superlatives when she called Siré later.

Invaluable, inestimable and irreplaceable.

Oh yes, they wouldn't believe how invaluable it would be to restore Biera's memories, but it was the new ones Máriddja was interested in. They were the ones that got away from her, she thought as a jolt of pain seared through her gut. Out of habit, she massaged the knot of cancer cells beneath her skin in an attempt to lessen the searing ache.

Biera had retreated into a world he didn't share with her, and he spent less and less time in their lives as they were now. In some ways, she could understand it; heaven knows she would have liked to escape this wretched existence herself, but there were a number of pressing matters that required her input before she could rest.

The fact that she had taken the gun off him hadn't helped, not when she had been careless enough to simply throw it in the bin outside. But it had been a spur of the moment decision; she sometimes felt a little anxious about what the old man might get up to next. And if she were honest, it was lucky he had brought it back in again; it had been incredibly useful when she'd shot the elk.

Máriddja nodded to herself, thinking about the knives she had hidden, the matches, the car keys . . . She sighed and shook her head to help dilute her thoughts, and her eyes came to rest on the printed text in front of her.

Sissel Jarre wrote about documentation, about historical abuses and reparations, pleading with Biera to get in touch so that she could interview him. He was one of only a handful of living people to have first-hand experience of being forcibly relocated from Sweden's northernmost Sámi community, after all.

Máriddja found herself thinking about the *akkja* in the attic. Perhaps the sled might be of interest to the project? It wasn't like she and Biera had any use for the old thing, after all, and if the Sámi Parliament wanted it then they may as well have it. The original plan had been to burn it, but that hadn't felt right, so this was a satisfying solution. Compensation for the conversation Ms. Jarre sadly couldn't have with her husband. It was lucky Máriddja hadn't managed to drag it down the steep stairs yet, to carry the debris out to the heap of other things waiting to go up in smoke on the charred earth outside. There, where the remains of their barn lay in state.

How she would manage to hand the *akkja* over to them, intact, without having to haul the damn thing down herself was something she could work out later. She could start by writing a letter to Jarre, offering her the heirloom. Yes, may as well – everyone knew the Jarres were a headstrong bunch; they never gave in before they got what they wanted.

If she hadn't managed to get a good look at lieutenant colonel Hägg and determined that he was an ordinary Swede, she might easily have mistaken him for a Jarre. The very picture of a stubborn, impossible man, she thought to herself. It wasn't her damn fault if kids sent cheeky letters to the army from time to time. Didn't they have a sense of humor?

64

Biellorássi

Mimmi was waiting outside the local Sámi school.

It was a warm day, and she pulled off her gloves and sat down on a kick sled by the bicycle racks. She took off her hat and felt her hair spill down onto her sweaty forehead and cheeks. She pushed it back and closed her eyes, enjoying the eager heat of the sun on her face.

What an afternoon!

The bright sound of the kids playing in the yard made for pleasant background noise, though it also egged on the sharp beak of longing she felt for a child of her own, causing it to peck away at her heart.

Mimmi had told Micklas she would take Johánás to see his great grandmother in the care home where she lived, both to drop off some dried meat and to collect his eighth birthday present. The twisted scraps of meat were in a canvas bag on her lap, smoked and dried so that they could be eaten as toppings or snacks. Their flavor was incredible, and Mimmi thought it was sweet that Micklas cared for his old mum to send her treats like this. He didn't have time to visit her himself today, had to take the dog to the vet in town.

The spray from a wet snowball splashed up onto her legs.

"No, not her! Don't throw them at Mimmi!" she heard Johánás shout, and when she opened her eyes she saw a group of boys whose backpacks looked like clingy koalas on their backs. They were all forming snowballs in their bare hands as they walked, hurling them at the trees and rooftops with impressive accuracy. Johánás peeled away from the others and came towards her with a slightly embarrassed smile.

"Why, is she your new mum or something?" a tall boy in a pair of thermal Powerboots asked mockingly.

"Shut up, Teo," Johánás replied without looking back. He rolled his eyes at Mimmi to hide his embarrassment.

"Hi, buddy," said Mimmi, getting up from the sled with her gloves and hat in hand. The boy smiled and took the canvas bag from her.

"I can take that. You're so weak I feel sorry for you."

She gave him a teasing nudge in the side, and they started walking. The old people's home was on the next street over.

Johánás held the door for Mimmi, ignoring the button to make it swing open automatically. He shoved his gloves into his pockets and unzipped his overalls a little as they stepped into the turquoise corridor. The boy said polite hellos to the staff as he moved through the building, and they welcomed him warmly.

"Hi Johánás! She's just about to have her afternoon coffee. Shall I bring another two cups?" asked a woman carrying a load of washing.

"Yes please," he replied for both of them, opening the door to the little self-contained apartment and stepping inside.

An elderly woman with a shawl around her shoulders looked up as they kicked their shoes off in the hallway.

"Hello! Oh, how lovely! Micklas said you might be stopping by."

She got to her feet on unsteady legs and slowly made her way towards them. Mimmi had managed to take off both her shoes and her padded trousers by the time the old woman had made it the few meters to the hall.

She held out her hand in greeting.

The old lady gripped it and exclaimed: "Good grief, your hands are as cold as ice, my dear!"

She wrapped her old hands around Mimmi's and rubbed them for a moment before letting go with a laugh. She then gave Johánas a long hug and took a step back to get a better look at him, stroking his chin with her thumb.

"Your cold sore is back, I see. Have you been moisturizing your lips properly? Spring's a terrible time for the skin. Can I see your hands?"

She took them and stroked the backs of both. Johánas sighed, though on the whole he seemed to enjoy the attention.

"Crow pecked," the old lady muttered.

It was a term Mimmi had never heard before, despite her years of medical studies. She peered down at her little friend's hands and saw that they were red and chapped.

"I'll find you something to rub in," Johánas's great grandmother announced, tottering away into her granny flat. "Come in, come in!" She waved a hand over her shoulder as she weaved her way between the furniture.

There was a quiet knock at the door, and one of the carers popped their head into the room. Mimmi turned around and thanked them for the extra cups, setting them down on the little dining table where Johánas was already sitting. The old woman was on her way back from her bedside table with a tub of some sort of cream. She smiled politely as Johánas's great grandmother rubbed a generous amount of lotion into his hands, finishing off with a soft pat on the cheek.

"What a lovely apartment you have here," said Mimmi, running her hand over the grey crochet tablecloth and taking in the lush houseplants in ornate pots on the windowsill. "Is that a Cypress Peperomia?" she asked, nodding to a trailing plant that had spilt over the sides of its low pot.

"Yes, it is! It grows so fast in that south-facing window," said the older woman, turning to the plant with a smile. "The girls who work here, they're always taking cuttings to stop it from swamping all the others. Would you like one? Take it when I'm not looking if you do – they grow better when they're stolen."

She winked at Mimmi, who laughed. Mimmi liked this woman. She seemed so capable and kind. And she was clearly very fond of her great grandson.

Johánás himself didn't speak. He just fiddled with the dials on the radio and munched absent-mindedly on a cookie.

"And how are you, young man?" his great grandmother asked.

"Good. Grandpa waxed my skis and Tobba's not well."

"Uff, that's right, the dog. Hmm." She nodded. "Yes, Micklas mentioned that. Something about her ear?"

"Yeah, she got frostbite and it went all black and horrible."

"Sounds unpleasant." said the old lady, eyes still on her son's son. "And . . . how are things at home?"

Johánás hesitated, giving Mimmi a fleeting glance. "Good, except Mum isn't back yet. Something about the tour. She didn't come back at Easter like she said."

"Oh, no?" The old lady gave him a solemn nod. "Have you told Mimmi that your mum is an actress?"

Mimmi shook her head in surprise.

"She's part of the Sámi theatre; they're doing a play about that skull measuring business at the moment."

Micklas's mother seemed proud on behalf of her great grandson, and Mimmi saw the boy sit tall, but she also got the sense that the old woman was boasting about Aile for Johánás's sake. The boy would probably have benefited from having his mother around a little more often, Mimmi thought to herself.

"And what about your dad? Do I need to give him a clip around the ear?" the old lady joked with a glimmer in her eye, making it clear that she was perfectly capable of such a thing.

"Nah, he's OK. He just hasn't been home much . . ."

"So you're living with Grandpa now?"

The boy inhaled affirmatively and tried to look like it didn't bother him.

"Well, it's lucky you have your own room there, isn't it," the old lady said warmly. She turned to Mimmi and explained: "It's my old house, you see. Micklas took it on when I came here, and Johánás has had his own little nook there since he was just a tot." She smiled and cocked her head at the memory. "His father, Peter—"

Before she had time to get any further, Johánás interrupted her by pointing to a painting over by the window, leaving Mimmi wondering what the old woman had been about to say.

"Look! That's the flower I told Kaj about!"

He was pointing to a small, beautifully framed painting of a bluebell.

"Mimmi has one just like that!" he explained.

"Oh?" said his great grandmother, slightly taken aback.

Mimmi had got to her feet and was standing on the rug by the wall, studying the painting. It was unsigned, but she didn't need a signature to recognize her mother-in-law's work.

Laura's distinctive style, the colorful edge at the bottom of the flower, was something she had seen countless times before. It was one of a number of recurring motifs in the flowers.

"Ah, I've had that a long time," the old woman said after a moment. "I think it's so beautiful, and it acts as a reminder to be brave . . . to be compassionate."

Mimmi turned to her with a look of curiosity.

To her, the delicate, unassuming little flower was more a symbol of something that needed protection to avoid being broken by the breeze of a passing butterfly.

"I was given it as thanks, you see, for helping a girl escape a violent man."

"Then I can understand why the painting makes you think of bravery and compassion. What happened?" Mimmi asked, putting all thoughts of how the girl in question had got hold of one of her mother-in-law's paintings to one side. What an incredible coincidence.

The old woman was quiet for a moment, lost in the brush-strokes on the canvas. "I helped to save that young woman's life, and her son's. I won't utter their names, a promise is a promise – but the boy's father was a real brute, and he beat her black and blue. So when I spotted an opportunity to help the lass, I took it and made sure she got away . . ." Johánás's great grandmother looked sad but proud. "I've often thought about her older brother and his wife. For them, life was probably never the same again. They were incredibly close, you see, brother and sister. Despite the age gap. And when she disappeared, it must have broken their hearts – especially because they lost the little one at the same time. He lived with them, you see. Couldn't be with his parents with everything as it was . . . so his aunt and uncle took him in as though he was their own. No, life was probably never the same again for the Rijás. I still feel guilty about that to this day . . . The lad was so sweet and kind, a bit like our Johánás. I don't even want to think about what their lives must have been like once they lost him. Some people end up shouldering the most unfair of burdens. And the girl, well, her brother had taken care of her since she was just a little thing herself."

The old woman slowly shook her head, eyes downcast. Mimmi's sympathy for the couple who had lost their beloved boy made her face crumple.

Johánás gave her a searching look when he saw the expression on her face.

"Yes, it was a real mess, all that business. The girl had made some bad decisions in her life, but her relationship with the man who almost killed her was undoubtedly the worst one of all," the old woman said.

"She sent me that painting later, with a brief note to say that they were fine. It cheered me up no end, and I've had it on my wall ever since . . . it's followed me everywhere." The woman smiled softly, and then continued: "I wondered whether she might get in touch with her brother after a few years, but I later found out she never had. She was too worried about what the brute might do to the old couple if he found out they'd been in contact."

Mimmi sat silently, waiting for more. Her gaze hung on the old lady's lips.

"I suppose you could say she paid a heavy price, having to stay away from what little family she had left. But the question is whether Biera and Máriddja would have thought it was worth it if they'd known. And the boy. He wasn't given any choice, poor thing . . . It was a wretched business through and through. Still, I make myself think about it now and then, as a reminder that the most important thing in life is to take care of one another. It means more than you might think."

Her words cut deep inside Mimmi, who couldn't help but give Johánás a quick glance. The old lady noticed, and she smiled with her whole heart.

She peered out through the crack in the open door to the past and met young Risten's frightened eye in the backseat, hugging her boy to her chest. The boy she could see so much of in her own great grandson, Johánás.

A little dandelion, sprouting up despite the cold, barren scrap of land fate had dealt him. She hoped there would be other hands to cup sweet Johánás once she was gone, just like she had once protected Risten and her boy.

"I'm afraid I've managed to forget your name already," Mimmi said with an apologetic laugh, though Johánás's great grandmother hadn't introduced herself when they arrived.

"I'm Unn," the old lady said with a warm smile. "Nice to meet you."

65

The Old Bachelor Comes In

The Nilssons' Nuffe opened the door with the little frosted window in it and trudged inside with his shoes on. Stood beside the firewood box, fingers brushing the dog hair caught in the rough grain and the nail heads sticking up out of the old wood.

Nuffe sighed and looked at his mother and father, who were sitting at the kitchen table. His father lowered the weekly magazine he had been flicking through, and his mother tore her eyes away from the magpies outside, flapping around the net cage where the meat had been hung to dry, giddy on spring air.

"There's something I need to say," Nuffe announced, voice faltering as his parents watched him, his mother over the top of her reading glasses and his father with his half-empty coffee cup resting against his chest.

His mother smiled and clasped her hands. She stared at her son, seemingly so moved that she had developed a few extra chins, and Nuffe felt his heart huffing and puffing in his chest, like an achy old dog trying in vain to get comfortable.

"OK. Shit, I don't really know how to . . . say this."

"You don't need to say anything, Nuffe, love. We already know," his mother said with a fond sigh.

His father glanced at her, still not lifting the warm embrace of the mug from his chest.

"No." Nuffe swallowed. "I mean, I don't think you do."

"We do." The woman who had birthed him gave a motherly smile. "A mum just knows these things. Haven't I always said so, Sören?"

Her husband mumbled something inaudible, studying his adult son, who was now twisting his woollen hat in his hands. The reflective stripes of Nuffe's postman's uniform caught the light, flashing around both legs, and his father mumbled again as his mother nodded, smiled and sighed happily.

Nuffe seemed to have lost his tongue, thought Sören, though he didn't say anything. Instead his wife picked up where she had left off.

"Gosh, I can't believe this day is finally here . . . Your father had his doubts, but I've always *known* you would confide in us eventually! I want you to know that we couldn't be happier . . . You have to be true to yourself," she said, sitting tall and giving a solemn nod to a postcard of a crucifix on the spice rack, propped up against a pot of fennel seeds.

"Let the boy say what he has to say," Sören said with a glance at his wife, who nodded and turned to her son, who – blushing furiously – seemed incredibly uncomfortable.

Nuffe Nilsson swallowed and massaged the back of his downy neck.

"I just want to say," his mother butted in, "that whatever it is, we're ready. Whatever your secret is, we understand . . . Oh, sweet child." She had tears in her eyes.

"Sally . . ." growled Sören in warning, nodding encouragingly at his son.

"Yes, yes, I just wanted to put that out there. That we'll still love you all the same."

Sören sighed.

Nuffe stared down at the floor as though his neck was no longer capable of holding the weight of his head.

"You're going to be shocked, I'm afraid . . . it's not what you think," he said in a gravelly voice.

Sören was starting to get an inkling as to where this was heading, and he blinked a few times and then pushed back from the table with a loud screech, making space for him to swing one leg over the other. He leant back with his arm draped over the back of the chair, demonstrating a state of relaxation that bore no relation to how he actually felt.

"I can't live like this anymore," their son muttered to the floorboards. "I just need to get it out."

"Come on, Nuffe; you know nothing can shock your old mum and dad. We already know, just come out and say it . . . for your own sake!" Sally encouraged him.

Sören's back was now sweating, and he cast a slightly anxious glance at his wife's expectant face. Then, at long last, his son looked up at them, lower lip trembling. He spoke quickly, as though he wanted to blurt it out now that he had finally made up his mind.

"I'm not gay."

His mother flared like a newly lit match, only to fade and go out. Sally shook her head as though she didn't understand what her son had just said.

"But . . . you are, aren't you?"

Sören placed a reassuring hand on his wife's, which seemed to have frozen on the table. He had suspected this might be coming and had spent years trying to clear a path for his son to speak his truth.

"No, Mum, I like girls . . . women, I mean. I know how much you've been hoping, so you must be really disappointed in me, but that's the truth. I can't keep pretending. Can you forgive me, Mum?" Nuffe had tears in his eyes.

Sally Nilsson sat perfectly still, a frown hovering just above the bridge of her nose.

"God, I knew you'd take it like this," Nuffe whimpered, slumping down onto the firewood box and clapping his hands to his face.

"Come on now, it's not like anyone has died. I think it's a good thing you've told us how you feel, Ulf," his father reassured him, patting his wife's clenched fists again. "We've talked about this, Sally," he went on. "That it might not be how you hoped—"

"But you've been sweet on boys," Nuffe's mother interrupted him. "You've been in love with your colleague since . . . well, since you first got the job at the post office!"

"No, Mum, you've got the wrong end of the stick. Tommy's just a good friend . . ." Nuffe sounded defeated.

"But you stay over at his house. Surely men don't have sleepovers unless they're in a . . . a romantic relationship?" His mother's voice grew shrill towards the end of the sentence.

"Sally, love, I've told you it was probably just so they could go out for a drink in town! He couldn't exactly drive home if he'd been drinking, could he?" Sören said wearily.

Nuffe himself didn't speak, he just sighed from the depths of his big, heavy body.

Sally got up and, true to habit, shuffled over to the sink. She lifted the soap dish to wipe the surface beneath it, then did the same with the draining rack. Her shoulders shook softly as she carried out the familiar movements, trying to calm her nerves.

"Mum . . ." Nuffe pleaded with her. "Can't you try to see the positives instead? I don't see how this makes any difference? It's just how I feel . . ."

Sören interjected: "Plus, not all daughters-in-law are like Liselott's, you know. They're not all kleptomaniacs and . . . whatchamacallits . . ." Sören searched for the right word.

"Vegans!"

Sally sobbed with her back to them, tipping the yellowed soap into the sink and scrubbing hard at the residue in the old enamel dish. She blew her nose on her apron.

"Right, vegans . . ."

"Have you ever heard of a man living on that kind of diet?" She had turned to face them now, with a wild, sad look in her eye. Her reading glasses had fogged up, and she took them off and threw them to one side. They skidded into the sink, which only made her sob even harder.

Sören and Nuffe moved over to the trembling woman, wrapping their arms around her from either side. She tipped her head from one to the other, and then said:

"What are the girls at choir going to say?"

"I'm sure they'll understand," said Sören. "It's not the end of the world . . . Their sons are all straight too."

"Yes, and their daughters-in-law are all crazy! You know full well that Mona's daughter-in-law *tricked* the boy into moving to Partille! Partille! Dragged him and the kids down there, all that way *south*! To all the crime and the concrete and the . . . the nonsense."

"Didn't Josef get offered a management job down there?" Nuffe interjected.

"Yes, that *she* forced him to take!"

Nuffe gritted his teeth to prevent yet another objection as his mother continued to babble away. About Åsa, whose son was married to a fiery woman who wouldn't let his mother iron his pants, and Lisbeth's Jonatan, who had been talked into buying a car without a roof by his crazy Stockholm partner.

It seemed clear that the women in the choir used their practice sessions to vent about their sons' unwelcome independence. And that Sally, in turn, had boasted about her son's homosexuality – which liberated her from the yoke of any daughter-in-law.

"I think we need to pull ourselves together now, Sally," said Sören, reaching for his wife's glasses from the sink, drying them off and perching them on her nose. "There, now. Let's look at this rationally. Surely you can see that it's not sustainable for the boy to keep pretending to be something he's not, just to make us happy?" her husband said, making himself seem like a co-conspirator when in actual fact he was nothing of the sort.

Because the truth was that Sören had been fairly confident that his son was straight for a long time.

He gave Nuffe a firm pat on the arm and then nodded to show his approval.

"Does this mean you're going to move out . . . now that you're not gay?" his mother asked in a weak voice. "That we won't get to keep you here in the house? I know it's selfish of me to hope for something like that, but it's been so nice having you here."

"Mmm, maybe at some point," said Nuffe. He had stopped rubbing his neck, anxiously wringing his hands or letting his lower lip tremble. "And if it's any consolation, Mum, I promise not to shack up with anyone who won't eat your food. That's assuming I can even find someone who'll have me," he laughed. "Still, at least I can start looking. Now that you know what's what, I mean. And you know, Mum, with you as a role model, it's not going to be easy to find someone who measures up. No one's smoked sausages are as good as yours!"

Sally laughed, and Sören used his finger to rap a little tune on the table, showing his agreement.

In his hand, Nuffe was clutching a shopping list of ordinary, everyday items. But on the back, in black ink, it read:

Better a lion in the kitchen than a dormouse in the mirror.

She was an *oracle*, old Máriddja. Completely out of her mind, yes, but an oracle all the same, Nuffe Nilsson thought to himself, feeling his heart rate slowly settle.

66

Domestic Threat

There had been a stranger at the door.

A woman with permed hair and a grin like an angler fish – plus all the charm of a barracuda.

Máriddja had taken up her usual spot behind the plastic flowers in the hallway window when she saw the car. She had raised a finger to her lips and shushed Biera, who was chuckling to himself at something only he knew, but he hadn't heard her, so it was all the same.

The door was locked and the bell broken.

Despite that, the curly-haired stranger had pressed her finger to it repeatedly before trying her luck by knocking instead. Máriddja had crouched down against the door, knees creaking, wishing their visitor would toddle off on her way.

"I'm from social services," the unwanted guest had shouted through the sturdy door, giving the handle a try. "Hello?"

Máriddja stayed as quiet as a wood mouse, and Biera squinted up at something on the ceiling and clapped his hands in delight. His hearing aid was on the table.

The door handle was in bad shape, provisionally repaired with fishing line, and as she hunched on the floor, Máriddja hoped it would stand up to the stranger's attack.

Fortunately, the messenger from social services had given up after a while, scribbling something down on a sheet of paper that she pushed into the mailbox on her way back to the car.

She had paused to study the badly damaged mailbox and then peered around the yard one last time. She stopped by the broken garage door. Squinted in at Máriddja's heap of junk and at the remains of the burnt-out barn, before – thank God – she shoved herself back into the car and drove away.

Still on the floor, Máriddja shuddered. *Dodged a bullock there,* she thought. She used the door handle to drag herself up, groaning as another sharp pain seared through her gut.

"Damn busybodies," she muttered to herself, popping a King of Denmark into her mouth to help with her nerves. She was trembling with indignation and terror.

Who would have thought that being allowed to mind your own business could be such bother!

She perched on the armrest of Biera's chair and lowered her head to his shoulder. He smelt like old man and tobacco, and she filled her lungs with his scent. That alone seemed to have a reinvigorating effect on her. Biera stroked her head through her hat, but he didn't speak.

"We're always going to be together, aren't we?" she asked him in a weak voice. "Aren't we?"

Biera patted and stroked her with his trembling hand.

"Course we are, Máriddja. Where else would we go?"

The perm from social services would probably have a whole host of unwelcome suggestions about that, Máriddja thought, swallowing hard.

"True," she said with a deep sigh. "We're fine here. We don't need anyone else."

"Though *Isá*'s probably going to need help with the reindeer soon," Biera conceded.

She looked up at him. "For God's sake, Biera. Your dad is dead and the herd has been sold. You need to pull yourself together! People might catch on, and then they'll come and take us away. If we end up in a home, we won't be together anymore! You've seen what happens on the TV box!" Her voice was thick with barely repressed tears, held back by the floodgates of her lips. "We need to stay here, where we can be together. Anything else is out of the question! We don't have children to look out for us, or even to fight with the authorities to let us stay together in a home. I was hoping . . ." Her voice gave out on her.

"I know, *ráhkis*. But it'll be nice for Heaika-Joná and Risten to spend some time together, won't it? He's always wanted to go to the circus! Besides, we've got all the baking to do, so it'll be good to have them out of the way."

Máriddja squeezed her eyes shut so hard that it made her cheekbones ache, and Biera gave her a reassuring pat on the hand.

"You take the sled, I can carry it. We'll get the grouse later."

He smiled at her, mumbling something in Sámi about hiding Easter eggs and sealing the smokehouse while they were still fit and young.

The cancer in Máriddja's belly clawed at her like some sort of prehistoric beast, and she gave Biera a strained smile.

"Yes . . . you're right. Let's do that."

As she locked herself in the toilet to let out every last tear she had been holding back, she heard Biera cheerily call for the dog. The same dog that had been dead for twelve years.

Máriddja sobbed uncontrollably and dug out the phone.

"Siré? Are you there?"

"I'm here," said Siré.

"I'm so scared. So alone," Máriddja cried quietly.

"You can always talk to me," said Siré, which only made her cry harder.

67

Liejbbeålmåj Receives Visitors

No one could have guessed what awaited them when they pulled up outside the little house on the mountain, not least Viveca the social worker and Palle from transport services. Viveca had decided not to take no for an answer after her last visit and had come back ready for battle, but *this* was something else entirely.

Standing on the front porch was a tiny old woman with a woollen hat pulled down over her forehead, swinging an antique bear spear from side to side.

"No one's coming in here, so you might as well clear off right now!" Máriddja shouted at Viveca and Palle as they got out of the car. "We're not going anywhere . . . and I won't let the state come an inch closer than it already has."

Viveca and Palle exchanged a startled look over the roof of the taxi. The old woman was ready to fight like an old Valkyrie, and clearly had no intention of letting them in.

"Hi, Maria," Viveca said softly, taking a few steps forward. Palle was right behind her, prepared to provide help if she needed it, though he had really only come in his capacity as a driver. They had left the doors of the car open.

"My name is Máriddja," the guardswoman growled.

Viveca turned around and mouthed "call for help," and Palle discreetly pulled out his phone. He spoke into his headset, seemingly without moving his mouth, and then nodded to Viveca to let her know the deed was done.

"I'm Viveca Orrhammar, I'm from social services. We've been trying to get in touch with you and your husband for a while now." She thrust out both her palms and her underbite toward the old woman in an attempt to show her good intentions.

Máriddja didn't let them out of her sight, and nor did she lower her bear spear. *Damn the cops for taking the gun off me,* she thought, forgetting her own part in that story. It would have been a damn sight more impactful to be aiming at them with a firearm instead of her *áddjá*'s old spear. Still, there was something quite nice about defending herself with the same weapons her grandfather had once used to hunt.

Máriddja Rijá felt the spirit of *Liejbbeålmåj*, the God of Blood and Hunting, take over her, and she smiled to herself as the powerful presence gave her renewed strength.

She drove the blunt end of the spear into one of the wooden boards on the porch, pointing the still-sharp tip towards the yard. Like a bear hunter, waiting for the furious animal to charge out of nowhere and throw itself towards its own death.

"I don't care where you're from, I want you to clear off right now! And leave us in peace!" Máriddja explained with what was, in her opinion, a dignified, terrifying, thunderous voice.

Right then, another car pulled up behind the taxi. The police, Palle thought with a sigh of relief, though deep down he was also thinking that they must have teleported to the mountain, because it had been no more than a few minutes since he had called to ask them to come.

But it wasn't the police.

It was a green military vehicle with black and yellow number plates.

The army? Palle thought in confusion. Everyone stared at the pot-bellied man who opened the car door and studied the scene in front of him.

"Platoon chief Hägg," Máriddja blurted out, resisting a sudden urge to salute him.

Like hell! *None* of these poxy messengers of the state would be getting any marks of respect from her today. She tightened her grip on the spear.

"What's going on here?" Hägg asked with all the authority his job title conferred.

Palle clicked his heels together and stood to attention. Viveca responded calmly.

"We're just having a chat with Maria here," she said, giving a warning nod towards the aged Valkyrie on the porch.

"Why is she armed?" asked Hägg, turning to Máriddja a moment later to repeat the question.

"None of your damn business. I'm the one asking the questions here! Why are you back?"

Platoon chief Hägg looked slightly troubled, though after an embarrassingly long silence he replied: "I came to ask about the coffee and the . . . uh . . . cookies."

He held his head high like a stubborn child with pockets full of stolen apples he believed were rightfully his.

"What?" Máriddja snapped. "I've got no plans to invite anyone in for coffee, surely you can see that? I'm under siege here, for God's sake! Why don't you get these strangers out of my yard instead of bothering people for a cuppa in the middle of a war!"

She used the spear to point at Viveca and Palle.

"Why do you want coffee and cookies right now?" Palle asked. He had been following the exchange closely and couldn't help but ask.

"Top secret! Not something that concerns . . . civilians," Hägg snapped. "But if you really must know, the coffee I drank here did wonders for my prostate. Got everything back in order down there," he said, gesturing to his crotch. "And the almond cookies . . . well, they're probably the best I've ever had – outdid my ex's inedible baking by a mile. I was passing by, so I thought I'd ask for the recipe."

Palle's jaw dropped.

Viveca's did the same.

But Máriddja laughed. "Oh, I'll tell you! Those were girl scout cookies, from when they came round selling them a year or two back!"

She nodded to her audience with a look of triumph.

"But there haven't been any girl scouts in the area for years," said Hägg, trying to work out how long it had been since the local group in which his daughter was active had been disbanded.

Máriddja shrugged.

"We bought a whole crate of them, and I must say they were good, lasted forever."

She seemed incredibly pleased with her unrivalled stockpiling skills.

Hägg was starting to look a bit green around the gills, but he forced himself to swallow and whimpered: "And the coffee? Dare I ask?"

"Ah, that," Máriddja snorted. "Good old-fashioned boiled coffee, of course. The trick is not to rinse the grinds out of the pot; you just keep adding more. The pot gives a certain character to the coffee once it's been cooked in for so long."

This time Hägg was powerless to stop himself from retching.

"If we could get back to the matter at hand," Viveca spoke up once the lieutenant colonel had managed to compose himself. "We'd really like to come in and have a look around inside, talk about the future."

"No one's coming in here," Máriddja barked. "You've got nothing to offer us. We won't let you split us up, I hope that's very clear!"

As she spoke, a small car pulling a trailer appeared on the driveway, and a plump young woman in a pair of trendy glasses and a woollen skullcap announced her arrival with a cheery: "*Bures!*"

She paused and took in the scene with wide eyes.

"What in the name of hell!" Máriddja sighed. "Are all the spirits on the loose today? Be gone! Home! Back in that car with you!"

She used the spear to demonstrate where the latest arrival should go.

"Biera and Máriddja?" the chubby young woman dared ask.

"Present," said Máriddja, sarcastically holding up her hand.

"Great, we spoke a few weeks ago. I'm Sissel Jarre, I'm here to pick up an *akkja*? But if now isn't a good time . . ." she said hesitantly, taking a step back when she saw Máriddja's furious face, the queasy lieutenant colonel, the nervous curly-haired woman and the terrified driver.

Máriddja closed her eyes and seemed to be gathering her strength.

"It's up in the attic," she said with forced calm. "I couldn't get it down the stairs on my own."

"We can help!" Viveca offered.

Palle couldn't help but admire her perseverance. Personally, all he wanted was to jump back in the car and get away from this madhouse as fast as his tires would carry him.

"Absolutely," Hägg spoke up with a formal nod.

The old woman actually seemed to be considering their offer, so Viveca went on:

"We'll just help you carry it down from the attic, Maria . . . and then we'll leave."

"Fine," Máriddja agreed, her chin held high. "But no funny business! The old man and I aren't going anywhere with you, is that understood?"

Everyone nodded, some more hesitantly than others.

Máriddja turned around and unlocked the door.

"No strangers have crossed this threshold in years," she said, as though to emphasize just how lucky they were, marching into the house with her group of visitors following at a safe distance behind her.

"My God . . ." Viveca mumbled once they were inside.

No one else spoke, but they were all thinking the same thing. My God . . .

68

The Old Soul Under the Rug

The sight that met the visitors to the little house was both startling and heartbreaking. Viveca from social services lost her composure, gaping so much that her underbite stuck out like a stubborn drawer.

Máriddja stood on the trapdoor to the cellar, still wielding her spear, though she suddenly seemed a little softer around the edges somehow. Close up, they could see just how thin she was, how sunken her cheeks were and how hollow her insolent eyes seemed behind her smudged, old-fashioned glasses.

She was clutching one arm to her stomach, as though she was in pain.

The floor where they were standing was so dirty it looked more like a well-trodden earth floor in a barn. There were a few shabby pieces of furniture, all held together with electrical tape, and the stove looked like it hadn't been used in years. That was probably the case, as there was also an ancient hotplate on the shabby worktop, crowned by a rusty coffee pot with dried-on gunk right up the spout.

Hägg looked like he might need smelling salts to prevent himself from swooning like a Victorian lady.

The windows, the table, the little fridge were covered in a thick layer of dust. In the middle of the table, there were a couple of grubby plastic boxes of almond cookies. Máriddja stared at her visitors with a defensive look in her red-tinged eyes.

"Hellooo?" a weak voice suddenly called out from beneath her feet.

The old woman looked like she had just been given an unexpected suppository. She glanced down at the rag rug as though it had done something inappropriate, then cleared her throat.

"What was that?" asked Palle, studying the rug – the original color of which was indeterminable – as though it might get up and introduce itself.

Máriddja glared at him, but she didn't speak.

"My God . . . is there someone in the basement? You haven't shut your husband down there, have you?" Viveca cried, slapping her hand to her décolletage.

"Of course I haven't," Máriddja snapped back. "He's actually down there of his own free will."

The rug started talking again:

"Máriddja? Do you have people up there? Is it the Nilssons' boy?"

The old woman rolled her eyes and turned to the strangers, ignoring the rug's questions. "See, you can hear he's just fine. He likes the cool air . . . you've got to be careful not to get too hot at our age."

"But it must be freezing down there?" said Hägg.

"No, no," Máriddja cut him off. "He's got a reindeer hide to sit on, and I threw him a blanket."

"Surely you must see that this is madness? Move to one side so we can help the poor man out!" Hägg's tone sounded suspiciously like an order, though it had little effect.

Viveca tried a different approach: "Please, Maria. He's old and cold. Let him come up here where it's warm!"

Máriddja shook her head, though she seemed to relent a moment later. She took a few hesitant steps to one side, and Palle and Sissel worked together to pull back the talkative rug so that Viveca could open the heavy trapdoor.

Little by little, a thin old man emerged from the darkness of the cellar. The first thing they saw was a dirty mop of hair, impressively thick for his age, followed by a pair of innocent child's eyes peering up at them. A mouth whose three teeth were very much in the minority, and a wrinkled tortoise neck, thin shoulders and a sunken belly. He stepped out onto the kitchen floor on his unsteady legs and big feet. The man was wearing a hide over his shoulders, like some sort of prehistoric mammoth hunter, and he peered up at them with an absent smile before turning to Hägg.

"There he is! Did you get the right soured milk this time? And did you remember to buy yourself a few sticks of gum with the change?" He gave platoon chief Hägg a mischievous wink and pressed a finger to his lips.

Everyone had said no to the coffee that Biera, thrilled to have visitors, had asked Máriddja to heat up. He was sitting on the bench beside his protective wife, who had left the spear leaning against the backrest and now had her hands clasped in her lap, awaiting their next move like a seasoned chess player.

"Well, the attic's over there," she said, nodding to a steep staircase in the hallway. It looked like it had probably been lethal even in its prime, and Sissel seemed to be debating whether or not the sled shouldn't just join the rest of the junk when it eventually went up in flames.

But the representative of the Sámi Parliament quickly came to her senses and remembered why she was there. She gave Máriddja a plucky smile and started her vertical ascent up the visibly disloyal stairs. Palle went up after her, and they worked together to bring the heavy object down, lowering it to the floor with a soft thud.

The others remained where they were at the kitchen table, reflexes and muscles primed in case the poorly repaired chairs gave way beneath them.

Viveca had attempted to make conversation with Biera, but had given up following a glance from Máriddja. She hadn't managed to get anything but a few words of Sámi out of the old man – that and a brief drinking song.

"Deep down, you know the two of you would be more comfortable elsewhere, don't you, Maria? If you moved to the care home in town, there'd be help and support for both you and Per."

"Out of the question," the old woman had snapped, though her gaze did waver a little.

"Your husband," Viveca nodded to Biera, who was trying to prise the lid off one of the plastic boxes to get at the almond cookies inside, "is clearly suffering from dementia, and you're in no fit state to care for the two of you anymore."

Máriddja avoided their eyes, taking the box from Biera and giving him free access to the dense little treats inside.

"Can't you see that you're living in misery?" Hägg blurted out, earning himself a sharp kick in the shin from the social worker.

"This is our home," Máriddja replied haughtily. "We've done the best we can. We're happy here, and we don't want to leave."

A number of barely visible creases had appeared on her old chin, an omen of looming tears.

"But maybe you could reconsider, for Per's sake? Do it for him, so he can be more comfortable. So he can get the care he needs."

Biera munched on a biscuit with an open mouth, following their exchange with unsuspecting interest.

And that was when it happened.

Máriddja's proud posture began to slump, and she swayed slightly beside her husband. She bowed her skinny neck in silent agreement, and it was as though they could hear her will snapping like a dry twig, only to be tossed onto the fire and become thick smoke in the breeze.

She put up a bit of a fight, for the sake of appearances, declining to pack their belongings into the old carrier bag that was held out to her. Ignoring their suggestions to put on a coat and refusing to get into the car, which she claimed smelt rotten.

Who would she be if she didn't act up a little, for the sake of appearances, now that she was falling apart in front of these strangers?

"What's this?" Sissel asked, lifting the paper bag containing Risten's school books out of the *akkja* before Hägg and Palle carried it over to the waiting trailer. She flicked through the pages with the reverence of an archaeologist.

"Oh, that's just my sister-in-law's old junk. Schoolwork and that sort of thing, I think. You can chuck it away, it's not worth keeping . . ."

Sissel had delved into the bag with the intensity of a racoon in a trash can and was now rifling through the books inside. Her eyes had lit up, and she practically cried out in ecstasy.

"Not worth keeping?! Do you know what this is? Wow, thank God you didn't get round to destroying these! There are family trees . . . registers, interviews! I recognize some of the names here. Oh . . . wow!"

Sissel sat down on a chair and used one of the sheets of paper to fan herself so that she didn't faint with excitement.

"This is invaluable for my work! For our work! For the whole Sámi people!"

"Invaluable, inestimable and incomparable, is it?" Máriddja asked with a wry grin.

"And then some!" Sissel gasped, giving her a teary-eyed smile.

Those Jarres, Máriddja thought to herself, with a not entirely unhappy chuckle. They always got what they wanted in the end.

69

Dandelion Child

Kaj was in the process of putting some of their winter clothes away when Mimmi called. He had her slightly campfire-smelling padded pants in his arms, and he scanned the hallway for somewhere to set them down.

"Hi, honey, how's it going?" she asked, sounding slightly pressed for time.

He could hear her fingers tapping away at the keyboard in the background.

"Yeah, not bad, but I'm starting to realize we have an insane number of coats. I don't even know where to put them all. I keep having to move the box of sandals there's no room for anywhere. It's like a Rubik's cube in these closets," he said.

Mimmi hummed in reply. "Listen, Micklas just rang. Johánás's school called to say that he has a fever and earache. Probably a middle ear infection."

"Uff," said Kaj, opening a drawer full of socks and thinking about where else he could put them to make room for all their sunhats and caps.

"I told Micklas we'd take care of it, so he doesn't have to drive back to town. He's busy launching the boat today, but he said he'd take Johánás to get checked out tomorrow morning."

The sunlight was filtering in through the patterned glass on the front door, painting the socks on the floor in a riot of colors and making them look like the work of an unsupervised three-year-old with a new pack of crayons.

"OK. Yeah, it'd be a while before Micklas got back even if he did leave now," Kaj agreed. "What about the kid's dad?"

"He didn't mention him. I guess he can't help."

"I'll go and pick him up," Kaj said with a sigh, starting to clear a path to the front door so that he could get out to the car.

"You're the best, you know that?" Mimmi sounded relieved, and Kaj could practically hear the corners of her mouth curling downwards in the special way they did when she smiled.

"You haven't left me with much choice," he said, digging out the keys. "Just come straight home once you're done. Please."

Kaj pulled up outside the gates to Johánás's school and, after some effort, managed to open the childproof latch.

An older woman in a pair of Wellington boots and tinted glasses came out to meet him. She started talking, fast and sing-song. Reached out and gripped Kaj's hand, gave it a firm shake. He felt embarrassed when he blurted out his name and admitted that he couldn't understand a word she was saying.

"Whoops, I thought you were . . . Ah, OK. Johánás is just getting his coat on. He's a little subdued and could probably do with a nap, maybe a bit of TV. He often gets these infections at this time of year." Her voice was deep, her vowels sounded different to Kaj's.

"I'm sure we can arrange that," he said, giving the teacher a polite smile.

"I'm glad to have met you, actually . . . Micklas said that you and your wife are friends of the family?"

"Yes, we—" Kaj didn't have time either to confirm or deny what she had said before she took a step closer and lowered her voice.

"Look, I'm going to level with you. If a child is suffering in any way, we have a duty to report that, and I'm afraid Johánás isn't doing well. He hasn't brought in a single piece of fruit to eat all term, and he doesn't have any spare clothes on his shelf – he has to borrow from the lost property box just to be able to play outside with the others during break. His father, Peter, *never* answers the phone when we call, and I can't seem to find the right number for Aile."

"She's on tour," Kaj said with a frown. "I've never actually met her."

"That doesn't surprise me; Johánás barely has either. Considering how things are at home, I have to say I think it's tragic she isn't around more. He needs his mother."

Kaj swallowed, a strange new weight on his chest. "I had no idea . . . What about Micklas? His grandad? Surely he can—"

"His *áddjá* does his best, there's no doubt about that," the stubborn little woman interrupted him.

The May wind was mild, and Kaj noticed a single yellow dandelion growing by the wall of the building. The teacher went on:

"The problem is that Micklas isn't well himself. He works far more than a man his age should, to support himself and Peter's family and help keep their heads above water."

Kaj felt a powerful sense of shame creeping up on him. The image Johánás's teacher was painting wasn't a pretty one. He should have noticed before now.

"I understand," he said quietly, clearing his throat and nodding. "It's not a good situation for a little boy."

The woman was quiet for the first time since they met, and she studied him. Her eyes looked almost black behind her dark glasses.

"Yes, we're just thinking of the boy," she said. "Would you tell Peter and Aile to get in touch with us or the headteacher *as soon as possible*?" She underlined the last part with the sharpness of a scalpel. "Because we're going to have to submit a report to social services about this . . . For Johánás's sake."

Kaj nodded, unable to do anything else. Over the teacher's shoulder, he saw a small figure being led out the main door. A young man helped Johánás put his backpack on and pulled a hat onto his dark head. The boy was drooping like a little flower, he looked pale and serious.

Kaj waved to him, but Johánás's fingers barely straightened out as he returned the gesture. He slowly made his way down the steps and over to them.

The woman in the Wellingtons said something in Sámi and gave Johánás a rough pat on the head. Johánás mumbled something almost inaudible in reply and moved so close to Kaj that Kaj could feel the heat of his fever through his thin windbreaker.

"OK, goodbye then," said the teacher, giving Kaj a lingering glance before she turned around, retrieved a forgotten spade from the straggly grass and headed back inside. The birds sailed overhead, giddy with spring, and the sun was warm on their backs.

Kaj gave Johánás an aspirin when they got home, then tucked the sickly boy up beneath his own quilt, which he had brought through from the bedroom. It was soft and floral, a little threadbare, and as one of the few things he had chosen to keep from his childhood home, something he also associated with the loss of his parents.

The boy's eyes were big and feverish beneath his heavy eyelids, and Kaj switched on the kids' channel and put a glass of water on the floor by the leg of the sofa. With a sluggish gaze, Johánás watched the animated figures chattering and driving around on screen.

Kaj tiptoed out to hang the boy's coat somewhere in the messy hallway, and as he searched for a free hook, he heard a weak voice from the next room. It was as light as fog, creeping around the corner.

"You're not going anywhere, are you?"

Kaj stood perfectly still with the boy's damp shoes in his hand. Looking down, he saw that the lining was so worn that it was like string stretched over the smooth tongue.

"No, I'm right here," he replied, frozen to the spot.

The sound of his own quiet voice felt like a tender bruise in his chest.

"Good." That solitary word came out like a whisper.

Kaj didn't speak, lost in thought in front of the hallway mirror, his mother's flowers visible from the corner of one eye. The house was so quiet he could hear the clock ticking in time with his own pulse as he half gazed at his own reflection.

Through his blurred eyes, he looked like a skinny little kid with a mullet and trousers that were wet at the front.

"You have good snacks here," he heard the sickly voice say. "But that's not why I like . . . coming here."

Kaj didn't speak.

"It's hard being at home, because . . . my dad's not very well."

70

Ready and Waiting

Did he have time for a coffee? Kaj glanced down at his phone and decided that he could probably manage a few mouthfuls of much-needed caffeine.

He had been on call overnight and was nearing the end of his shift, but before he left he needed to deal with an urgent case.

Until now, his shift had been relatively quiet, but he hadn't managed to get any sleep. His conscience was still smarting at the way he had behaved towards the little boy who had turned to them for help. The things the lad had mumbled in his feverish delirium, together with what the teacher had said, had left Kaj shaken.

As the reasons for Johánas's uninvited visits became clear, Kaj had begun to understand his own reactions and feelings around having him in the house.

He had to admit that the child had been partly right in what he had said, that Kaj saw himself in him and that that was one of the reasons he had displayed such pathetic antipathy towards the boy. But that simply wasn't acceptable. He had been a real shit, and he felt a powerful urge to put things right. There was something about the boy that touched a part of him, some kind of echo between them. Kaj's parents hadn't been absent in the way that Johánás's were, but the boy's loneliness still reminded him of himself. Laura and Hans had been there for him and given him everything he needed. Everything but answers. That meant his life lacked a proper foundation. In some ways, perhaps, it was as though his mother had always slipped out of his grasp whenever they touched upon anything away from the art, literature and creativity they shared. Laura had been plenty of things, but maybe, just maybe, his own insecurities stemmed from everything she didn't want to share with him.

He would call Johánás after his post-shift nap and ask whether he wanted to come over and help drain some of the meltwater from the lawn. Though maybe the boy wouldn't be feeling up to that yet, even if his fever had broken . . . Maybe he could borrow Palle's gaming console and invite him over to play on that instead? He thought they still had some jelly raspberries and fizzy pop in the pantry. Yes, the little guy would probably like that. The decision helped ease his mind slightly, enabling him to refocus on his work and the task at hand.

This was a meeting that had been eluding him since he first arrived in Guovddo.

It was one of his very first cases, and every time he logged into the system he came face to face with a blinking reminder about his lack of follow-up.

It concerned a couple of complex personalities who had got up to all sorts of things at home, and Kaj was willing to admit that he was quite curious to finally meet these people, who had managed to evade him and his colleagues within social services and the health system for so long. He fiddled with the phone as he sipped his hot coffee from a paper cup. Wrote a message to Palle about the gaming console – not that he expected a reply any time soon; his friend was working.

Noomimmi, as Palle called their girlfriends, had plans for their partner-free morning, and Kaj suspected they were already hard at work papering the guest room at home. He scrolled through his Instagram feed and hit "like" on a picture of Micklas's dog, a Finnish Spitz, taken from a worm's eye view.

He then checked the time again.

Why weren't they here yet?

He paced around the room, slumped into his desk chair and leant back with a sigh. Turned his head so that his cheek was on the headrest and peered outside in search of blue flashing lights.

Kaj fiddled with the buttons on his scrubs and thumbed the badge on his chest.

71

The Final Caravan

Lined up on the neglected road, the cars looked like they were forming a funeral procession.

In the first car, with Palle behind the wheel and Viveca in the passenger seat, Máriddja sat slumped beside an excited Biera. Hägg's green military vehicle was next, followed by Sissel Jarre, bumping along in her little Golf with the *akkja* secured safely in the trailer.

You're part of the caravan yet again, Biera. Part of another move your people have been forced to make, Máriddja thought sadly, her eyes on the old sledge in the rear-view mirror. *And you, my gieres, are being forced to tear up your roots once more, to tag along because you don't know any better. The first time it happened you were in your mother's belly, and this time you're strapped in tight under social service's seat belt.*

She studied Biera's profile as he gazed inquisitively out through the car windows. In her hand, she was clutching the telephone machine device.

As they'd hauled the *akkja* and the couple's few belongings out of the house, Biera had sat happily on the kick sled outside. It had stayed behind as a monument to spring on the thawing mountain. He seemed to be enjoying all the fuss and the warmth of the sun on his cheeks.

Hägg had, without quite knowing how, become involved in evacuating the elderly couple, and had marched around barking orders. As he passed the old man on the sled, he heard him speak up:

"It's the cat you should thank."

Biera smiled up at Hägg, who had stopped in his tracks and was looking down at the shabby old uncle in his woollen cap.

"Rubbing the blood of an inbred field vole into the skin does wonders for the plumbing." He nodded to himself and then added: "Old trick."

Hägg stared at Biera as though he were a gospel singing pepper, then hesitantly moved on, casting the occasional thoughtful look back at the old bloke.

Was Biera referring to the incident with the mouse he had stepped on the morning he came over here for the first time? Strange. As he sped up to continue directing this circus of scatterbrains and madmen, he heard the old man's voice behind him:

"Damn smart cat . . . you should take good care of it."

The ravens circled above the caravan of cars like a gaggle of professional mourners. Máriddja didn't need to look at them as they landed in the trees on either side of the road to know that they were an omen of death, and that it was her bodily remains they planned to feast on.

In a whisper, she tried to get through to Siré. Too beaten to ask for help, as she had originally planned.

"Siré, are you there?"

"I'm always here."

Máriddja closed her eyes in gratitude at her friend's reply. "It's over now, Siré. They're forcing me and the old man to move into a home, and they're going to separate us."

"I'm sorry."

"Me too." Máriddja sobbed quietly, wiping her nose with the back of her hand and trying to compose herself. "It's probably just as well. For Biera's sake, since I don't have much of this life left. It'll be over soon. I'm tired to my bones."

"Do you want to sleep?"

"Yes, dear. I think that's what I want."

72

Unexpected Passengers

Noomi had received a text message, and she read it aloud from the stepladder where she was busy cutting in at the edge of the wallpaper.

"From Palle," she said to Mimmi, who was crouched over by the bucket of paste. "Listen to this."

Mimmi looked up, her interest piqued.

"On the way back from Sarvesoajvve. Wildest drive I've ever done. Finally managed to get Per and Maria Rijá to come with us, but you wouldn't believe the state of their place. The old bloke is away with the fairies and the woman is, like, dying and crazy. Tell you more once I get home. Driving now xx."

"God," said Mimmi. "Working for the transport service is clearly more exciting than it sounds."

The two women laughed and shook their heads.

Mimmi realized that Kaj, who was still at work, would have a dramatic last case to deal with before the end of his shift, and she hoped for his sake that the old couple weren't in too bad a state.

"Their surname, Rijá . . ." Noomi sounded like she was deep in thought. "That's not such a common Sámi surname. Where have I heard it before?"

Mimmi stirred the wallpaper paste with her stick. "Sounds like one of Kaj's mum's middle names. Laura Kristina Ria. I've never come across anyone else called Ria before. Made me wonder whether her parents were drunk and misspelt Pia when they went to register her birth," Mimmi joked.

"Maybe they were as demented as these old fogeys on the mountain?" Noomi retorted, and they laughed as they continued their work, putting up a stubborn sheet of wallpaper with an old-fashioned medallion pattern. Mimmi paused as she held out the next length to her friend.

"Hold on, did you say Rijá . . .?" It did sound familiar. She was sure she had seen it somewhere recently. Among the things Kaj had inherited from Laura? That was it, wasn't it?

Their faces flushed, and Mimmi lowered the paper and pushed a wad of tobacco beneath her lip. Noomi did the same. Various fragments of memories and thoughts started coming together, forming a surreal, warped image.

Hadn't Johánás's great grandmother mentioned the Rijás, too? The old couple who lost the little boy and his mother? Though their first names had been different, not Per and Maria. Mimmi racked her brain for what Unn had said. Máriddja, was that it?

Noomi seemed to have read her mind: "Máriddja and Biera are the Sámi equivalents of Maria and Per."

"Oh my God, then maybe they're the same people? Which would mean that Laura's brother and his wife . . . are the old couple who were left behind when the young woman fled her partner with her son?"

Mimmi's eyes were like spheres, darting around the half-renovated room as she thought aloud. Noomi gave her an admiring look that encouraged her to go on.

"Which would mean that the young woman must have been Laura . . . and the child . . . Kaj!"

"Seriously, my head's spinning!" Noomi said flatly, changing her position on the ladder. "And they're in Palle's car now?"

"Shit!" Mimmi swore quietly.

Noomi agreed, adding a Sámi expletive of her own.

"I need to call Kaj!" said Mimmi. Then it hit her, like an oversized icicle straight to the brain: "But he's at work . . ."

The two women gasped, and Noomi clapped both hands to her head in a gesture of horror.

"*Älä helvetissä!*" Mimmi muttered to herself in Finnish. The moment required something far stronger than Swedish swear words could provide. She knew that much, Mimmi Rajala.

73

Nameless and Rootless

Unfamiliar places
Unknown faces
Shackled and broken by distant suits
Forcibly chained to others' roots

Laura and Kaj hadn't hopped out somewhere along the way as they drove south. They had stayed in the car with Hans until he reached his final destination, the small flat where he lived in Sundsvall.

In a whisper, Kaj had asked when they would be going back to Máriddja and Biera, said that he missed them, missed home. And with an ache in her gut, Laura had replied only to say that he shouldn't speak Sámi.

She had told Hans that her son's name was Kaj that terrible night in the car. It was her nickname for the boy. Heaika-Joná revealed far too much about their Sámi background and would only provoke questions that should never be asked – for everyone's sake. She never got round to filling in the paperwork to make the change official, but from that day on, he became Kaj. When Hans asked her name, he hadn't caught the "Risten" part, unfamiliar as it was to him, and she had decided that that was probably just as well.

They were on their own now, Laura and Kaj, and if they were going to survive in this strange new world then there were a lot of things they would have to put behind them.

All the dangers, the memories, the roots and the sense of safety, buried beneath spadeful after spadeful of earth and lies. It was the only way she could be sure Bill would never find them, nor hurt Biera and Máriddja. She told herself that her brother and his wife would be safe from Bill's violence and his thirst for revenge if she left them in the dark about where she and Kaj had ended up, though she had only ever managed to half believe that. She refused to acknowledge Kaj's desperate cries for them, refused to give in.

She was broken, damaged and afraid, and she was also anxious about how she and her son were going to make a life for themselves away from Sámi lands. She had told herself that her parents had managed it, all those years ago, back when their skis and sleds had carved wounds into the snow on their forced journey south.

She and Kaj would create a new life for themselves, too. Just like their displaced kinsfolk, they would have to learn how to live in a different culture, among people who were not theirs, speaking a different language. Above all, thought Risten, now Laura, they would have to forget everything that came before if they were going to manage what lay ahead.

For a long time after that, she was unable to sleep through the night without waking up in panic and scanning the darkness for danger. The period of withdrawal from the highs she had lived with for so long proved negligible, paling in comparison to her shameful longing for Bill. Despite everything that had happened, he still tugged at the stitches that were holding her together inside, tempting her to come back so insistently that she felt like screaming. He was the real drug she had been addicted to, she realized; all the rest was just background noise.

She could see that now.

Laura strained her ears in the dark. In the glow of the street lamp outside the little room that she and Kaj shared, she curled up behind him, despair like a stranglehold around her throat. She whispered his *luohti*, the *joiks* they had left behind.

Máriddja and Biera. The *joiks* she had pressured her mother and father into teaching her. The *joiks* they had given her, bled out through taut lips for her.

As Risten, she had been greedy, wanting to hear all about the places they had once belonged. Not places that had belonged to them, but that they had been a part of. About their forefathers, their friends, their relatives and legends. In remembering through the *joiks*, her parents painted a picture of the people and the earth where their roots dug deep with equal parts resignation and pride. Of the wide, snow-covered landscape where her relatives had sown the seeds of life and got them to grow, where they had been laid to rest and now walked the paths of eternity in peace.

Kaj's mother quietly sang her family's *joiks* for the last time. She wanted to etch them into his soul, to wrap them around both him and her alike as protection against anything bad that might happen.

She knew she would never sing them again, in the same way she knew she had to let Biera and Máriddja fade into the past – so much so that Heaika-Joná eventually forgot them entirely, for his own sake.

And she was afraid, so afraid that nothing would grow in the cold. Without the life-giving rays of the Sámi father's sun, in land where the ground frost maintained an iron grip on all life.

She had no roots here, nowhere for her severed rootlets to take hold. But maybe that was a good thing? They had left their names behind; would anyone ever truly get to know them without those names? She had to believe so. And she also had to believe that her actions would be forgiven by the spirits and forces around her, the ones that saw everything, because she knew they would also see that she hadn't grabbed the boy and run for her own sake. Away from the people who represented safety and home to him.

Her big brother had known, hadn't he? With a sudden clarity of vision, Laura finally understood the stories Biera had told her son, the same ones he had told her when she was just a girl.

She could hear the echo of his voice inside her.

Stories about the *háldi* who was planted in a patch of earth, in a world where she didn't belong. The children whose seeds of life had been sown in something that would never last. The *háldi* who would disappear if you said her name, if you called her what she really was.

With a shudder, Laura understood what the powers inside her brother had been trying to tell them, trying to prepare them for.

She was the *háldi*. Bound by mystery for the rest of her days, in a world where she didn't belong.

74
Heaika-Joná's Joik

The call finally came to tell him they were on their way.

Kaj stood in the doorway of the examination room and saw the woman from social services approaching with a husk of an old man clinging to her arm. He was surprised to see Palle just behind her, pushing a thin old woman in a wheelchair. She looked like someone had hacked away every last ounce of flesh from her body, and she didn't look up when Palle raised a hand in greeting. The old man was acting like he was out for a walk with an old friend, the childlike innocence of dementia plain to see on his face, and he gave Viveca a toothless grin as she said something, nodding politely to every single painting they passed in the hallway.

The old woman in the wheelchair raised her chin higher and higher the closer they came. Eyes closed and nostrils flared, she seemed to be sniffing the air for something – like a hunting dog following a scent. Strange.

When she reached the doorway where Kaj was standing, she suddenly looked up at him. From her deathly pale face, her eyes gazed steadily at the doctor without blinking. She closed them again a moment later and drew in a deep breath through her nose, smiling to herself. A single tear then rolled down her cheek, like a boulder down a mountain.

Something began to stir inside Kaj, and he found himself unable to do anything but stare at the two sickly old people in front of him. His head was spinning, and his eyes darted from the senile gentleman to the little old lady, who was still loudly sniffing the air around her.

"Heaika-Joná," said Máriddja Rijá, with such warmth that he was almost bowled over by the emotion in her voice. "I remember your scent, my boy. You've come back to us!" she said, her eyes welling up.

The unfamiliar sound of his birth name felt so right in this woman's mouth.

"I thought we'd never get to see you again," she said, letting out a laughing cry that teetered somewhere between sadness and joy. "Your *eanu* isn't in the best shape, unfortunately . . . I'm afraid our reunion has come a little too late for you to get to know him again, but you should know that he has *missed you* every day since you left." The old woman didn't bother to wipe away her tears as she glanced over to her husband.

Viveca from social services had guided him into a chair, and the old man was now busy looking down at his hands in his lap. He mumbled to himself, slowly linking his fingers together. He was wearing an old animal hide over his shoulders, and it smelt musty and rancid.

Suddenly, as though a door had opened, letting all the world's spirits and animals into the room, the old man started singing. Brief, melodious sounds and lingering notes. His voice rose up towards the ceiling before sinking again, hitting Kaj like a blow to the chest and making him gasp as though the song had struck him square in the solar plexus.

Máriddja smiled and closed her eyes. Absorbing the *joik*, breathing it in.

Kaj could hear himself in the old man's fumbling tones, could feel his innermost being in Biera's song, which painted

Kaj's essence in such bright colors that he almost felt like he could reach out and touch it. His name, Heaika-Joná, fluttered by once or twice, making his soul shiver.

From time to time it felt like the *joik* was about to peter out, only to take on such power that the old man had to pause and gasp for air.

It was nourishing, it was affecting, and it was unspeakably beautiful in its raw, delicate nature.

Before the elderly man finished, he looked up at the young doctor and smiled. And Kaj remembered. A small boy who had been hidden far away in a dark cellar of forgetting, he remembered them both. There were no clear images for him to cling onto, no memories that could explain who they were to him, but he knew that the old couple had been missing from his life for a very long time.

That wordless sense of what they had once shared filled the gaps inside him with strong, vibrant colors; the voids that had hollowed him out were suddenly brimming with emotion.

Just like a *joik*.

Exactly like the *joik* that had coaxed Heaika-Joná into the light and brought him back to himself.

75

Thank Heavens

Mimmi had used her key card and was now hurrying down the corridors at the health center. Towards a door with a nameplate that read *Kaj Bäckmark, Resident Doctor*.

One of her colleagues stopped to chat outside the visitors' toilet next door. "Do you have a shift today, Mimmi? I thought you had a few days off. Saw on Instagram that you were doing some renovations. Where did you buy that wallpaper?"

"Yeah," a harried Mimmi said to the chatty nurse. "I just need to speak to Kaj."

Before her friend had time to reply, Mimmi had knocked, opened the door and slipped into his office, all at lightning speed.

"He's got patients . . ." the nurse said to the closed door. She hesitated for a moment, then clip-clopped down the corridor in her white uniform clogs.

And thank heavens Mimmi arrived when she did. The shabby old lady in a woollen hat was swaying on her thin legs, and Kaj seemed to have frozen, tears running down his cheeks. He looked like he might collapse at any moment. Viveca from social services appeared utterly lost, standing beside a chair holding a man so old he was almost mummified. The elderly man was peering up at Palle, who opened his mouth to speak only to close it again, blinking in confusion. It was almost as though he was trying to send some sort of Morse code message using his eyelids, and the old man seemed to agree, leaning forward in his chair to get a better look.

Everyone turned towards the door when Mimmi came in, and with a few quick steps in her neon running shoes, she reached the shaky old lady.

"Why don't we sit down?" she said, raising her voice in an attempt to wake Kaj from his trancelike state. She led the patient over to the metal examination stool beside the old man and managed to push her down onto it with no more than a slight pressure on her shoulders.

Mimmi reached for Kaj's stethoscope, gently lifting it from around his neck and putting it on. She held the chest piece to Máriddja's skin and listened. Glanced up at Palle, trying to get him to do something about Kaj, who had slumped to his knees on the grey linoleum floor. Palle hurried over with a cup of water for his friend.

"Is there anything I can do . . .?" Viveca from social services asked, her voice a little unsteady. She wasn't quite sure what she had just witnessed, nor what was appropriate after such an experience.

Mimmi didn't reply until she had taken off the stethoscope. As she pressed her strong fingers to the elderly woman's thin wrist, she asked Viveca to fetch a nurse. The old lady looked up at the ceiling, eyes full of old woman's tears, and mumbled something in Sámi. Words that Mimmi, with her knowledge of Meänkieli, understood as some sort of thanks.

Once she had finished examining her, she held out a hand.

"You must be Máriddja Rijá? My name is Mimmi Rajala, I'm a doctor here at the health center."

"Mimmi?" Máriddja repeated, neither confirming nor denying her name. "Heaika-Joná's Mimmi?"

"Yes," Mimmi replied, casting a quick glance at her fiancé, who was now back on his feet, steadying himself against the washbasin. Trembling, with one hand on the bun on top of his head.

"I saw the notice. The engagement notice." Máriddja's voice was weak and weary. "In the paper. That's how I knew he was back. But I realized he might not remember . . . us. He was so small."

"Oh? That's good," Mimmi replied confidently. She assumed her professional role and, in a few simple steps, managed to bring order to the chaos.

When Viveca eventually returned with a male nurse, Mimmi ushered her and Palle out of the room, telling the latter to call Noomi for an explanation.

"Are you OK, Kaj?" Mimmi asked. "Arne can take over and help with Máriddja here," she said with a nod to the new arrival.

He looked so small in his doctor's coat.

Arne had already begun his examination, and the old man – Biera, presumably – looked like he was about to doze off.

Kaj got up and cleared his throat. He shook his head with a teary laugh, then slowly, as though he was crossing oceans in time, moved over to the couple and crouched down between them. He took their furrowed hands in his, like a child beneath his parents' protective wings.

Máriddja peered down at the grown man in front of her with a look of astonishment and joy. Biera's rough thumb moved slowly, absently over his cheek.

He was in shock, there was no doubt about that, but Mimmi had never before seen her partner so alive.

76

Portrait Pieces

They straighten up their crooked spines
Shaking ice from stalks and vines
& despite the expanse of frozen white
Unfurl their leaves in bright sunlight
– The people who sow in snow

Somehow, the big bubble of circumstance, catastrophe and coincidence had burst, breaking like the ice in spring. Despite Máriddja's stubborn resistance. And from the trembling chaos of desperation, nerves and shock, the gale had abated.

Heaika-Joná was with them again, in the eye of the storm, but time was running out and there was plenty that remained in shadow. Despite all that, Máriddja was so overwhelmed with gratitude that she could barely speak. She still had so many questions, but the answers were now within reach.

Heaika-Joná had come home.

Biera and Máriddja underwent various examinations and received prompt, appropriate interventions. Before they knew what was happening, they had been transferred to a cosy little apartment in an assisted living facility. Together. Máriddja had also been given an urgent referral to the regional oncology department. She would be offered – and hopefully even accept – treatment and help with her pain.

As soon as Máriddja had processed their new surroundings, she hurried to call Siré and tell her everything, with all the confidence and cheer of a summer's day. She rounded off by triumphantly announcing that they had a balcony with views across to the supermarket and the pharmacy – just imagine, being able to get hold of more of her favorite herbal mouthwash whenever she wanted it!

Heaika-Joná and his Mimmi were coming over with takeout food, too.

Máriddja was happy, and Biera was happy because she was happy, though the only changes he seemed to have noticed were that his snow shovel was missing and that Máriddja had changed the curtains.

When Kaj and Mimmi turned up with two bags of what was, according to Máriddja, the most *thrilling* food, they sat down at the kitchen table. Silence filled the room. Máriddja had been saddened to discover that the boy had forgotten his mother tongue, but she took comfort in the belief that it would soon come back. It was still in there somewhere, after all, and he was back in his rightful environment. Of course it would stir to life.

She refused to call him Kaj; Risten was the only one who had ever used that name at home. Heaika-Joná had told them about his mother's death, and Máriddja had cried at the lost opportunity to ask her sister-in-law for forgiveness.

And then they had started to fill in the gaps in their lives up to that moment. Little by little, they worked together to complete the jigsaw of their years apart, felt the pieces fit into the nooks and crannies, answering previously unanswered questions.

Biera contributed with advice on repairing fenceposts in marshland and seemed to be enjoying himself. Kaj was sad that his uncle's dementia was so advanced that he couldn't follow the conversation, but Máriddja saw the way her husband glanced at his nephew, almost shyly pushing the fresh almond cookies over to him, and she knew that some part of her husband understood that their boy was back.

Kaj had bumped into the postman when he went up to the mountain to collect a few things for Biera and Máriddja. After introducing himself, Nuffe had run over to his mail van with an excited look on his face. He returned with a tote bag full of stamped letters and handed it over to Kaj.

"I didn't have the heart to stamp them all *Return to Sender* and give them back . . ." Nuffe Nilsson explained, sounding embarrassed. "They didn't have an address for you . . . just your names," he added with an apologetic glance.

Kaj had peered down into the bag, stuffed full of words from a despairing woman, a mother without a child. Someone who must have known her letters would never arrive but had needed to write them anyway.

"Thank you," Kaj had said, gripping the bag tight.

"I thought maybe it was better this way," the plump postman added. "Deep down, she must've known what was what, but I guess she just needed to get all that longing out."

The two men's eyes met, and they nodded.

"She's a good person. They both are," Nuffe said, making his way back over to the van, which was parked by the mailbox. "We're so pleased that you're back, my folks and I!" he said as he was leaving, closing the door behind him and skilfully steering away from the verge, driving to his neighboring house with a feeling of satisfaction.

Kaj thought in wonder that the letters, marked with names that hadn't been used in decades, could easily have ended up anywhere – most likely in a receptacle for combustible waste. Yet here they were, back where they were supposed to be. And though the names felt unfamiliar, he could tell that they were his and his mother's. Heaika-Joná and Risten-Laura Rijá.

Kaj hadn't read any of the letters yet, but they were now sitting on a chair between him and the old couple, a testament to the many obstacles they'd had to overcome.

He and Mimmi had spent every spare moment since meeting Biera and Máriddja on putting the pieces of the story together.

Laura's collection of knives her big brother had made, fragments of Unn's story about "the girl" who sent a painting of a flower in thanks. Laura's inability to share her memories of her son's early years. Her reluctance to talk about the past.

They had managed to come up with a near-complete portrait of one woman's determination to protect her family at all costs. Laura had helped Biera and Máriddja stay afloat over the years by anonymously buying her brother's crafts, objects she had later left to the son they had once shared.

Her efforts to shield them from the truth she had been convinced would destroy them, through Bill's revenge, were heartbreaking. Because what his mother hadn't known – and they all agreed that this was probably for the best – was that her great sacrifice had ultimately been unnecessary. Her tormentor had died just a few years after she and Kaj had run away.

The pale, long-necked spirit of Risten-Laura soared above the open balcony door, and her family came together in grief over the tragedy they had all been forced to endure as a result of a string of unfortunate circumstances.

Kaj had called his brother Gustav and told him and his family to immediately book flights north to meet their long-lost aunt and uncle.

And, not least: face the new portrait of their mother which, through their combined brushstrokes, had revealed a soul that was more tortured, and brave, than any of them ever could have imagined.

77

Routes of the Forcibly Displaced

A woman stepped forward onto the dais. Eyes fixed straight ahead, she walked over to the microphone stand. She was dressed like a politician, in sensible heels, and her glasses were perched on the tip of her nose. Her mouth was small but firm as she spoke.

"To the Sámi people, to Sweden . . . On behalf of the Swedish state, and the country as a whole, from the bottom of our hearts: *Ándagassii*, sorry. For the terrible suffering and the conflict we caused with the forced displacement of your families. To those families who were separated, for the roots we severed and the deep wounds we left in Sámi history, we apologize . . . To the family of Ante Niila Juhán Rasti . . ."

Johánas stood perfectly still, the familiar itch to keep moving now nowhere to be felt. Once the minister had gone through the list of every family who had been forced to leave the northernmost part of Sweden a hundred years ago, he saw the chair of the Sámi Parliament step forward. The minister lowered her head and took the chair's hands in hers. Johánas wouldn't have known she was the chair if Mimmi hadn't bent down to straighten the tassels on his woven shoe bands. With her mouth to his ear – he could smell the Thai food they had stopped to eat on the way here on her breath – she had explained that the chair herself had roots in Karesuando, relatives who had been displaced. The woman was visibly moved by the occasion, and started speaking in their own language, talking about the importance of redress, of repatriation and forgiveness. Words that were occasionally hard to follow, but with enough emphasis that even Johánás could feel their weight. Things would, where possible, be put right.

The chair then cut the ribbon that had been set up in the town square in Karesuando, declaring the memorial to the routes of the forcibly displaced, *Bággojohtin bálgat*, officially open.

A trail had been marked out, following one of the most frequently used routes, with text in Sámi, Finnish, Swedish and English on beautiful silver signs wherever it crossed the main roads. In a number of particularly memorable locations, these signs told stories. Like where the Beavrrit family had lost half their reindeer when the animals turned back to the place where they were born. Or where Garen Rohkos had lost her unborn twins as a result of the gruelling journey.

The names of the families that had been driven out of the north were inscribed on memorials in the places they had been sent, alongside those of the hard-pressed Sámi families already living in the area, forced to accommodate them on insufficient land. Johánás knew that his own ancestors' names were written there, ditto Kaj's crazy aunt Máriddja's.

"We stand together, side by side in unity as the singular people we are. No longer separated by the colonial power." said the woman on the stage. Or something like that, anyway; Johánás was struggling to keep up, and he wondered whether he dared ask Mimmi if he could go and sit down on the edge of the curb. It was a warm day, and he was desperate to get out of the sun.

Kaj had promised that they could walk some of the trail if they had time, and Johánás had seen him pack a Thermos of chocolate milk in his backpack. Then again, it was a long way back to Guovddo – around 250 miles – and they would have to set off in good time if Johánás was going to make it to soccer practice. The boy fiddled with the hem of his new *kolt*. It was the first time he had ever owned one that had been made specially for him – in the past, he'd always inherited his older cousins' cast-offs – and the colors were so bright, the fit so comfortable around his shoulders. Kaj had arranged to have it made for him, at the same time he had one of Biera's old *kolts* tailored to his slim frame. Pretty nice of the loser, but Johánás was sure it was worth it – given the number of kisses Mimmi had showered upon her fiancé.

Johánás looked around the crowd as another person addressed those gathered, someone from the audience this time. The minister struggled to unhook the microphone from the stand and then passed it to the man so that everyone could hear what he said. He seemed to be the chair of a local Sámi organization, and he talked about the importance of the ceremony, not just to those with roots in Karesuando but also to the descendants of more southerly families. It was an acknowledgement of the hardships they too had been forced to endure: made to share their land, their livelihood and their lifeblood with strangers. The project was not just a long-awaited apology from the state, it also represented the reconciliation and reunification of the Sámi people. Johánás knew that this part was relevant to his family, and he stood a little taller. It was nice that it was happening, and judging by the adults' reactions it was something they had been waiting for for a long time. He knew that many Sámi had been made to move south to areas where those who were already there had been forced to step back, but clearly there was more to it than he had thought. He listened patiently, with the sense that all these people with the microphones were actually speaking directly to him.

Doctor Kaj's eyes were fixed on the stage, and it seemed as though he was absorbing every new family name, every speech, memory and verse, making space for them inside himself. Johánás wanted to say that he liked seeing him like that, but he wasn't quite sure how to begin.

Once the man was finished and the microphone had been returned to the stage, project manager Sissel Jarre got up to read a poem by Risten-Laura Rijá, Kaj's mother and Biera's little sister. Johánás knew they were descendants of a Karesuando family, and he listened extra hard and shifted a few inches closer to Kaj. Glancing up, he saw that the older man's eyes were closed, which came as a relief – it meant the doctor wouldn't tease him for standing so close. The boy didn't know why, but it felt like his stuck-up new neighbor needed him there, like a heavy little anchor.

Johánás was good at reading the adults around him – life with a drunk father and an absent mother had made him attentive to everything that wasn't said – but the words now filling his ears felt so clear, like they were being spoken directly to him, that it was as though he was transfixed. Sissel Jarre's reading of Risten-Laura's words caused countless eyes to well up, but they felt like soothing tears, not ángry or hopeless ones. Not the usual kind, lonely and despairing.

Sissel closed her eyes as she recited the poem, allowing the words to sink in, to sink down into the earth and take root. Her hands moved as though she were singing a *joik* as she spoke:

> Lines of ink instruct command
> Fettered families fettered land
> Royal seal seared like a brand
> Tumbled from a furrowed hand

Salty tears metal taste
Icy wind that bites the face
Wayward herd the dogs guide forth
Turn hearts and antlers to the north

From mothers' bellies seeds do spill
Aged withered frigid still
Kin torn from all they've ever known
Trails of blood away from home

Unfamiliar places
Unknown faces
Shackled and broken by distant suits
Forcibly chained to others' roots

They straighten up their crooked spines
Shake the ice from stalks and vines
and despite the expanse of frozen white
Unfurl their leaves in bright sunlight
– The people who sow in snow

Without noticing it, Johánás closed his own eyes. He felt Kaj's hand on his shoulder, squeezing it in time with the words being read aloud. When the boy next looked up, he briefly met Kaj's gaze. The doctor's eyes shone, and Johánás couldn't quite manage to hide all of the emotions he felt. Something happened between them in that moment, between the grown man and the young boy. And then Kaj let go of his shoulder, and Johánás pulled away and rolled his eyes. Standing beside them, Mimmi sighed over their embarrassment at showing any vulnerability.

On the other side of the crowd, Johánás saw Viveca from social services with a couple of other women who worked for the authority he both feared and felt a vague sense of gratitude towards. The women waved, beaming so brightly at the sight of the doctor and the young boy that Johánás felt a rush of embarrassment. His immediate instinct was to throw sand at them, but that feeling passed when he looked up and saw Kaj's face. Mimmi's lame fiancé grinned down at him and winked.

78

Dear Siré

"It's over now, Siré. The mission is complete." Máriddja hesitated for a moment. "And I have to say, that's largely down to you. I wanted to thank you for being such a friend. You're a good woman, Siré. Never forget that."

"I'm not a—"

"Shh," Máriddja hushed her. "Not a word about what you really are. You never know what might happen if you start talking about things that should remain unsaid."

Author's Note

Dear Reader,

The Sámi are Europe's only indigenous people, and one of Sweden's official national minorities. The area the Sámi call their own is known as Sápmi, and spans four countries: the far north of Sweden, Norway and Finland, plus Russia's Kola Peninsula.

Sápmi can be divided into a number of language areas, its people to different subgroups of Sámi. Sweden, for example, is home to the Northern Sámi, Lule Sámi, Pite Samí, Ume Samí and Southern Sámi. Their language, traditional costume and, to some extent, cultures differ, but they still consider themselves to be one people.

Traditionally, the Sámi have made a living through reindeer herding (which, to some extent, requires a nomadic lifestyle), hunting, fishing and carving. Today, however, the majority have more conventional jobs to make ends meet.

Like many indigenous peoples around the world, the Sámi have been harshly treated by their respective states over the years. They have endured forced Christianization, scientific racism and the colonization of their lands, forced labour and, as you will read about in this book, forced relocation.

The Sámi see themselves as a people without national borders within the boundaries of Sápmi, and as such they have always moved over large areas. The Northern Sámi – the group to which my character Biera belongs – spent the bitter winter months around Karesuando, in the far north of Sweden, before moving their reindeer over towards Tromsø in Norway. The Karesuando Sámi had been making use of these summer pastures on the islands off the coast of Norway since time immemorial.

Following the dissolution of the union between Sweden and Norway in the early twentieth century, the Sámi who had made their homes on both sides of border suddenly found themselves unable to cross from one country into another. The Karesuando Sámi were left without summer pastures for their reindeer, and as a result the Swedish state made the decision to "relocate" a large number of families. They and their herds were forced to move some 600 miles south, to more southerly Sámi communities. No one had prepared these southern Sámi for their arrival, however, nor for the fact that it would mean sharing their already-scarce land with people with different traditions and practices in terms of reindeer husbandry. This led to major conflicts.

In certain locations, the local Sámi were forced to give up both their reindeer and their sense of cultural belonging to make space for the Northern Sámi. These forced relocations took place for many years, creating deep wounds for the Sámi people – both those who were brushed aside in favor of the reindeer herders from Karesuando and those from the north who never wanted to move in the first place. Families were torn apart, and the journey itself was incredibly gruelling, taking place on skis during the harsh Scandinavian winter, with herds of reindeer that wanted to turn around and head back home. Some spent years trying to convince their reindeer to migrate to their new lands, and there were severe penalties for those who refused. One family saw their entire herd forcibly slaughtered by the authorities.

As the Sámi are a people with powerful bonds with nature, their forefathers and the spirits they believe surround them, it was incredibly traumatic to be resettled in a new, unfamiliar setting where they did not feel welcome. The vast majority of those who were forcibly displaced never saw their families or their home territories again.

The distance between the fictitious community of Guovddo (where this book takes place) and Karesuando (from which Biera's parents were forcibly displaced) is around 280 miles. Guovddo itself is around 450 miles south of the summer pastures Biera's parents visited prior to their relocation. As such, his family is very much from the north, despite the fact that Guovddo and Máriddja's family lands are also in northern Sweden.

Today, reconciliation efforts are underway in various parts of Sápmi. The Swedish government has established a truth commission, and the Swedish Church is undergoing a reconciliation process and has published a white paper on its historical abuses. A Sámi Parliament was also established in 1993. It is primarily tasked with monitoring cultural issues, but has limited powers. At the most recent election in 2021, some 9,000 Sámi were registered to vote. The total number of Sàmi in Sápmi is estimated to be somewhere between 80,000 and 100,000.

Sweden has not ratified the Indigenous and Tribal Peoples Convention (ILO 169), which is – among other things – based on the principles from the UN's other declarations of human rights also being applied to indigenous peoples. As a result, Sweden has received extensive criticism from the United Nations, Amnesty International and the Swedish Equality Ombudsman.

Without these protections and recognition from the state, the Sámi continue to see their lands depleted and colonized. For indigenous peoples around the world, nature is sacred and traditional ways of life are bound up in protecting the land. This makes it particularly painful for the Sámi to be denied any influence in national environmental policy. Forestry, waterpower, mining and other industries are found across Swedish Sápmi today, and these developments continue at a rapid pace.

Warm regards,
Tina

Acknowledgements

Thank you to the lovely Rhea Kurien and the dream team at Orion, both for putting your faith in me and enabling me to live out my dream under your banner.

To First Edition Management, from the bottom of my heart: the biggest of thank yous. I'm so proud and humbled to be making this journey with such incredible women. And to Kaisa Palo, my agent: you have been – and continue to be – vital and indispensable.

Thank you also to Paloma Agency for your hard work.

A salute, fanfare and confetti shower to the most brilliant of translators, Alice Menzies. You have done so much more for this book than just translate it. I'm in awe of your skill and feel for the text!

Thanks to Tjallegoahte for the brilliant comments and tips.

Thanks to Katarina, who read this manuscript at every awkward stage and was nothing but enthusiastic and encouraging. Seriously, I thank my lucky stars for you.

Thanks to Ylva, forever my first reader, and also one of the last before the text went to print. You always know what I need.

Thanks to my big, messy family. To Mamma, for passing down the háldi story and so many other incredible tales.

To Farmor, for calmly but impatiently waiting for me to write this story and then welcoming every draft with open arms.

To my brothers, ErikSimonDavid-ArturLinusHannes, and my sisters-in-law: AnnaErinaSabrinaMariaEmma. You keep me sane, and that says a lot!

Thanks to Pappa, Harriet, Ivar, my parents-in-law, Momma, Lasse, Börje, my aunts and cousins, one big muddle of craziness. I love you, but if you don't sing this book's praises you'll be in real trouble. That also applies to you, Momma – and since a good chunk of Máriddja is based on you, I'm counting on you hitting back.

Thanks to my friends for their never-ending patience over the fact that I never call and rarely leave my mountain, but who still love me all the same. The feeling is entirely mutual and unconditional.

Thanks to my former colleagues at the library in Arvidsjaur for never getting sick of bouncing ideas with me, and for being impressively patient with me during this wild ride.

Thanks to all the wonderful people on social media for giving me the hubris I needed to write this book. Without your polite interest in my nonsense, none of this would have been possible.

A huge thanks to two wolves. Without you I don't know what I'd do, and you know I mean it.

Thanks to Flora and Ejvind. For coming along in the end, and for every precious day we get to spend together, forever and ever, Amen. I love you so much it drives me crazy.

And, of course, I'd never miss an opportunity to pay tribute to the love of my life: thank you, darling Ludde! For letting me read this text to you over and over again, for spending hours and hours discussing characters, plot and emotions without getting bored – and for giving me the keys to so much, not just in terms of my writing. I'm the luckiest woman on earth. Plus, you're shit hot.

Last but not least: thanks to Siri. For responding to all the twisted things I've ever asked – and for doing so without judgement.

RAISING READERS
Books Build Bright Futures

Dear Reader,

We'd love your attention for one more page to tell you about the crisis in children's reading, and what we can all do.

Studies have shown that reading for fun is the **single biggest predictor of a child's future life chances** – more than family circumstance, parents' educational background or income. It improves academic results, mental health, wealth, communication skills, ambition and happiness.[1]

The number of children reading for fun is in rapid decline. Young people have a lot of competition for their time. In 2024, 1 in 10 children and young people in the UK aged 5 to 18 did not own a single book at home.[2]

Hachette works extensively with schools, libraries and literacy charities, but here are some ways we can all raise more readers:

- Reading to children for just 10 minutes a day makes a difference
- Don't give up if children aren't regular readers – there will be books for them!
- Visit bookshops and libraries to get recommendations
- Encourage them to listen to audiobooks
- Support school libraries
- Give books as gifts

There's a lot more information about how to encourage children to read on our website: **www.RaisingReaders.co.uk**

Thank you for reading.

---

[1] OECD, '21st-Century Readers: Developing Literacy Skills in a Digital World', 2021, https://www.oecd.org/en/publications/21st-century-readers_a83d84cb-en.html

[2] National Literacy Trust, 'Book Ownership in 2024', November 2024, https://literacytrust.org.uk/research-services/research-reports/book-ownership-in-2024